# Orchestrated LOVE

# Orchestrated Love

## A.J. BUCHANAN

4 Horsemen
Publications, Inc.

I am dedicating the first MM novel in my own pen name (and the first in the series) to two men who have always had faith in my ability to write in this genre... Tal Bauer, a wonderfully gifted writer of brilliant MM romantic suspense and an early mentor, and Ron Perry, my friend, business associate, and now fellow MM author. I learned some valuable lessons from each of them that I will never forget.

Tal, you'll be pleased to know that my career as an MM ghostwriter, which you helped to foster in its infancy, has led to some stellar reviews of many of those twenty stories (even though I can't claim them) and a wealth of experience in writing MM romances, all of which I bring to bear on this first work in my own name.

Ron, thanks for helping me learn about covers, fonts, chapter headings, and all that. You're such a gem!

Thank you both for your friendship, for helping me believe I could do this, for holding my hand, as it were, for guiding, supporting, and encouraging me in the ways that you have while I found my own way. I will never forget your kindness and professionalism.

This one's for you, guys!

Heart eyes,
AJ

# Table of Contents

# Acknowledgments

This novel has been five years in the making. I started it back when I was ghostwriting MM romances, when I had the good fortune to be mentored by Tal Bauer, a master in the craft. Thank you, again, Tal. There aren't enough words to tell you how grateful I am for you.

Thanks also to Ron Perry for his early review of my outline and his questions that helped me move this to where it is today.

I can't forget Linda Culbertson, my writing partner, my friend, my sister from another mister. She's been with me on this journey since I started actively working on it again in 2021. She's listened and responded to every scene, every revision, every hesitation, all the sexy times—she really enjoyed those!—every overthinking moment. Because, you know, that's what writing partners, not to mention friends, are for. I love you, girlfriend!

And last, but by no means least, many, many thanks to Mia Gardiner for her careful attention and suggestions and for her kind words about the work. I truly appreciate you taking on the task of beta reading for me at such short notice, Mia.

♪ x ♪

# Prologue

*Noah*

*Ten years earlier...*

The words echoed in his ears, a punch to the gut that almost knocked Noah Santiago off his feet. They were the killing blow to his hopes, the thing he had most feared when he'd gotten the rather strained message from his music professor and tutor, Jackson Knox.

"We have to end this, Noah. We can't go on."

Jax's voice was hard, his face expressionless, no hint of emotion anywhere to be found. If Noah didn't know any better, he might have thought Jax really felt nothing for him. But he did know, just as he knew the why of Jax's decision. Last week's accidental meeting had been a close call. Too damned close to be comfortable, to be safe. Thankfully, they hadn't been careless enough to show any outward signs of affection, though while they'd been sitting together in their seats, they'd held hands for the entire performance.

But Noah had known Jax would break things off for certain after that. It wasn't in his nature to expose those he loved to slander or to endanger their welfare in any way. And if anyone discovered that they were lovers, Noah could kiss his scholarship and his chance at making a name for himself as a concert violinist goodbye. Not to mention what would happen to Jax, who was his professor. Why he had let himself hope that the love between them could blossom and grow, he'd never know. And why the hell had Jax let things go so far before he'd delivered the killing blow?

Somewhere in his deepest heart, Noah knew the fault was equally his. He'd been the one to push in the beginning, to flirt, and tease, and seduce. He could have called a halt at any point while Jax was still refusing to allow things to develop and hesitating. But he'd persisted ... when had he ever *not* gotten what he wanted out of life? No one said no to Noah Santiago. Well, no one had, until this moment. And what the hell was he to say to the man who had his heart? He could rail at him, sneer, and sling hurtful words, but what would that accomplish? He'd end up looking like every other rejected lover and prove to Jax that he was no more mature than any of the other students he taught, that he was an entitled, thoughtless, selfish twenty-one-year-old only out for himself and what he could get out of life.

He drew himself up to his full height and inhaled slowly, trying to bury the pain. When he felt more in control, he spoke.

"Sure. If that's what you want, it's fine." He instantly regretted his phrasing. *Way to sound grown up, Noah!* "I mean, I understand, and I appreciate you being straight with me." *Liar! You hate every fucking second of this.*

He watched Jax clench his fists before shoving them into his pockets. He knew what that meant, and it broke him wide open to know that Jax hated doing this as much as Noah hated him doing it. He wished, just for a moment, that Jax would give in to the urge he was fighting to hold him and just hug him, one last time, for old times' sake. But he knew Jax wouldn't. They were standing in his office, where Jax had summoned him earlier. He pulled his gaze away from the bulge in those pockets, his thoughts away from the hugs he would never again receive or return.

"I've asked Professor Parks to take over your lessons," Jax continued after a moment. "She's quite excited at the chance to train you. We both recognize what an exceptional talent you are. I trust her. She'll do right by you."

Noah didn't know what to say to that. He wondered what Jax had said to explain his sudden request, but he wouldn't ask. It didn't matter, or at least it shouldn't, so he wouldn't let it. It hadn't even occurred to him that this was a complete and utter break between them. Why hadn't he realized that Jax would not want to have any further contact with him at all? He wasn't stupid, so why did he think it would have been easy to break off their love affair but still maintain their professional contact? He knew how they felt about each other. It would have been impossible for Jax to keep tutoring him in private without them losing focus and then what would have been the point? *Fuck, this hurts!*

He cleared his throat to rid it of the tears crowding it. He refused to cry before this man who was breaking his heart. He was not a kid; he was a man as well. He would deal.

"Thank you, Professor Knox. Will that be all?"

He saw Jax wince at the use of his formal title and felt a zing of satisfaction and pain at the same time. He *should* feel some of the hurt raging in Noah's chest. Noah would not be sorry for inflicting it. Neither of them should leave that room without hurting. Losing the love they had found should not go unremarked. Jax—*Professor Knox now, remember?*—was speaking again.

"I'm so sorry, b— ... Noah."

*Babe ... he almost slipped and called me babe. Shit! Why, Jax, why? Why are you doing this to us?*

"I never meant to hurt you, Noah. Please know that." Jax's voice broke for a second and he stopped speaking. Noah watched him swallow, heard the click of his throat as he did, before he continued. "I know that you will be a fabulous addition to the music world when you graduate. You're a star and don't you forget it."

*Fuck, fuck, fuck! Don't cry, don't cry!* Another sharp inhale and a hard swallow of his own to help keep his rioting emotions in check. Noah knew if he opened his mouth, he'd beg Jax to change his mind, and he knew the other man wouldn't. He wasn't going to beg though; he was tougher than that. He nodded instead, turned, and walked out of Jax's office, his shoulders squared, his head held high, hoping he wouldn't meet anyone coming in. He wasn't in the mood to talk to anyone, to pretend to anything like normalcy when his heart was tearing apart inside his chest. He needed to get out, away from this building, away from Jax, away from his shattered dreams.

# Chapter 1

## *Jax*

*Sometimes, love hurt.*

The sun beat down on his bare arms as Jackson Knox strolled along the boardwalk in the picturesque lakeside town in upstate New York. Lake Ontario glistened in the midday sunlight, and boaters and skiers zipped along its surface, enjoying the summer heat. Jax had arrived two nights ago. He was keeping a promise to spend a few weeks with his longtime friend, Jim Bell, and his wife. They were expecting their third child after two miscarriages and Jax, who was godfather to the other two, had not seen them since the twins were a year old. That had been seven years ago.

"So, are you sure leaving the big city university for a little river town college is the right move?" Jim asked, looking keenly at Jax. "It seems like a step down, my friend."

Jax looked out at the horizon before answering. "It became more than I wanted," he said. "The competition, the infighting, the politics, the increasingly intrusive expectations. I'd had enough. And it didn't help that I was being harassed by a colleague."

Jim stopped and turned to look at him. "Harassed? How?"

Jax stifled a smile. Jim had always been protective of him, ever since their days as freshmen in college, when Jax came out as gay. He'd lost most of the people who had called him friend, but Jim stayed with him, supported him, and tried for the next four years to find him a guy to love. The thought made a chuckle escape him.

"One of the other professors was ... interested in me in ways I couldn't reciprocate." Jax didn't explain why he couldn't. It wasn't something he was prepared to discuss now, if ever at all. "He got a little pushy. I just needed to escape that without stirring up a shit storm."

Jim frowned. "So, what? You're running away?" Jim sounded incredulous.

Jax's smile was a brittle fake. "Hell, no. I just didn't feel like dealing with the ugliness of all that. Rejection is painful for both parties." His heart squeezed at the memory of the rejection that had broken his heart and that of the man he loved.

Jim sighed. "Will you miss the fast pace? The state university might seem pretty tame in comparison."

"No. I've had my time living the big-city, music-circuit life. I don't need Philly or New York or Boston as much now as I did when I started out. Something else is pulling me here ... peace. I can pass on my passion to students without sacrificing my soul."

"You make yourself sound like a very old man," Jim protested. "You're barely in your forties, Jax. You've still got the rest of your life ahead of you."

"I'm not retreating from the world, Jim. I'm just realigning my interests. This college has a nationally, highly respected music program, and I can do my thing and still enjoy living, traveling...-”

“Maybe you’ll finally find the guy you can spend your life with,” Jim interrupted him.

Jax laughed. “You’re never gonna let that go, are you?”

“Why should I? Everyone needs someone to love them. I’ve got Annie, and she has me. You, on the other hand, have no one. You need to stop running away from commitment, my friend.”

Jim’s words gave Jax pause. Is that what he’d been doing? After Noah Santiago, he had shut down his emotions, unwilling to feel again the ache of longing and desire, of love and affection that the younger man had engendered in him. He had done the right thing in stopping things from going any further than they already had. Although he had wanted with his whole soul to make Noah his in every way, it would have been wrong, and he wouldn’t have been able to live with it if anything had happened to break them apart once he had taken the final step. So he had pushed Noah away, breaking both their hearts. Sometimes, love hurt. He sighed. Who was he kidding ... love hurt all the damned time.

“Earth to Jax!” Jim’s voice broke into his musings. “Where’d you go, man?”

“Nowhere.”

The lie slid off his tongue with ease. He had never told anyone about the man he fell in love with and saw no reason to do so now. They hadn’t seen each other in more than ten years. Noah had probably found someone else and moved on with his life. Jax knew the younger man had made quite a career for himself, first with an orchestra on Broadway, then with a well-known philharmonic orchestra, before joining the wildly popular and immensely talented Barrington String Quartet. In his most vulnerable moments, Jax had found himself stalking Noah's Facebook page to keep up with the younger man's career. They had become Facebook friends while they were together, and while neither had ever used the connection much then, after the breakup they hadn't used it at all. Jax had no way of knowing anything personal about Noah, as the only things he posted on his page were career related.

"I was just admiring the view," he continued, desperate to get Jim's attention away from him. Searching frantically for something to say, he grinned when his stomach rumbled.

"I think that's a sign that what I need is food, not love," he quipped. "Let's go get Annie and find a nice restaurant for lunch."

Lunch was a rowdy affair, what with two rambunctious eight-year-old boys making eating difficult for their parents. Jax studied them in one of their quieter moments, and thought about how he was disappointing his mother, who desperately wanted grandchildren. She knew he was gay but still expected him to find a way to bring grandchildren into her life before she passed on. He didn't think he had it in him to raise children on his own, and he wasn't prepared to consider adopting any until he had a partner.

Unbidden, Noah intruded into his thoughts again. Jax hadn't seen any updates from him in almost six months, and he wondered what that meant. Had he gone off with the love of his life? It wasn't impossible. A lot of people disappeared from Facebook when they found love. Or maybe he was on tour … one of his most recent posts had been about trying for a guest spot with André Rieu on one of the conductor's concert tours.

Jax shook himself. It was pointless to keep thinking about a man he'd likely never see again, unless he was willing to send him a message on Facebook. He didn't know why

Noah was suddenly appearing in his thoughts, but he was determined to root him out before he found himself lost in memories and depression again. To that end, Jax turned his attention to his godsons.

"The first one of you to finish his lunch without making a mess gets to ride in my car to the festival tomorrow."

The boys' eyes widened. Jax had a red 1969 Ford Mustang with black racer stripes, and they had been asking him for the last two days if he would let them ride in it. He watched in amusement as they settled themselves in their seats and applied themselves to the hot dogs and fries they had ordered. He finished his own meal, pleased that he had managed to do something for Jim and his harried wife. He knew only too well how hard it could be to raise boys. His mother had raised four of them, and after his father had been killed, he had had to help her raise his three brothers and his baby sister. He nodded when Annie thanked him silently.

"No problem. I used to be just like them. My poor mother thanked God every day when we grew out of this stage."

They all laughed at that. Jax had never shared much of his life before college with Jim. All his friend knew was that Jax was one of five kids, that his father had been killed in a motorcycle accident, and that his mother now resided in Florida with his sister who was a schoolteacher. Jax hadn't shared the story of his brother, the ex-con, or of the other two who were Army Rangers. Jim had never asked, and it hadn't seemed important to speak of those things. He didn't want to encourage questions that he wasn't prepared to answer.

After lunch, both boys having been models of good behavior, Jax offered to keep them for a couple of hours so Jim could take Annie for her Ob/Gyn appointment. He took them on a boat ride, and by the time they returned, they were tired enough that he didn't need to keep calling them to stay with him. Jim and Annie were ready when they got back to the doctor's office, and they all went home together.

Jax's car was parked on the street in front of Jim's house, and he noted the small gathering of boys eyeing it from across the street on the lake side of the road.

"You boys into cars?" he asked like Captain Obvious, walking over to where they were.

A general murmur of agreement was his response. The twins had joined him and stood on either side of him like bodyguards. He could almost feel them preening with the importance that their particular acquaintance with him afforded them.

"How old is it, mister?" one tousle-headed boy asked.

"It rolled off the assembly line in 1969," Jax told him.

"Wow! That means it's..." he paused to calculate the answer in his head, but another boy beat him to the punch.

"It's fifty-three years old? Wow! It's as old as my dad!"

Jax chuckled. He was not a particularly outgoing guy, but his car invariably garnered him friendly conversation. He knew that if he had chosen to ride his Harley instead, the attention would have been even greater.

"Can we touch it, mister?" another boy asked.

Jax nodded and watched as they all gathered around to trace their hands over the car's lines, admiring with more than their eyes the beauty of the vehicle. He understood their awe and their enjoyment of the car. It was exactly how he had felt the first time his father had brought it home when he was a small boy. After the accident, the car had played a big part in his recovery from the shock of his father's untimely death, and he had channeled his rage and fear into learning everything he could about it—how to repair it, how to maintain it, how to drive it.

Eventually, the boys had to go home, and Jax took his two sidekicks in with him to dinner. Afterwards, he shooed Annie away when she went to clear the table.

"The boys and I have this, don't we, boys?" he told her. "Go put your feet up." He turned to Jim and added, "I'll bet she could use a foot rub."

Once the dishes were done, Jim called the boys to shower and Jax went to the guest room. Annie was asleep, and he didn't expect Jim to be available again for a while, so he checked his emails, and once that was done, he found himself logging in to Facebook and searching for Noah's page. There hadn't been any activity for a while, but he noticed a new posting. It was two months old. Apparently, Noah had been in an accident and was on leave from the string quartet. Jax read the comments on the post, the latest written a week ago, and the hairs on the back of his neck stood on end.

Robin Xavier said, "Noah, I've only just heard what's happened. I'm so sorry, sweetie? Where are you? Please be safe, and call me when you can. <3"

There was no response to any of the comments. What exactly had happened to Noah? Where was he? And who was Robin Xavier? Jax knew that Noah was from somewhere in upstate New York, but he couldn't remember where. He shut down the laptop and picked up his cellphone, lying back on his bed and scrolling between the two pictures he had kept there. Both were of Noah, and he let himself remember how he came to have each photograph...

*It was Thanksgiving Eve, and the college campus was quiet. No one was there, aside from diehards like Jax, who would leave later for his family's home. He'd get there by early morning and spend only a couple of days with his mother and any of his sib-lings who were able to make it back. In the meantime, he had one* last piece of data he needed to verify so that he could finish the article he was revising to submit to his editor for publication at the beginning of the new year. He sighed, wishing he could find a way to simplify his life. He had his fingers in too many pies these days and he was worn thin. Still, if he wanted tenure, he'd have to toe the line.

He'd finished earlier than he had expected and was exiting the library when he bumped into Noah coming in. They'd only just begun to explore the connection between them, but Jax hadn't asked about his Thanksgiving plans. He'd just assumed that Noah, like every other student, was heading home.

"Oh, sorry!" Noah apologized without looking up. "I wasn't looking where..." And then he saw Jax and got tongue-tied.

Jax smiled, his skin warming where they had touched. "No problem." He steered Noah back out into the crisp autumn afternoon, and led him around to the side, away from the sharp breeze and any prying eyes that might still be around. "Why aren't you on your way home?"

Noah blushed. "I spent the airfare on a concert, so I'm stuck here."

Jax frowned. "Why didn't you tell me? I would have..."

"No," Noah interrupted him. "It's fine. My pops says he'll come up tomorrow, and we'll go out for dinner here instead."

Noah's mother had died when he was a very little boy, and he'd been raised by his father, who'd spent his life as a conductor for Amtrak. Now retired, he lived for his son's concerts and for the golf games he could finally afford to play at the club in the community he had retired to.

"I thought you were going to your family," Noah added. "How come you're still here?"

"Finishing an edit for an article. It'll be one less thing to do when I get back," Jax told him, suddenly wishing they could spend even a little time together before he left. "Are you very busy right now, or can you stop by my place for a drink?"

Noah finally held his gaze, his eyes bright with feelings Jax could understand. The last time they'd managed to spend some time together, they'd made out like teenagers, with Jax having to struggle to hold himself in check even as Noah kept pushing him to lose control. The look in Noah's eyes said he recalled it all too well ... and maybe wanted it again.

"You know you don't need to ask, right, Prof?" A teasing smile accompanied the question, and the little dimples in his cheeks made Jax harden in his jeans.

"You like to tease, don't you?" he accused Noah, restraining himself from reaching over to kiss those dimples. "But can you pay the piper?" he wondered, returning the smile in what he knew was a far more predatory way.

Noah chuckled. "Somewhere in there is a joke about me being the piper!"

Jax laughed, his hot breath escaping in puffs of mist on the air. "Cocky bastard!" he said, making Noah laugh with him.

"And you're not?"

The question hung in the air, even as Noah's eyes slid down Jax's front to his tightening jeans. Jax felt the look like a caress, and he watched as Noah reached down as though to touch him. He wanted it more than he wanted his next breath, but he knew, in the part of his brain not overcome by lust, that they were out in the open, that anyone could come around the corner and see them, and that he owed it to Noah to protect him. He stepped away, inhaling deeply and shaking his head gently when Noah stepped closer.

"Not here. Come see me when you're done inside. I'll have dinner waiting for you. We can spend some time together before I leave."

"Deal."

Noah turned, and Jax watched him walk away, waiting until he could move without discomfort before heading out to his favorite Italian restaurant. He knew Noah liked comfort food, and because he also knew Noah's financial situation, Jax always tried to feed him well when they ate together.

Having food delivered on Thanksgiving Eve from a popular restaurant was an exercise in patience, so Jax called in his order ahead.

"Whatever you all have for today's special, for two," he told them, and then went back to his townhouse to set things to rights.

He put a bottle of wine to chill, tidied the magazine rack and cleared the coffee table. Then he set the dinner table ... Noah was worth special treatment, even if he was going to see his dad the next day. Jax thanked his mother silently for making him learn how to set a table, among other things, and as he placed the unlit candles in the center, his cellphone rang. The food was ready for delivery. They checked to make sure they had his address correct, and he wondered when Noah would arrive.

As though he'd conjured him, his doorbell rang and Noah stood just outside, a bouquet of flowers in his hand.

"Happy Thanksgiving! Thought you might like to dress up your table," he said, smiling shyly.

Jax stepped aside so he could enter, and as soon as he shut the door, he pulled Noah in for a kiss. "Thank you. That's really sweet. Happy Thanksgiving to you too. Come through. Food's on the way."

Noah placed the vase with the flowers on the dining table and smiled at Jax.

"Wow! You sure know how to make a guy feel special," he said. "Nice spread. I love that they're not your mother's china."

Jax laughed. "She wouldn't part with those, I'm afraid. Besides, I like these plates ... they're masculine."

"Don't think you need to worry about being masculine, Prof," Noah said, turning to look him in the eye.

*The shot of lust that speared through Jax at that moment matched the hunger in Noah's eyes, but he stayed where he was by the door and waited. He would let the younger man take the lead for now.*

*"D'you mind if I wash up?" Noah asked.*

*"Not at all. You know where to go."*

*While Noah cleaned up, the food came, and by the time he emerged from the bathroom, Jax had set out the containers on the counter.*

*"Buffet style, so we can have more room on the table," he told Noah, and went to get the wine from the refrigerator while Noah took their plates and began to serve them.*

*"You don't have to do that," Jax protested.*

*"I know, but I want to. You got me food. The least I can do is make a plate for you."*

*Jax poured the wine, and they sat down to a delicious repast, but he was too wound up to fully enjoy it. His eyes took in Noah's features, particularly his mouth as he ate and drank. And Jax knew the younger man was aware of his scrutiny, because Noah's heightened color gave him away.*

*"Do your other students know how unnerving your stare can be?"*

*Noah's question gave away his nervousness, and Jax chuckled. "Am I making you nervous?"*

*"I feel like a steak, and you're the starving homeless man on Thanksgiving."*

*Jax laughed out loud at that comparison. And then he almost choked on the wine he had just sipped when Noah added, "I'm ready whenever you are. Just say the word."*

Jax's whole body shuddered as the memory of the rest of that afternoon swamped him. They had kissed and frotted against each other, and Noah had given him the best blow job he'd ever had, before allowing Jax to return the favor.

They'd fallen asleep wrapped around each other, and when Jax woke before Noah, he'd taken a picture of the younger man, his body curled around Jax's pillow which he had drawn up against his chest when Jax had slid out of bed.

The other picture he'd taken as Noah was standing by the door, before he'd had to leave. Jax hadn't dared to kiss his lover before he exited the car at his apartment, but he had watched as Noah walked slowly up the steps to the front door of the house and turned to wave at him. He tooted his horn once and drove off as Noah went inside.

Dredging up the memories wasn't helping him. He was aching with a need that lived just beneath the surface of his skin, ready to pounce on him whenever his thoughts strayed to the man he'd loved and lost. He wouldn't sleep now unless he did something to wear himself out. Checking the time, he saw that it was just past nine. He could go for a run. That would do the trick.

Before he could talk himself out of it, he was jogging across the road to the beach and running along until there was no more beach and he had to take to the running path. He ran the whole length of it, about a mile and a half, and then turned around and ran back. His mind had been blank for most of the run, for which he was grateful. He would take a shower and collapse into bed, and hopefully, it would remain so.

But then he rounded a corner on the gravel path and bumped into another man also out jogging late at night. Jax put his hands out to steady the person, who was shorter and somewhat lighter than he was, noting the hoodie pulled over his head. He assumed it was a man, because he couldn't imagine a woman out running after dark up here where life shut down much sooner than in the city.

"Sorry," the other jogger said.

Jax froze and stumbled back. His mind refused to believe it, but his heart knew who it was. He caught himself before he fell and spoke a name he hadn't uttered in ten years.

♪ 13 ♪

# Chapter 2

## *Noah*

*Tears were for the weak. He was strong.*

It had been a long day, and Noah was tired. Funny how depression worked … some days, he functioned like a regular adult, his body under his control, and life was tolerable. Other days, he lost the plot a little bit, his body making him feel like he was his own ancestor, his mind a jumble of disconnected thoughts, his spirit suffocating under a weight of useless emotion. Which probably explained why he was so tired. He'd spent the whole day battling a sense of loss that even after all this time had swamped him when he wasn't even aware of the flash flood approaching.

Finally, in a last desperate bid to shed the burdensome feelings, he'd decided to go for a run. At least the only people who knew him in town were the older folks, most of whom didn't go out after dark, and almost all of whom were probably in bed if not asleep at the hour he chose to go out.

He looked up as the ghost from his past whom he'd bumped into said his name as though he were asking a question.

"Noah?"

*Shit!* The last person on the entire fucking planet that he had expected to see ever again in life was just sliding the big hands he had used to stop him from falling off Noah's forearms. The places he had touched burned, as though he had acid on his hands. Noah was stunned into silence. What the hell should he say? Should he acknowledge that he recognized the man who was looking as gobsmacked as he felt? Or should he pretend he didn't recognize him and keep running? Neither prospect thrilled him, but he was a grown-assed man now, not a wannabe of twenty-one. He didn't run from his problems or his fears ... well, not all of them.

"Professor Knox. What a surprise!" He may not be running from his problems, but he sure as hell didn't have to face them head-on.

Noah didn't look in the man's face as he offered the greeting. He didn't want to see how Jax—no matter what, he was still Jax to Noah in private—would react to being so formally addressed. Noah knew it was a slap in the face, but he wasn't feeling stable enough to be less aloof right now. He needed a bit of space between himself and the man who had broken his heart ten years ago, the man he had never stopped loving.

"A pleasant one, I hope, Noah?"

Jax's voice was pure sin ... deep and dark, like sexy hellos and midnight love songs. Noah shivered in reaction to the sound sweeping over him. How the hell did this man still, after all this time, have such power over him? He felt mesmerized by the sound and had to shake himself to make a response.

"It's been a long time, sir."

Maybe if he kept denying that they were more than professor and student, he could get through this unexpected meeting, and then he'd never have to see the man again.

Jax sighed, and Noah knew he had hit a nerve. It hadn't been his intention, but he would take it and run with it if it meant he could get away from Jax before he let all the words welling up inside him burst out like a torrent in a storm. He didn't want to be the guy who laid bare his whole soul to the man who had sent him away when he was a junior in college, the man who had given Noah away to a different professor so they would never have to meet for lessons, the man who had told him that they were over.

Noah knew why he had done it, and in the reasonable, logical, objective part of his brain, he knew Jax was right. He loved the man for wanting to protect him, for being willing to sacrifice his love for Noah's safety. But the part of Noah who had loved Jax with his whole soul was still as angry and hurt in this moment as he had been when Jax had turned him away. He still wanted to punch his lights out, to rail at him, to ask him if that was what he thought love was. But this wasn't the time ... there would never be a time for that, if Noah had his way. With any luck, Jax would be leaving town in the morning, and they'd never have to see each other again. He ignored the pain that twisted in his chest at the thought, as though they had never been apart long enough for him to be used to Jax's absence from his life.

Time had managed to cauterize the wound, and on the surface, it had healed. But now, ten years later, Noah had to face reality ... it may be covered by layers of determination and control, but the wound still throbbed, it still ached, and it would most likely burst open again if he spent any more time in this man's company. He couldn't handle the pain a second time … but he didn't want to let Jax walk away again without a fight.

"How have you been?"

Jax's question brought Noah out of his musing. A part of him wanted to be bitter. How the hell did Jax think he'd been? He'd had his heart handed to him by a worldly guy who'd probably gone on to conquer other young guys with his charm and sex appeal.

"I survived," he said, and then wished he'd kept his mouth shut. He hoped that Jax would think he just meant the breakup, because there was no way he was going to talk about the accident. Not with anyone, and especially not with this man. He wasn't ready to have *that* conversation with anyone. He didn't imagine he ever would be.

Silence greeted his words, and he looked up at last, taking in the man before him. Jackson Knox was maybe an inch over six feet tall, with hair as black as a raven's wings, though there was a scattering of gray in amongst the black these days. He still wore the sexy scruff that he had steadfastly refused to call a goatee on his square chin, and he noted how it now also rode up the sides of his jaw. The beard also boasted a few strands of gray, and coupled with the sweet little mustache he now sported that grew in a thin line down to his chin scruff, he looked even hotter. His high cheekbones seemed more pronounced, making his face seem leaner and his nose straighter than before. Noah found his eyes drawn helplessly to Jax's lips, the top one a thin bow that came to a sharp point in the middle, just enough to settle into the dent in the fuller bottom lip. Just looking at Jax's mouth was making him as crazy now as it had done the first time he had seen it up close.

*Fuck! I need to get a damn grip.* Noah upbraided himself even as he licked his own lips in reaction. Jax had yet to respond to him. Time to get a move on. He needed to finish his run, now more than ever.

"You haven't changed at all, have you?"

Jax's words, coming on the heels of Noah's own inspection of him, was almost comical. Clearly, they'd been looking each other over. He should be pleased that he still looked like the energetic twenty-something he had once been, but in addition to a broken heart, he was now also the bitter owner of an impaired limb and unable to play his violin for any length of time. Certainly not enough to handle the heavy demands of all-day rehearsals and endless performances that had made the last nine years of his life at once exhausting and exhilarating. His life had had meaning until six months ago.

"We all change, sir," he said bitterly. "It's just a fact of growing older."

"You're still as beautiful as ever, Noah," Jax said, holding his gaze.

Noah shivered in reaction. Whenever Jax wanted him to know that he was being as honest as he knew how to be, he held his gaze when he spoke. As he was doing now. And how that little gem of knowledge made Noah's heart skip a beat, even as his mind said "Whatever, man!" He shrugged a mental shoulder.

"Thank you." Noah still knew how to be polite, even in the worst of circumstances.

"Well, I'd best let you get going, huh? It was great running into you."

"Same here. Maybe we'll see each other again."

*What the hell is wrong with me? I don't really want to see this man again, do I? After how we ended? After I ran away? After we never talked again?* It seemed his heart was not on board with his brain's demands.

"I'd like that. I'll be here for a couple of weeks."

Noah's heart thumped in his chest so hard he thought he might pass out from it. He nodded, because he couldn't speak, and then turned and ran back the way he had come, sprinting as fast as he could to get away from the man who had managed to break him wide open again with just a few words. By the time he got back to the cottage his father had bought and where they had lived for as long as he could remember, Noah was exhausted. He locked the door after himself, patted his ancient German Shepherd on the head, and went to get a bottle of water from the refrigerator. He swallowed it in a few thirsty gulps and threw the empty bottle in the recycling bin by the kitchen door.

Klinger clacked over to him as he made his way to the bathroom. The dog butted his hand as if to say, "One pat isn't enough," and Noah laughed as he stopped and gave the dog some loving. Klinger was a big dog, but he loved to roughhouse, despite his advanced years. Noah let the dog push him over and ply him with doggy kisses until he was laughing madly. Somehow, Klinger always seemed to know when Noah's mood was blue, and he always came through with doggy therapy.

"Alright, monster, I have to take a shower now. If you're a good dog, I'll give you a treat when I'm done. So sit."

Klinger sat immediately, cocking his head to the side in inquiry.

"Good dog! Now stay!"

Klinger lay down, his head on his paws, and prepared himself to wait. It never ceased to amaze Noah how much the animal seemed to understand. He walked into the bathroom, leaving the door ajar, and set the water temperature while he brushed his teeth. Then he stepped into the shower and ran his hands all over his sweaty body, rinsing off the dog hairs before lathering a washrag and scrubbing his body. He squirted shampoo into his palm, rubbed his hands together, and reached up to wash his hair. From nowhere, the memory of Jax standing before him, eyes closed while Noah washed his hair, made him instantly hard.

He and Jax had only ever showered together a few times after they made love. He'd slept over at Jax's place on a couple of those occasions once they'd finally gone all the way. It was a revelation to Noah, and he had loved opening himself to Jax in that way. And when, just before dawn that last time, Jax had let him top, Noah had fallen all the way in love with the man who had begun to steal his heart from the very first moment of their meeting.

Inhaling sharply, he finished washing his hair and stepped out of the shower, drying off hurriedly and stepping back into the hallway with the towel wrapped around his middle. There was no way he was rehashing any of his past with the sexy professor. It wouldn't make a difference. They hadn't seen each other in ten years, and both had moved on. Jax must surely have found someone else to love by now, someone to replace him. That thought made Noah gasp, as though he'd been punched in the gut. Klinger heard the sound and stood up, bumping him in the leg and looking up into his face.

"I'm fine, boy, don't you worry!"

He dragged on a pair of shorts and a tank top, fed Klinger a treat from the not-so-secret stash he kept in his bedside table drawer, and threw himself across his bed, suddenly unable to form a coherent thought. Reaching for the remote, he switched on the television and scrolled through the channels, looking for something to distract him until he fell asleep. Reality shows and animal antics couldn't hold him, and even BBC America's documentary series on Earth's habitats and life forms, which normally he loved, left him cold. He wasn't in the mood for police procedurals, or vintage comedy, and the pseudo-porn on Cinemax and HBO made his skin crawl. His mind just would not settle.

Finally, he got up and went for a bottle of water, chugging it on his way back to his bedroom. Why wouldn't Jax leave his head space? He needed to do something, or he'd be a wreck in the morning, and he had scheduled his first private lesson for ten o'clock. He grimaced. He wasn't looking forward to teaching anyone to play an instrument he no longer could play for more than half an hour at a stretch without suffering for it. Maybe he should have offered piano instead of violin lessons. He could play enough for kids to take their exams and enter college with more than enough expertise to study it. He was no classical pianist, nor a virtuoso, but he could hold his own.

Turning back in the doorway of his bedroom, he went back to the small living room where his instruments lived and sat before the upright piano. His grand piano was in storage until he decided what he was going to do with his life. And the violin leaning against the wall in its case was not the one he used for performances. He let his fingers trail over the keyboard, trying to lose himself the way he used to be able to do, back when he was principal violinist understudy in one of Broadway's finest orchestras, before his work with the Barrington String Quartet took off. Back before the accident, before he was crippled.

Hot tears stung his eyelids as the memories rose up like ghouls to shout at him in impotent fury. He swallowed them. Tears were for the weak. He was strong. He had survived a horrible crash and debilitating rehab. He would survive this pain as well. He struck a chord and let that guide him in what to play. But the music was all wrong, the notes jangling like broken wind chimes in his ears.

*"Let go, Noah. Feel the notes. Feel the rhythm. Feel them like rain on your skin, like fingers in your hair, like kisses on your lips. Let them touch you where you want to be touched in this moment. Let go and let them be in you. Let them be you."*

Jax's voice spoke quietly into his tortured mind, his presence almost as real as the stool on which Noah sat, as powerful as the tears that slid unbidden down his cheeks, as seductive as the man who still had his heart. Noah relaxed and wept as he played through the pain in his hands and in his heart. When the piece ended, he closed the piano quietly and curled up on the big old leather couch, dragging the soft throw over himself. He didn't know when he fell asleep.

Mr. Pyle's rooster's morning refrain, followed closely by Klinger's wet tongue on his face, woke Noah much earlier than he might have been awake on a regular day, but he felt no ill effects from less sleep than usual. In fact, he felt almost energized. His hands were sore, his forearms aching, his fingertips still a bit numb, but the weight of the night before seemed to be lifted. He wouldn't look a gift horse in the mouth. He needed to meet his new, and so far only, pupil with a fresh face and bright smile. Whatever had caused the change in that last hour before bed, he was grateful. Rising slowly, as his body still needed time to adjust after a night spent curled up on his couch, he did all his stretches, and went to relieve himself in the half bath reserved for guests. Then he made some coffee and let Klinger out while it perked.

By the time he had showered and changed, the sun was bright in the sky, and he was ready to take Klinger for his morning walk, knowing he wouldn't need to scoop any poop. He was grateful that his dog knew to keep the solid stuff to their yard. He didn't know how he would manage to clean up after his pet with his clumsy hand in public without drawing attention to himself. And the last thing he wanted was anyone's attention. That always came with a hefty side of pity, and he wasn't in for that.

The path he ran at night was the one he took by day to walk the dog. It was long enough that Klinger would get enough exercise, and short enough that he wouldn't be exhausted when they got back. The dog was fourteen years old, and though he was in good health, he had already exceeded his life expectancy by a year. Noah was grateful for the animal's presence, especially since his dad was away and wouldn't be coming up for the holidays for another two weeks.

"Morning, Noah lad!"

Mrs. Pyle's cheerful greeting pulled a reluctant smile from Noah. She was probably the cheeriest person he knew, always humming and smiling, and had been so since he was a small boy.

"Good morning, Mrs. Pyle!"

Noah waved as he walked away, glad that she was not much of a talker before noon. The streets were beginning to come alive with locals on their way to work as well as vacationers. Noah let Klinger lead the way and followed the dog slowly, letting the peace of the morning enfold him. In the light of day, his encounter with Jax became less threatening, though he was still unsettled by it. Would they meet again? Where was Jax staying? His thoughts wandered as aimlessly as his dog did, and before he knew it, they were standing together on the end of the pier, looking out over the wide lake.

"Good to see you out and about, Noah! How's your father doing?"

Another cheerful voice broke into his thoughts, and Noah turned to see his dad's drinking buddy, Herbert James, walking his little Pomeranian.

"Dad's fine, thank you, Mr. James. He'll be up in a couple of weeks."

"About damned time, too," the older man retorted. "How am I supposed to win at poker if he's not around to beat?"

Noah laughed. The men played for beer, and one or the other of them always ended up paying the tab on their nights out. Noah wished he had even one friend like that. Mr. James and his dad had been friends forever, it seemed like, and nothing but death was likely to break them apart.

"How long are you staying this time, son?"

Noah winced. In the last eight years, his summer stays had been shortened by his hectic performance schedules, and he had barely had enough time to spend the odd weekend with his dad. Now, he'd be there for the foreseeable future. He had never spent a winter in the cottage, but no one else needed to know that he was thinking hard about doing so for the first time. Swallowing the ache in his chest, he said, "All summer this year, Mr. James."

The older man smiled. "I'll bet your dad will be thrilled."

Noah smiled, not knowing how to answer that comment. His father didn't know that he was no longer with the orchestra. That was a bit of news that he had not felt ready to share in an email or over the phone. He didn't know how his news would be received, and he admitted that part of his anxiety was dread at having to tell his father, who had worked and sacrificed to get Noah to where he had once been, that his son had failed, and that he would no longer be the concert violinist his dad had been so proud to show off to his friends.

"I'd better get going, Mr. James," he said, suddenly unable to be in anyone's company. "Have a real nice day, sir."

He hurried away, not waiting for an answer, hoping the older man wouldn't be offended by his sudden and hasty retreat. When he got back to the cottage, Klinger was panting madly, and Noah felt a surge of guilt that he had rushed the dog back home with no concern for his aged limbs and heart.

"Sorry, monster," he said, crouching to hug the dog before pouring food and water into his bowls.

Not knowing what to eat, he chose cold cereal, and after adding too much Frosted Flakes to the bowl, he poured cold milk over it and went to sit before the television again. The news was on, and Noah ate distractedly, watching the latest madness in the world and wishing he could feel something other than despair. Switching it off, he rinsed his bowl and spoon, set them to dry in the dish rack, and went to gather the things he'd need for the music lesson. The little girl would arrive at ten, and because she had already begun to learn the violin, he'd have to test her first to see how far along she was so he could tailor the lessons to suit her needs. He prayed silently, as he tidied the living room, that this would be enough to distract him from sad thoughts, at least for an hour. Once she left, he'd have to figure out how to spend the rest of the day without thinking about Jax and what might have been.

# Chapter 3

## Jax

*I'm looking for someone I used to know.*

"Settle down, you two," Jim scolded his sons as they tussled in the back seat of Jax's car. He shot them a reproving look, and the boys sat back. "Strap yourselves in," he added, and waited until they did before turning back around.

Jax looked at them in the rearview mirror. The booster seats they were sitting in raised them high enough that he could see the happy grins on their faces. He remembered being this excited about going out when he was a kid, so he couldn't help the grin that creased his cheeks. Summertime was the time for carefree ways and fun days, and today the boys were going with him to see the start of the Windjammer festivities.

"If I have to keep calling to you guys, you're grounded for the rest of the weekend."

Jim spoke sternly to his sons, who stared back at him wide-eyed. The Windjammer Festival was one of the highlights of summer on the lake, and if they were grounded, it meant spending their days with their next-door neighbor Mr. Morris, a crotchety old man who would make their little lives miserable with work around the house and yard. Jax watched as they nodded solemnly and prayed that he'd have no reason to complain. They could be rambunctious, but they were just a couple of cool little boys who simply needed an outlet for all their pent-up energy. And with Annie so close to giving birth, Jim's attention was rightfully centered more on her than on his sons. Jax was happy to help in any way he could.

Annie appeared just then at the front door. "Don't forget the snacks!" she called out.

Jim hurried back to get the bag she held, kissed his wife soundly, whispering something in her ear that made her blush, and then came back to put the things in the trunk. Jax touched the horn and they all waved as he moved off. He headed to the side parking lot by the hotel that was on the lakeshore, knowing they'd opened it for a small fee for visitors to the festival. He parked as close as he could to the pier, and Jim led the way down to the gate where they paid their entry fee, got their arm bands, and sauntered in. The place was already hopping with crowds of tourists and locals, but Jim insisted that the boys take a potty break so they wouldn't have to stop too soon.

Jax enjoyed the friendly atmosphere and the energy of the event. He stood by the railing and watched as a big yacht flying a Jamaican flag maneuvered itself into position alongside an equally big one with a helicopter perched on an upper deck.

"Dad! Look!" Jake, named after Jax, pointed to the big boat with the helicopter. "Do you think it really flies?" His voice was filled with awe.

"I'm sure it does, buddy," Jim said.

"Why do they need a helicopter when they have such a big boat?" Jude wanted to know.

"I dunno, son. Maybe they want to be able to fly over and see the ocean from the air."

The boys kept their eyes trained on the chopper as though willing someone to get in and lift it away. Jim eventually got them to move on, bribing them with ice pops when they stopped for the third time to watch the big yacht with the chopper. They wanted to know if the people on the boat were the owners and if they could go talk to them. Jim managed to dissuade them, and Jax followed along, losing himself to the carefree spirit of the place.

From nowhere, thoughts of Noah invaded his mind, and he found himself wondering what it would be like to hold hands with his man as they strolled along the pier, admiring the boats, inhaling the smell of greasy foods and sugary treats, enjoying the artworks on display. They had never had a chance to be together in that way before he had called a halt to their affair. The closest they had come to enjoying public time together was when Jax had gone to see Noah at the annual students' Christmas concert, a few months before he had called things off between them. The faculty had mingled with the student musicians, and he had managed to spend a few precious moments with Noah where he could let the younger man know how deeply he was coming to feel for him …

"You were brilliant this evening, Noah," he said, smiling at the gorgeous young man standing before him, his violin case in his hand. "I couldn't be prouder of you."

"Thanks, Prof," Noah said, mindful of the people milling about.

Jax could see that he wanted to say more, and he himself was barely managing to resist the urge to lean in and kiss Noah's plump lips. He stepped back a pace and turned to look around. People were moving about in the hall, chattering and laughing happily.

"Let's go get something to eat. Maybe we can find a quiet place to chat for a few minutes."

Noah nodded and followed Jax out of the auditorium to the tables set up with food. "What would you like?" he asked. When Noah began to object, he added, "No refusal. You can't serve yourself and carry your violin."

Eventually, after they'd each made their choices, Jax had found a quiet spot on the balcony outside the hall. There were one or two other people also there, but he managed to situate them so they would not too easily be seen. He didn't want to examine too closely the reason he'd chosen the spot, and he was grateful that Noah didn't object.

"So, what are your plans for Christmas?" he'd asked, watching as Noah dug into the food on his plate.

"Since I missed Thanksgiving, I'm going to my dad's for Christmas. But I have to come back right after New Year's because there's that public concert I promised I'd do with the school district's concert orchestra. We'll need to rehearse with them for it."

"Yes, you will. That's a good thing you guys are doing. The kids will love that they're playing with a college orchestra."

Noah lowered his eyes for a moment, then looked up at Jax again. "Will you be back in time for it?"

The question was shy and tentative, and Jax could hear the hope he was trying to disguise in his voice.

*"Would you like me to come back for it?" He'd already decided that he would return in time for the concert, but it would be nice to hear Noah say he wanted him there.*

*Noah smiled. "You know I would. Why do you even ask?"*

*"Maybe I want to make sure. Youth is fickle, you know."*

*"If you say so, Prof," Noah teased, knowing Jax hated it when he called him that in private.*

*"Don't forget payback, babe," Jax said, raising a brow at him, and chuckled when Noah pretended to pout.*

*And then his blood pressure soared when Noah added, with a sly grin, "What makes you think I've forgotten?"*

*Only the fact that a group of students wandered past just then stopped Jax from pulling Noah into a hot kiss. His body hummed with the need to kiss the younger man on his pretty mouth, to devour him and own the grin that creased Noah's cheeks…*

This wouldn't do. He hadn't come all this way to lose himself in thoughts of a man he had given up. Jax refocused his attention on his surroundings. Unbeknownst to him, they had come to a halt at the barricades that separated the pier from the main road, along which the parade was to pass. He could hear the marching bands and craned his neck to see where the floats were. People had begun to gather, and he and Jim put the boys to stand in front of them. Jim had bought them extra-large ice cream cones, and they were busy making sure that not a drop was wasted. Jax grinned as he saw their tongues busy lapping up every stray drop of the multicolored ice cream in the huge waffle cones they held.

"They're gonna be a handful later," Jim said. "Unless we can find a way for them to work off all the energy this sugar rush is gonna give them."

"I wouldn't worry too much about that," Jax told him. "The parade will last a good couple of hours at least, and after that maybe we can let them loose to swim before lunch. I saw a sign about swimming as we were coming in."

"Okay. As long as when we get back home, they're too tired to harass their mother. I just spoke to her, and she's loving the quiet."

Jax laughed. "When is she due exactly?"

"Another month, but if this one is anything like the boys were, she'll be at least a week early."

"I guess you're not gonna leave her side much for the next few weeks, huh?"

"Nope. In fact, you're on your own after today, my friend. I need to keep close to her, in case she needs me."

"No problem. I'm sure I can find enough to occupy me before I have to leave."

He looked back up the road where the sound of music grew louder, and he could see the first of the marchers approaching. It was a band, and he felt his spirits settle as he let the music wash over him. This band was clearly experienced, and their playing was flawless. He smiled as he recognized the tune they were playing.

"They're pretty good, aren't they?' Jim said, nodding toward the band.

"Better than that, Jim. These guys are masters. Have any idea who they are?"

Jim shrugged. "I dunno. Probably the college band."

Jax's heart sped up for some unknown reason and he glanced around him sharply. Someone was watching him, but he had no idea who or where the person was standing. He kept looking around but could see no one, and when Jake tugged on his shirt to get his attention, he looked down at the little boy.

"Did you ever play in a band, Uncle Jax?" he asked.

"For a while in high school, yeah, Jake."

"Did you like it?"

"It was fun, until I got bored with it, yes." Jax chuckled at the memory of how quickly he lost interest.

"What did you play?"

"The clarinet," he said.

The marching band was much closer now, and Jax could see their brightly-colored uniforms. They were executing a dance move as they played, keeping time with the rhythm of the music while showing off their finesse with their instruments and their ability to multitask. Jake had turned his attention back to them, and once again he felt eyes boring into him. Jax turned away from the advancing group and concentrated, searching through the thickening crowd around him, turning to look everywhere ... and then he saw him. Noah.

He was standing almost directly behind Jax, his eyes boring into him, dark and unreadable. Jax felt the immediate reaction to Noah that had always kicked his heart rate up whenever they were together in the past. The fact that even after ten years he was still so susceptible to the younger man did not bode well for his resolve to move on with his life. Noah was no longer his, had not been his for a decade, and he would not let any unresolved emotion send him hurtling back into the dark place that had taken him years to free himself from. He'd been too old for Noah back then, and his chance with him was certainly long gone now, wasn't it? It was best he remembered that.

He closed his eyes, willing his body to calm down. It had heated up even more, and he was almost dizzy with the combination of his emotions and the heat of the day.

"You okay there, buddy?" Jim's concerned voice had him opening his eyes at once and clearing his throat.

"Yeah, just a little hot. I'll go get something to cool me down. Want anything?"

"Water's good," Jim said, turning back to listen to something Jude was saying. Jax walked away, avoiding going anywhere near Noah. He remembered passing by a shaved ice truck to his left, down on the boardwalk as they were coming in. He headed over and stepped gratefully up to the window, thankful no one else was in line.

"I'd like your largest mixed flavor shaved ice, please, and a bottle of water."

After he paid for the items, he stepped away from the window and took a big bite of the icy treat, letting it melt on his tongue before swallowing, hoping to cool the fever of his thoughts before he had to return to Jim. He walked slowly back to where his friend stood, sucking on the sweetened ice, aware that Noah was still somewhere in the crowd, probably watching him. Resisting the urge to look for him again, he handed Jim the water and resolutely looked at the passing parade. But when he swallowed the last of his icy treat, he turned to see if he could find Noah in the crowd, because he couldn't bear the need pulsing in him to look his fill on his last chance at love, even if he had lost it.

"Parade boring you, bro?"

Jim's sardonic question brought his focus back around to the spectacle passing by them. There was a float going by now, though Jax had no idea what it was supposed to represent. He scrambled for something to say to explain his distraction.

"No." *I'm looking for someone I used to know.* "Someone bumped into me."

He looked over his shoulder again, and Jim gave him a look that said he was full of it, following his gaze to where Noah had last been standing. Relief shot through Jax when he couldn't see him there. He wouldn't have to explain anything; he could keep his secret. Unless and until Noah showed any sign of wanting to renew their acquaintance, despite his words from the night before, Jax wouldn't make any moves. He'd given up that right when he'd walked away all those years ago.

"Bound to happen at these kinds of events," Jim said, smirking at him.

Jax shot him the bird but smiled, glad for the brief respite from the tension riding across his shoulders and down his spine. Noah was here. Why the hell hadn't he thought of that? He would at least have prepared himself for the possibility of seeing him again. It wasn't as though the town was so large that they could miss each other at this festival. He tried to focus his attention on the float that was now approaching, but a few minutes later he felt that same prickling at the back of his neck, and he knew without having to look that Noah was back.

He looked around again, trying to be surreptitious about it, but Jim turned with him, following his gaze.

"Who was the hottie glaring daggers at you, bro?" his friend asked.

Jax hunted around in his suddenly vacant head for a convenient lie but before he could fashion a believable one, he heard his name called and he swung in the opposite direction and came face to face with one of the last people he had ever expected to meet again.

"Jackson Knox, as I live and breathe!"

The man calling him by his full name was a handsome, burly man with a full head of thick silver hair and a beard that was as dark as the hair on his head was not. Jax sighed and plastered a smile on his face. Gordon Monroe was Emeritus Professor of Music at The Prescott School and Jax's one-time mentor. He was a harmless enough fellow these days and a brilliant jazz musician, but Jax could never forget how the man had made a pass at him that had left him not only disgusted but reeling from disappointment.

*And yet, despite all that, you went and had an affair with a student!* The thought slammed into him unbidden, and he gasped at the pain it caused, prompting Jim to turn to him and ask, "You okay there?"

Jax nodded and caught his breath before saying, "Just lost my wind for a second." No way was he going back to those memories here or now. He turned to the older man standing there clearly waiting to be introduced and said, "Jim, this is Professor Gordon Monroe, virtuoso jazz pianist. Gordon, my friend Jim Bell."

"A pleasure to meet you, Mr. Bell," Gordon said, shaking hands enthusiastically.

It had been decades since Jax had seen the man standing before him, but he could still feel the residual disgust he'd felt when his then-mentor had groped him backstage after a rehearsal. He was reluctant to shake hands with him now, wondering if the professor had overcome the impediment—rumor had it—that had ultimately led to his being forced to retire.

"It's good to see you again, Jackson," the older man said, bringing Jax back to the moment.

He had his hand outstretched and Jax stiffened his spine before taking it. He kept the handshake brief and slid his hand away as soon as he could.

"How have you been?" the man continued, ignoring the parade going by. "I've followed your career since you graduated. A doctorate from Eastman and a stellar career. I always knew you had it in you."

Jax didn't know what to say and settled for "Thank you." The thought that this man knew anything at all about him was unsettling at best, repulsive at worst.

"Rumor has it that you've left Rochester. Where are you headed?"

Jax was damned if he'd tell this man anything he didn't already know. "Just taking a break for now," he answered casually, but turned his eyes to Jim's face, hoping his friend would get the message and not offer any further information.

"Uncle Jay, can we go see the boats now?"

Jax's shoulders heaved in relief at his godson's interruption. "We sure can, Jude."

He turned back to Gordon. "Well, it was good catching up, but I promised the boys I'd take them to see the boat show. Enjoy the rest of the parade." He managed another fake smile and said to Jim, "You coming?"

Jim nodded and said his farewells, only speaking again when they were standing in the boatyard and the boys were entranced by the pictures of the boats currently berthed in the harbor. Jax kept an eye on them even as Jim said, "Hmm ... you have anything you'd like to share?"

Jax shrugged. "Like what?"

"Oh, I dunno ... like why you hauled ass away from the oily professor just now. Or why the sexy dude was glaring at you like he'd happily murder you."

"Oily professor?" Jax glommed onto that. "What makes you say that?"

"He was eyeing you like the finest New York steak, and you barely gave him the time of day." Jim paused, then asked, frowning, "Is he the guy who was harassing you?"

Jax chuckled. "No. That guy is my age. Gordon ... happened earlier, when I was still a student."

Jim's eyes bugged out of his head. "Are you saying what I think you're saying, bro?"

"I don't know what you think I'm saying, but it's probably not as extreme as you're imagining. He just had a bad case of the wandering hands. Google him … you'll see all the stories. Just know, they're probably all true."

"Dad, can we go on this one?"

Jake came and tugged at his father's hand. Jim looked down to see which one the boys wanted to tour and nodded. "Wait just a minute," he said and turned back to Jax to add, "We'll finish this conversation later. Come on, before they cause an international incident."

Jax nodded, grateful for the reprieve, even though he knew it was short-lived. He'd have to come clean to his friend about Noah. The question now was how would he keep Jim from finding out that the feelings he had buried for so long were not dead?

# Chapter 4

## Noah

*He had thought he'd be over Jax by now.*

"Sorry!"

Noah sidestepped the man carrying the toddler while the woman walking beside him pushed a stroller with an infant asleep under a parasol. The man nodded absently, listening as his son asked for whatever treat they were passing by. He kept walking, trying not to think about why he had stopped to stare at Jax who had been with another guy and a couple of boys. Why hadn't he thought about the fact that the man would be here at the parade? For Pete's sake, this event was one of the highlights of the summer season in town, so why *wouldn't* Jax be there? The town thrived on the income that the three-day festival brought with the increase in visitors who spent a lot of cash.

He should never have stopped to look, but the sight of the man he still loved—even if he'd never admit that to another living soul—drew him like a magnet. What had Jax thought when their eyes had met? Had he been as poleaxed as Noah had been? They were bound to meet again before Jax left to wherever he was headed, and Noah needed to figure out how to deal with that. He wanted to avoid the other man as much as possible, but he also wanted to get his attention, get him talking, tell him everything he'd kept in his heart for the past ten years while he'd made a name for himself as part of the acclaimed Barrington String Quartet.

Making a snap decision, because he knew thinking too hard on it would send him running again, he turned back but Jax had gone. He was determined to find him this time, though, so he made his way methodically through the crowd, enjoying the warmth of the sun on his face and arms. He'd always been a sun-lover and today it seemed the heat was loosening the chains that he'd wrapped around his heart.

The crowds around him made his body hum with a kind of excitement he usually only felt when he was preparing to perform. And since he hadn't done that in months, he was hard pressed to understand why that was. Surely it couldn't be because he'd seen Jax again? He'd run away the first time they'd bumped into each other, and he'd been determined to keep his distance, but now he was almost impatient to find him again. Which made no sense whatsoever. The parade was winding down, but there were still a few floats left. Hopefully, Jax and his companion would still be around watching it.

Had he moved on? Was that guy his husband? The thought filled Noah with renewed pain, after his meltdown a few nights earlier. He had thought he'd be over Jax by now, but if the way his body was reacting was any indication, he'd been fooling himself for the last ten years. And even the anger that still simmered in him languished behind the other more pressing ones that had been bombarding him since that fateful meeting on the jogging path.

A cheer rose up from the crowd to his left and he turned to see what all the fuss was about. A performer on stilts was juggling and making balloon animals which he was passing out to the children gathered around him. Moving closer, Noah scanned the group and found the man he was looking for smiling down at one of the boys who had been with him earlier. The child said something that made Jax laugh and then, as if he sensed he was being watched, he looked up and their eyes met a second time.

*Holy Mother of God!* The impact of those dark eyes on him remained as potent as they'd ever been, overlaid by a flash of pain that Noah could well understand. Noah unglued his feet from where they were stuck to the ground and walked to where his former lover stood, never taking his eyes off him. *What the hell am I gonna say to him?* Drumbeats of tension pulsed in his chest, and he knew that his sucking in air like a drowning man had nothing to do with the escalating temperature of the summer day.

"Noah! Hi."

Jax's awkward greeting pulled Noah's lips into a reluctant smile. *Well thank fuck! At least he's as lost for words as I am.* He was sure he could do better than that.

"Hi. I saw you and your..." Well, maybe he *couldn't* do any better because was he really going to low-key fish for information about Jax's marital status?

"My best friend Jim and his kids."

Jax's smile widened as though he knew Noah's secret, but he only turned to his friend and made the introductions.

"Jim Bell, meet Noah Santiago, a former student."

Noah refused to let that hurt. Jax hadn't lied, and maybe it was better for the two of them if he didn't offer up any further information about how they knew each other. Besides, he shouldn't be wanting Jax to introduce him as anything else. Too many years of silence had passed between them for there to be anything other than professional interest. And even though they had been lovers before Jax had painfully yanked the rug out from under him when he'd ended their affair, no one else needed to know how far along that forbidden path they had traveled.

"It's a pleasure to meet you, Mr. Bell," he said, summoning up a smile.

"Same here, Mr. Santiago. And just Jim, please." Jim Bell's wide grin was infectious as he turned to the boys standing between him and Jax. "These two are my boys, Jake and Jude. Say hello, boys."

A simultaneous "Hi!" greeted him before the boys turned their eyes back to the juggler on stilts. He was moving around the circle now handing out tickets to the circus show later in the day. Stepping forward eagerly to get their own tickets, the taller of the two by a smidge—Jake, he thought—asked,

"Can we go, Dad? Please?"

His brother joined in the chorus of pleading, and Jim relented. "I'll text your mother and see if she'll be fine for another couple of hours."

He stepped away to send the message, leaving Noah standing with Jax, utterly at a loss for words. This was not like he had imagined their reunion would be in those early days after the breakup. There was no kissing, no strong hugs and tears of relief and happiness. There was only caution and a healthy dose of fear, intermixed with a powerful, reawakened need to return to the way things used to be.

"Are you enjoying the festival?" That was better. At least they could talk about what Jax liked for a minute before silence would swell between them again.

"It's a great day out, sure," Jax said, his eyes steadfast on Noah. "The boys are having a blast and their mother is loving the quiet at home."

Before he could say more, Jim came back. "Annie says it's fine as long as we bring back dinner for her."

"These boys won't last until dinnertime. Maybe we need to feed them now."

Jim chuckled. "You aren't wrong. So, Mr. Santiago, are you from around here?"

Noah felt his face heat up and ignored it. What did he have to be embarrassed about? "Noah, please. Yeah, kind of. My family moved up here when I was little, but I haven't lived here since I went off to college more than ten years ago."

Jim's intelligent eyes lit up. "Ah! So, you know Good Eats, yeah? Care to join us for lunch?"

This hadn't been in his plan, but Noah nodded anyway. What better way to ease back into an acquaintance with Jax than in the company of Jim and his sons who would help keep him out of his head and kill any awkwardness that might spring up between them? He had no way of knowing what Jax was thinking or if he was even interested in more than catching up, but it was probably for the best anyway, if they just tried to renew the friendship that they'd lost.

"Excellent!" Jim rubbed his hands together. "I already know what Annie will want. Jax, you're in for a treat." He turned to get his sons' attention. "Come on, boys! We're heading out for lunch." He looked back in Jax's direction. "We may have a bit of a wait if we don't get there before the rush, but I promise it'll be worth it."

As predicted, there was a line of people waiting to get into the popular eatery when they got there. Jim went in to request seating for five outdoors and within minutes they were being led to the very last empty table, close to the sandy walkway that led down to the beach. The umbrella over the table gave some shade from the sun, but the heat was relentless. Only the breeze off the water made it bearable.

"So, Noah, are you a music teacher as well?" Jim's eyes were curious as he looked across the table at Noah.

How to answer without going into details he wasn't sure Jax wanted shared ... that was the question. "I'm a professional of a different sort," he began, choosing his words carefully. "I've played on Broadway and in a string quartet."

"Broadway! Wow! That's impressive. Do you still work in New York City?"

*That's not the question you should be asking.* Bile rose in Noah's throat at the bitter emotion welling in his chest. "I...I'm on hiatus." Which wasn't a lie, exactly, though he knew Jax had noticed his hesitation. He *was* taking a break, right? That he had no idea what he would do with the rest of his life because the accident had made it impossible for him to continue to play professionally was moot at this point.

"What's your instrument?"

"I play violin professionally, but I also play piano."

"I can imagine if you're working every night all year long that your hands and arms need a break once in a while."

Noah smiled. In a way, Jim was right. Violinists often suffered from nerve pain, carpal tunnel pain and other work-related injuries, and not just in their hands and arms. He had tried his best to take care of his body, but since the accident, he'd let his fitness routines lapse and despite the physical therapy he had had in the first few months after the accident, he knew he wasn't in the best shape. Even if there was a chance that he could still play a sustained piece of music for any length of time in the future, he couldn't do it now.

"Most folks don't realize that," he agreed, hoping the man would let the subject go.

Their server arrived just in the nick of time, and between settling his sons down and placing orders for them, his wife, and himself, he was distracted from further questions. Noah ordered his favorite childhood meal from the restaurant ... a Johnny Marzetti with a side of Caesar salad.

While they waited for their food, Noah learned that Jax and Jim had known each other since they were kids, but had grown even closer when they'd ended up in the same college and Jax had come out as gay. Jax had never shared this story with him, and he felt a momentary prick of jealousy that Jim knew things about him that Noah didn't. *Don't be an ass, hijo. There's stuff he doesn't know about you, either!*

"Did you play in a marching band like Uncle Jax?"

Something *else* he didn't know. How had he thought he loved a man he didn't know such basic information about? Had it just been lust? After all, he hadn't been quite twenty-one the first time he'd met Jax, and it wasn't as though they'd had a torrid love affair. They had only been to bed twice before Jax called it off, and outside of that, they'd talked mostly about work and Noah's life. He looked over at the boy waiting for his answer.

"No, I wasn't that cool. I only played in my school's orchestra."

He had never been interested in the marching band, but the kid didn't need to know that. Better to let him believe that Noah thought that band was cooler than orchestra if that would keep Jax as the cool uncle. But Jax's sardonic chuckle washed over him like ocean waves on a summer day.

"Don't let him fool you, Jake. The cool kids were all in orchestra, and they knew it."

"So you only played in the band? I assumed you were an orchestra kid, Prof."

The nickname slipped between Noah's lips without a thought. What was he supposed to call him? How much would it take for his friend to know that Jax and Noah had been more than teacher and student together? Was that something either of them wanted him to know? Noah sure as hell didn't.

He looked up to find Jax's eyes on him, a sparkle of amusement and something more shining in them. Jax's lips quirked upwards slightly before he turned away at the approach of the server with their drinks. Wishing he could think of something to say to steer the conversation away from himself, he sipped his drink and savored the sharp, refreshing tang of lemon.

"I'd forgotten they also make some of the best lemonade I've ever had," Jim commented as though he was reading Noah's mind, releasing a loud sigh of approval after he swallowed *his* first mouthful.

"Can't argue with that," Jax echoed him.

The boys kept it from becoming more awkward, for which Noah was grateful, though he did wish they weren't as curious about him as their questions proved.

"Do you like playing piano?"

Noah smiled. Even if it hurt to play sometimes, he loved it almost as much as he loved his violin.

"I do. Do you play an instrument?" Time to pull the attention away from his life.

Jim snorted before either of his sons could reply. "You'd sooner catch them playing stick ball on the street than sitting at a piano."

"Aren't there any music programs in their school?" Noah knew that the arts were taking a beating in public schools these days.

"Yes, but it's nothing like what you're imagining," Jim answered with a shrug. "There's a band—not a marching band—in their school and a choir, but that's it. And the boys didn't want to play the only instruments available when they went to try out."

By the tone of his voice, Jim didn't seem too broken up about that. It wasn't a surprise really. Back when he was in elementary school, he'd been picked on because he played an instrument instead of ball.

"They can always pick it up later, if they're interested. What did they want to play?"

"I wanted to play the drums," one twin said while the other chimed in with, "the tuba."

Noah grinned at that. "Yeah, those instruments are tough to get into. In fact, I don't recall the tuba being a choice back when I was in grade school."

The server brought their food just then, and the next few minutes were spent passing around each person's meal. Jim spared an extra minute to remind the boys of their table manners and then they dug in. It had been years since he'd last had a Johnny Marzetti and the creamy mac and cheese combined with the well-seasoned minced beef and Italian sausage mix had him closing his eyes in food bliss. Maybe he should order another serving to take home for dinner, so he wouldn't have to figure out what to make.

"Good, is it?"

Noah opened his eyes then, embarrassed that he'd forgotten where he was in the throes of food ecstasy. Jax's eyes were on him, gleaming with something like what Noah used to read as desire. But that was years ago. A lot of water had passed under the bridge since then, and he was under no illusion that the older man wanted him. He'd made his position abundantly clear on that fateful day when he'd sent Noah packing with his tail between his legs like a whipped puppy. He cleared his throat and sipped his lemonade to give himself time to let loose of the bitter thought.

"Very," he replied and went back to his food.

Jim and Jax carried on a conversation without him, but he heard snippets of what they were discussing. Some older guy had been a perv when Jax was in college ... a professor. Wow! Was *that* the reason Jax had broken things off? The guy had been a repeat offender, apparently, and the behavior had been going on for years before someone squealed and the university put its foot down.

Noah wondered idly if that was the kind of thing the boys should be listening in on, but when he turned his attention to them, they were busily playing some kind of finger wrestling game and managing to get ketchup all over themselves. Maybe he should step in before their dad noticed and they got into trouble.

"You guys better watch it or your dad will get mad that you're making a mess."

He spoke just loudly enough that Jim heard him and turned his eyes to his sons. They immediately straightened up and went back to their food and the conversation became general again.

"You know," Jim pointed a French fry at Noah. "I've been puzzling over why I feel like I recognize you."

Noah stiffened but tried to keep a straight face. He had been happy to remain incognito, but he should have known it wouldn't last long. People may not know him from his Broadway work, but anyone who loved most kinds of music had at least heard of the Barrington String Quartet, because they formed a bridge between the classics and contemporary music and had made a name for themselves in the States and around the world. Thinking of the quartet now and about what he'd lost sent a sharp pain lancing though him and Noah winced, despite his best effort to remain cool.

"You're that virtuoso violinist in the string quartet that's been taking the world by storm lately. Your dad lives over on Pinehill and Crescent, right? A really cool old guy with a lot of stories about the places he's been to in his work. I'll bet you have some stories of your own, huh?"

"Probably not as cool as my dad's," Noah answered with a self-deprecating chuckle. He was nowhere near as good a storyteller as his father, and he hadn't paid as much attention to many of the places he'd been to as he should have because he'd been too caught up in his work, too married to reaching for perfection to stop and smell the roses. "He's the storyteller in the family."

"What's been your favorite place to visit?"

Noah was stumped. He'd been to Europe at least once every year for the last six, usually on tour with the quartet. They'd played concerts in the usual big cities—Athens, London, Paris, Rome—as well as in the Caribbean and across North and South America. The quartet had had to postpone its planned tours of Russia and Dubai because of his accident, and he had been too bitter to participate fully in the choice of his substitute. The woman was only going to be there for the duration of those tours, but Noah had barely had anything to say to her once she'd been auditioned and chosen. They'd spent the last six months getting her up to speed and within the next month or so, they would resume their schedule without him.

Now was not the time to wander off into a pity party. Jim was waiting for his answer, and he suspected that Jax was, as well. He wondered how much Jax knew about his life. He had not tried to find out anything about Jax. He'd had to keep his heart free of that pain, which was why he'd been so focused on work, first in the Broadway musicals and then with the quartet.

"It's hard to choose," he began, stalling for time. "I liked all the places we played in for different reasons." Not a lie at all, but still an evasion and he knew it. What did it matter which country he chose? Jim would forget about him soon anyway. "I really enjoyed it when we played in Athens. I loved Greek mythology in high school, and it was a thrill to actually be able to visit some of the places I'd only read about in English class until then."

"Annie, my wife, will love you." Jim grinned at him. "She's an English teacher and lover of all types of mythologies. And she loves to read fiction that uses them as the base for their characters."

"I take it you couldn't care less?" Noah guessed.

"Let's just say I'm not as … invested as she is," Jim replied diplomatically.

Jax snorted and Noah looked at him. His dark gaze held Noah's own for a moment, and he swore he could almost see Jax's thoughts in them. But he knew he no longer had any idea what his former lover was thinking. It had been too long since they'd looked at each other as more than strangers, and he'd be damned if he let himself hope they could return to those days. He'd been rejected once, and that was more than enough.

# Chapter 5

## *Jax*

*He did care, even if he couldn't
do a damned thing about it.*

Jax was doing his best to keep his eyes off Noah, especially because he could almost see the tension radiating off him like heat off a hot engine. He wished he could help him relax, but as he himself was on a knife's edge, he knew it was best if he kept his mouth shut and his eyes to himself. He kept an eye on the boys instead while Jim quizzed Noah, and he got to hear about the life he had lived these last ten years. Shocked at Noah's apparent lack of excitement about his travels, he'd looked up in time to catch his eye and did his best to keep his emotions off his face.

"Maybe someday you can go back for fun instead of work," Jim suggested.

"Maybe," was Noah's non-committal response.

Jax wanted to butt in, to ask why he wasn't more enthusiastic about his life and the opportunities that he'd enjoyed.

Noah didn't seem to be happy, but Jax couldn't imagine it was because they'd broken things off between them. Well, *he'd* broken things off. Noah was barely into his thirties, and he'd clearly been living a wonderful life professionally, so why was he so … subdued?

"When are you going back on tour?" he asked, intruding into the conversation in which he hadn't taken part so far.

Noah flinched. What the hell was *that* about?

"Not this year. I'm taking a break."

His tone was almost defensive, as though he was daring anyone—Jax—to question his decision. Somewhere in those last four words was a story that Jax was suddenly dying to hear. Noah had disappeared from social media about six months ago, so Jax surmised that something had happened back then that affected his decision to take a break. But what? Jax let his eye roam over Noah, for the first time unconcerned about whether or not Jim would notice. The younger man didn't appear to be sick and from the little he'd said, it didn't sound like he was losing his love for performance. So what the hell was going on?

"The yacht club is offering boat rides in an hour. Who wants to go?"

Jax looked at Noah, who shook his head. "I'm a flaming landlubber," he said almost shyly. "I'll swim, but boats give me the heaves."

"You go with the boys, Jim. I'll stay here with Noah. We can catch up. It's been a long time."

He wasn't going to hide his intention, even if all he wanted was to find out what was going on with the man who was a shadow of the vibrant person he had been in college. Guilt threatened to swamp him at the thought that this might all be his fault, before he gave himself a mental slap. *This isn't about you, Jax!*

"You don't have to..." Noah began, but Jim interrupted.

"Please, you'd be doing me a favor if you let him stay with you. He hasn't been away from us since he got here and I'm sure he needs a break from the boys."

Jax laughed. "When have I ever complained about being with these boys? How about never!"

Jim rolled his eyes at his friend. "Precisely my point. You're not likely to complain because you're in protector mode right now, and you'll do anything to wear them out so they won't burn Annie out." He glared at Jax. "Tell me I'm wrong," he dared him.

Jax laughed again and Jim nodded. "Uh huh! Thought so." Then he turned to Noah and added, "I'm sure you two will have a lot to talk about, both being musicians and all."

They finished up and walked down to the pier where the boat tour signups were located. Jim managed to get three seats on the boat that was getting ready to depart. They'd be out for a couple of hours, which was more than enough time for Jax to get to the bottom of whatever was going on with Noah. He grinned and waved to the boys as they shouted their goodbyes as though they were setting sail for the New World.

"They're hilarious," Noah said, his eyes squinted against the bright sunshine. "How old are they?"

"Eight."

"Why does their mom need time away from them? Is she sick?"

Jax knew what Noah was doing. It wasn't illogical that he'd want to know about the family he'd just had lunch with, but he could also hide behind that interest and keep a wall between them. And while Jax didn't think there was a chance of more than friendship going forward, no matter what his heart might be thinking, he also didn't want there to be any more strain either, especially not now that they'd reconnected.

"She's pregnant. The baby's due soon."

Noah looked up then. "So you're going to be an uncle again, huh?"

Jax chuckled. "Something like that. I haven't seen much of the boys since they were babies, but now that I'll only be a few hours away from the family, it'll be easier."

He'd been steering them toward a bank of benches in the little park alongside the pier and now he sat down, facing the water, his legs stretched out in front of him.

"Have a seat and tell me what's been going on with you."

Noah sat as far from him as he could on the bench, making Jax's heart squeeze in his chest. He supposed it was too much to hope that he'd been forgiven, even after all this time. He would do what he could to mend the fences and hope they could at least go back to being friendly.

"Nothing more to tell than I told your friend. It's been a busy few years, and I'm taking a break."

Jax studied him, wondering if Noah realized that he could still read him even when he tried to keep his guard up. A sure sign that he was lying, or at least not telling the whole truth, was the way he avoided eye contact. They might be on the outs as lovers, but even before they got physical with each other, Jax always knew when Noah was prevaricating.

"Why now? You were never the one to take a break, even when…" he paused, trying to find a comfortable way to say what was on his mind. "Even when you were stretched to the limit by academic and personal issues."

There … that was good. No mention of the times when Noah had fallen dead asleep in the breaks that Jax gave him during their practice sessions. Or the bags under his eyes from insufficient sleep when he'd been burning the candle at both ends with his job and the academic load he chose to carry. No mention of the time Jax had let him sleep as long as he could at his place before taking him back to the apartment that Noah had shared with three other students. No mention of the way he'd been reduced to a ghost of his former self after their breakup yet still managed to graduate *summa cum laude* from the program.

He hated that Noah didn't trust him or want to have anything to do with him beyond being superficial acquaintances. He wanted to be there for him as much as an older friend could be, even one with no special benefits from a more intimate relationship. He knew it wasn't in the cards any longer, but even after all these years, he still cared deeply for the man sitting next to him clearly trying to find a way to shut down the conversation.

"Look, I know you're likely still angry with me about the decision I made," he began and raised a hand when Noah opened his mouth to speak. "And yes, I know the last thing you want to talk about is us, but I just can't believe you're taking a whole year off without there being something seriously wrong, Noah. That's not the man I knew and..."

He bit back the rest of that statement. Even though he knew it to be true, the very last thing he would ever do is admit to Noah that his feelings were more than just deeply caring for him, that he was still as completely in love with him as he'd ever been. Because it wouldn't do to get his hopes up if Noah was kind and didn't rebuff him. Jax was eleven years older, and those years had begun to take their toll in subtle ways. He was under no illusion that a man like Noah, who had only grown more attractive with time, would be hurting for companionship with men his own age or younger.

"I was in an accident," Noah finally said when the silence stretched between them as taut as a trip wire. "I'm on hiatus to recuperate."

Jax sighed. "Is that why you're not touring? How long will the rehab last? Has the quartet postponed going on the road until you're well again?" The way Noah's jaw tightened with each question made Jax fear the worst. "Talk to me, Noah."

"Why? There's nothing you can do about it. And it's not like you care, anyway."

The stinging words of accusation crashed into Jax, breaching the emotional walls he was trying to keep up to protect them both. He *did* care, even if he couldn't do a damned thing about it. Why couldn't he be the man Noah could lean on during what seemed like a grueling time? Why did Noah think he had to go through whatever it was alone, or at least without a friend who would understand his trauma?

"Let's not bring personal feelings into this right now," he heard himself say. "I can be concerned about a fellow musician who is unable to do the thing he loves the most, can't I? Especially when he is a former student of mine?"

*That will definitely put the final nail in the coffin, Jax. He won't even want friendship after that little speech.* Noah's hesitation spoke volumes for his reaction to Jax's words, but there was nothing Jax could do about it now. He really should have been honest about his interest rather than couch it in those terms. How did he expect Noah to regain any trust in him when he couldn't even be honest about his feelings? He wasn't a callow boy, but he sure was acting like one at the moment.

"Look, you don't have to tell me anything you don't want to, but you can at least acknowledge that my curiosity is reasonable. We were ... close once, and I don't want you to think that you're alone in whatever is going on." A thought crossed his mind and the sharp pain it caused had him dragging a hand over his chest. "Unless you're with someone, in which case, I apologize for being pushy."

Why had he just assumed that Noah was currently single? Obviously, he'd be reluctant to share deeply personal problems with anyone other than his lover or close friends. Jax no longer fit into either of those categories, and it behooved him to remember that. The privilege of being let into Noah's confidence had been lost to him that fateful afternoon in his office.

"Are *you* with someone?"

Noah's question took him by surprise. It definitely wasn't anything like what he imagined Noah's response would be, and he was too shocked by it to react as sharply as Noah had reacted to *his* questions earlier. And anyway, what was he keeping a secret? That he was alone and lonely at forty-two? Why did he think Noah would care? His question didn't mean he'd suddenly developed an interest in Jax. *Get over yourself, Prof!* He could almost hear Noah's voice saying those words. He cleared his throat.

"No. There's no one." Least said, soonest mended. He would take a leaf out of Noah's book and offer up as little information as he could. They weren't back to being friends ... yet.

"I'm single as well."

Another silence, broken only by the voices of passersby and sea birds. Jax waited. Noah would tell him, or he wouldn't. If he didn't, Jax didn't know how they would spend the next couple of hours. They had nothing in common anymore except their love of music, and something was making Noah give it up, at least for a while.

"The accident exacerbated some issues I was already having, and I can't play for long periods of time anymore without significant pain, even with therapy and daily exercises. So I won't be rejoining the tour or the quartet, at least, not as the violinist."

Noah's tone was determinedly neutral, but Jax knew at once how deep his anguish must be. Playing wasn't just his job. It was his vocation. It was an extension of who he was as a man. Jax understood that only too well. And the Barrington String Quartet had taken him to heights very few other young musicians had ever reached.

"Damn, Noah! I'm so sorry."

Totally inadequate, as far as responses went, but what the hell else was he to say? What *could* he say that would make the utter desolation Noah must be feeling any less agonizing or the loss any less devastating?

"It's fine."

Jax watched as Noah arranged his features into the caricature of a smile and his heart broke. It was clearly *not* fine, but he wouldn't call him on the lie. Even though he could no longer offer emotional support, at least he could pretend he believed it.

"What will you do now?"

Noah shrugged. "Dunno. I've advertised to give private lessons, and for now that's as much as I can face. Long term, though, I have no idea."

What could Jax say to ease the hurt he could feel seeping through Noah's tightly-held control?

"What are the others saying? Do they have any suggestions for you?"

"We decided to table that discussion until after the concert tours we had scheduled. They were delayed while the guys found a substitute whom they wanted to work with, and now they're full steam ahead for the tour. When they come back, after Christmas, we're supposed to meet to talk about ways that I can continue with the organization."

He shook himself, almost like a dog shaking off water, then finally met Jax's gaze, a rueful smile playing around his lips. Jax stifled the urge to get close enough to wrap his arms around him and kiss that smile wider.

"Well, it's good to know they have your back," he said instead. "In the meantime, you know practice is key, even when you're not performing. And keep up the exercises your therapist recommends." It was easier to slide into instructor mode than allow inappropriate thoughts any room in his head.

"Aye, aye, Captain!" Noah's tone turned sardonic, and the sassy salute he sent Jax's way was full of piss and vinegar. "What about you?"

What about him? "I'm headed up to start a new job at the Riverdale Conservatory."

"Still teaching performance?"

"Yes."

Noah eyed him curiously. "Why did you leave the city?"

Should he be completely honest, or should he fudge the truth? How would Noah react if he told him that aside from being tired of the academic rat race, he was, in fact, avoiding a potentially explosive relationship issue? How would he even explain it without reminding Noah of *their* history? He didn't want to do that, but he also suddenly needed to be transparent. Noah had opened up, so he should, too.

"I needed a change of pace, and I needed to avoid a potential problem with another faculty member." There ... that was not a lie.

"Problem?"

Was it Jax's imagination or did Noah's expression become darker? What was he thinking? The reaction might just be more curiosity, but it might also be more. The thought that Noah might be feeling protective of him warmed Jax's insides, but he couldn't let himself hope. It was too soon, and they hadn't really said anything to make hope a viable option.

"He wanted a relationship, and I didn't."

Noah's face fell before he schooled his features to reflect aloofness. *Shit! You could have said that better!*

"I mean, we weren't *in* a relationship, but he kept pushing for one. And after a while, he began to become aggressive."

"Why didn't you just report him to the university?"

"I wasn't up for all that that would entail. I didn't want the kind of attention it would inevitably bring. Distinguished professors don't make waves unless they're the sort that will bring accolades, not notoriety, to the institution."

Noah shook his head. "I can't believe that kind of thing happens between professors. I mean, you hear of it happening between professors and students, but..."

His shock would have been comical if it weren't for the fact that the rest of the world made the same kind of assumptions about harassment in the workplace. Very few people thought men were ever the victims, and Jax hadn't wanted to have to keep explaining his decision or defending his actions. And he sure as hell hadn't wanted to get into it with people who wouldn't have taken his accusation seriously.

"I'm sorry that happened to you. I'm happy to say it never happened to me."

Noah's eyes went wide almost as soon as he stopped speaking. Was he extending an olive branch to Jax? Were they about to initiate a truce? He was more relieved than he could say that even after all these years, Noah hadn't talked himself into believing that Jax had taken advantage of him. The fear of that had lessened over time, so he hadn't realized that he still carried residual traces of it until Noah's declaration. He fumbled for what to say to encompass the breadth of the emotions he was feeling.

He settled for, "It wasn't fun, so I'm glad you were spared that. I absolutely hated it, so I can't imagine how a younger person must feel. The balance of power in that case is untenable."

Noah reached down for a pebble that sat in front of the toe of his left sneaker. It had an opalescent hue and he twirled it around between his thumb and index finger for a long time as if trying to decide what to do with it.

"It's hard even when there's no harassment."

The comment was a shot to Jax's heart. He *knew* that, God, but he knew that! He'd had no illusions about the effect his actions had had on Noah, but even now, he knew it'd been the right thing to do for both of them. And although the pain of pushing away the man he had fallen for still echoed in his bones, he knew that he had come out stronger, and based on Noah's career, so had he.

"I'm sorry, Noah." The apology slipped out unbidden, unplanned, uncensored. "If I could have found another way to protect you, to protect us both, I would have chosen it. You have to know that."

He'd never had the opportunity to truly apologize for breaking the younger man's heart until now, and he wouldn't be sorry that he'd taken the chance, even if it hadn't been his intention. Noah needed even this much of the truth from him, no matter what happened next between them.

"I know."

Noah swallowed, and Jax watched his Adam's apple slide up and then back down in the elegant column of his throat.

He'd always loved to nip him in that spot where it stuck out like a light switch waiting to be flipped. The memory of Noah's reaction when he did, hit him hard and he looked away. He had to get control over his thoughts and feelings before he made an ass of himself over a few words that probably meant nothing.

"Maybe we can move on now? I never expected to ever see you again, so I have to think that this means we're not meant to hate each other."

Hate? Noah had hated him? *Shit!* The thought shattered what was left of his control but before he could speak, Noah added, "I didn't want to miss you either, but I did, so this is good for that as well."

He had been speaking without looking at Jax, his eyes fixed on some point out in the bay. He turned finally and locked his gaze with Jax's. "So, pax?" He extended a hand and Jax braced himself for his touch.

He managed to withhold his shudder when their hands connected. "Pax."

# Chapter 6

## Noah

*I just wanted a break.*

"That was fun, Uncle Jax!"

One of the twins, Noah thought it might be Jude, raced over to where he and Jax still sat waiting for them. Jax grinned at the boy as he began an excited account of their time on the boat. Noah breathed slowly, deeply, watching the interaction between man and boy and letting his mind wander. Did Jax want kids? Why hadn't he found someone? Had that guy at his last college been the only one to try for something with him? Noah couldn't credit it ... Jax was too damned handsome and charismatic, not to mention talented and in demand, to want for a companion. Did he stay single by choice, or was he just picky?

*Would he have looked at you twice if he'd been picky?* The thought was unwelcome. He wasn't without confidence, but Jax's rejection had done a number on him and now he second-guessed himself about every date, every emotion, every desire. He wanted to blame it all on Jax, but he was also grown enough to know that that would be a lie he told himself so he could feel better. They had both grown older and, in his case, he hoped he'd grown wiser. Maybe this time, they could hold onto friendship.

"Well, I'd better get these boys home." Jim's hearty voice broke into his musings. "Annie just texted that she's ready for her dinner." He smiled at Noah. "It was really great to meet you, Noah. Don't be a stranger. Let Jax know when you can come by for dinner."

Noah nodded, not quite ready to admit that he had no way of contacting Jax. He could remedy that now though. But Jax beat him to it.

"My number hasn't changed, if you still have it."

A flush heated Noah's cheeks. Why did he still, after a decade, remember Jax's number? His burning anger and hurt had made it easy for him to delete it from his cellphone the very same day that Jax had broken up with him, but he hadn't been able to delete it from his memory. It might as well be wired into his DNA.

"I remember it," he confessed, his voice raspy.

He avoided looking at Jax as he got out his own phone and sent him a message:

[Noah: This is Noah.]

Jax pulled his phone out of his pocket and looked down, then looked back at Noah and nodded. "Thanks."

Even after Jim had herded his still-excited sons back to their car and he and Jax had said their goodbyes, it took almost half an hour for Noah to get back home. Klinger was overjoyed to see him and since he hadn't been out all day, Noah took him for a walk. It gave him time to process his afternoon, to think about how it had felt to be where Jax was again, and to obsess over whether or not Jax would call him first. He didn't know what he would say if he chose to break the silence, and part of him still felt the need to hold onto the hurt of their first parting.

The sun was starting its descent, but the sky was still bright with sunshine as he walked along the sandy shore of the lake. A cooling evening breeze blew off the water, and when Klinger bestirred himself to chase after a gull, Noah let him off the leash and watched as his dog played with the birds. Could he ever feel that light-hearted again? Meeting Jax after all these years had managed to upend all the control he'd kept in place once the shock of the breakup had worn off. How could he feel so undone after only a few hours together? And was Jax feeling this way too?

Probably not, he reasoned as he found a piece of driftwood and threw it for Klinger to chase once the gulls flew off. Jax was eleven years older than he was, and a guy in his forties surely had better control of himself. Not that thirty-one was that much younger. Klinger brought the stick back and wagged his tail vigorously in invitation.

"Alright, buddy, go get it!"

Playing fetch with his dog was just what he needed to do to settle his mind. When they finally returned home, the dog was tired enough that he bypassed his bowl after only a few seconds to suck down some fresh water before flopping onto his bed. *Down for the count!* Noah chuckled as he regarded his pet, grateful for the beast and his ability to help keep Noah on an even keel. Maybe *he* should take a nap as well. He was beat after a long day in the sun.

His cellphone vibrating on the nightstand woke him and he scrambled to pick it up, dragging a hand over his face as he did so.

"'Lo."

"Noah? It's Jax." Noah snorted. As if he'd ever *not* recognize the man's voice. "Are you okay?"

"I'm fine. Just woke up from a nap." *Now why the hell did you have to go and tell him that? TMI, man!*

"Summer sun got to you too, huh?" A quiet chuckle accompanied those words. "Just wanted to check in to see if you'd like to go for a drink later." When Noah didn't answer at once, Jax added, his tone carefully neutral, "If you're not already occupied, of course."

Noah huffed. "What exactly do you think I would I be doing? I already told you I'm alone." He hadn't meant to sound quite so pissy. It really was beyond time he reined in the drama queen attitude.

"So, is that a yes?"

And why did Jax have to be so patient with him, like a mature adult, while he sounded like a brat? Biting back the urge to be defiant—because why would he refuse?—he said, "Yes. Where do you want to meet?"

"Jim tells me there's a really nice pub in the hotel by the lake on Overlook Way."

"I know the place." Depending on the night, it would be great for an intimate date ... but he wasn't going to give voice to *that* sentiment because this *wasn't* a romantic date. It wasn't even a regular date. It was just two people catching up, hoping to renew an old acquaintance and perhaps establish a new friendship.

"I'll meet you there at eight?"

A pause ... was he about to change his mind? "How about I come and get you so we don't both have to drive?"

"If it's no trouble, sure."

"It's no trouble, Noah." Jax's voice was almost a purr that Noah could feel stroking his nerve endings. "Text me your address."

That's how Noah found himself rushing to shower and run the razor over his stubble before standing in front of his closet stressing over what to wear out for drinks with his former lover. His former still-sexy-as-hell lover. Jax would look good in anything he chose to wear, while Noah was sure he would look like a hot mess, like the way he felt, anticipating Jax's arrival. Eventually, with fifteen minutes left to go before Jax showed up, he settled on a pair of stone-washed jeans and a band T-shirt. His dark hair needed a trim, but he wasn't about to try to style it with product now. A quick comb through and a damp hand over top to smooth the flyaways, and he was ready.

And not a moment too soon as a knock and the doorbell sounded at the same time.

"Coming!"

He felt his cheeks warm at where his thoughts took him with that word. He hadn't cum in the shower, banishing thoughts of Jax before he did something stupid like jack off to memories that should be long dead by now. He would bet good money that Jax would never jerk off to thoughts of him. Doing his best to calm his fluttering pulse, he opened the door and tried for a nonchalant smile.

"Hey!" *Smooth, Noah, real smooth!*

"Hey yourself! Ready?"

"Yeah. Gimme a sec to check on Klinger."

He didn't really need to check on the dog, who'd raised his head curiously but hadn't moved. He did need the time to talk himself down so he could make it through the evening.

"You be a good boy until papa gets back, buddy," he told the dog, stroking his head for a few seconds before heading out the door.

The sight of Jax's car unglued his tongue from the roof of his mouth. "Wow! I'd forgotten that you had this sweet ride, Prof!"

He didn't even register that he'd used the nickname because he was so busy checking out the muscle car's exterior.

"How old is she again?" he wanted to know after he was strapped into his seat.

"Fifty-three." Pride colored Jax's response.

"She sounds like a girl half her age," Noah said. "How long have you had her?"

He sensed a shift in the air even before he turned to look at Jax's profile.

"Almost three decades. My dad gave her to me as a birthday gift when I was sixteen. I learned to drive stick shift with her and how to repair anything that went wrong, even the big stuff like replacing the clutch when I burned it out. She's my baby, for sure."

Noah's eyes wandered to Jax's hands where they gripped the steering wheel. They sure as hell didn't look like the kind of hands that knew how to do complicated car repairs, but he supposed that if they could play the piano as masterfully as Jax did, they could do anything their owner set his mind to. Involuntarily, his mind went to what those hands had felt like on him, and he shivered. Best not to let himself get mired in memories that would do him no good now.

The hotel parking lot was fairly packed, but Jax managed to find a spot closer to the retaining wall that separated the property from the beach. Noah watched as another couple walked ahead of them into the building, holding hands and smiling at each other. His heart twisted with an impossible desire. He had never held hands with Jax, and suddenly that lost intimacy was threatening to undo the calm he was fighting to build.

"Noah? You okay?"

He looked up to find Jax standing next to him, eyes trained on him in curiosity. "Yeah ... sorry. I'm fine."

The entrance to the pub was separate from the hotel's, brightly lit and inviting. Red and gold neon lights behind the glass, as well as a bright white awning, announced the establishment as The Lake and Inn, a play on the name of the hotel, Inn on the Lake. It was a gastro pub offering homier comfort food choices and fast food for clients who didn't want the fancier French fare served in the hotel's main restaurant, as well as the traditional service of a bar. The dimly-lit space was roughly divided into two parts ... the bar and some intimate booth seating, with not enough space between them for the few drunk dancers who were stumbling around and getting in the servers' way. Noah followed Jax to the bar, where two spots had just opened up and hiked himself up onto the stool.

Loud music poured from a jukebox in the corner close to where they sat, and a couple of customers were hoofing it to the energetic sounds coming from the old-school machine. The waiter, an older guy with a shock of red hair and piercings on each brow, earlobes, nose, and bottom lip, smiled at them as they got comfortable.

"Gentlemen, welcome to the Lake and Inn. I'm Lenny. What's your poison this evening?"

Jax looked over at Noah. "What would you like to drink?"

"I'll have the house dark brew, please." He wanted something robust, but wasn't up to hard liquor at the moment.

"Two house brews, please," Jax echoed him and looked up from the menu to add, "and some loaded fries, if you still have that."

"Coming right up."

The bartender went off to fill their order while Noah looked around, noting that there were several people in the pub whom he knew on sight, mostly older guys who were his father's friends and acquaintances. He had been kept so busy with his work that time at home had been brief, even under the best circumstances. Once he'd left for college, he had only come back for long breaks, especially because those were the times that his dad made sure to be home for him, until he retired and spent half his time in Florida where his family had a homestead.

"What do you do for fun when you're home?"

Jax's question startled him. "Nothing much, really. Usually when I'm home I'm so tired I spend half the time asleep or just lazing around. I try to get in some swimming, though not usually in the lake ... the water's too cold, even in August, and I'm not usually home much in the summer anyway."

"And have you been here since the accident?"

The bartender brought their beers, two glasses, and a plate of fries loaded with gooey cheese, crispy fried onion chips, ginger sticks, and bacon bits. Noah reached for one, popping it into his mouth and closing his eyes at the deliciousness. Mmm ... he could probably eat the whole plate by himself. He'd much rather eat than talk about himself, but that wasn't how friendships were formed, so he swallowed and answered.

"I spent some time at a friend's while I was in active therapy. I've only been home a few weeks."

"And where's your father? How is he taking this turn of events?"

Noah knew that Jax wasn't a fool, and that he had admired the relationship that Noah had with his dad, so he should have been expecting the question. Jax knew his dad spent the summer here so he could spend any time that Noah was free with him as well as do any maintenance on the house that was necessary before he rented it out long-term on his way back down south. When he hesitated to answer, Jax turned on his seat so his knees bumped Noah's thigh.

"Does he know you were in an accident? And does he know what that means for your career?"

Noah sighed. "He only knows about the accident. I haven't told him about the rest."

He could feel Jax studying him. Was he judging him? He probably thought it was a bad idea to keep it from his dad, but what was he going to say? *I failed, Dad. I'm a washed-up has-been. I don't know what I'm going to do with the rest of my life.* Was he being overly dramatic? Possibly, but that was how he felt. Jax couldn't understand what it felt like to lose your only vision of your future because there was nothing else to look forward to but the music. He was a tenured professor, had been made a distinguished professor a couple of years earlier, was still in demand and would remain so for as long as he chose to be.

"Why not?"

Noah ate a few more fries, wishing he could ignore Jax's question. "How do I tell my dad that my dreams have been shattered, that I'm washed up, that I can't do what I spent half my life doing anymore because I was stupid enough to get into a car with a guy who was impaired at the wheel?"

Jax's eyes widened and the shock registering in them was a fresh blow to Noah's heart. The only other people who knew what had happened was the driver, whose life was also forever altered, the members of the quartet, and the doctors and nurses who had looked after him while he'd been in the hospital. Not even his physical therapist knew what exactly had caused Noah to need his services. The quartet's publicist had deemed it wisest to keep specific details out of the news, for which Noah would be eternally grateful. Now he would have someone else shaking his head in disappointment at his foolish behavior.

"Did you know he was drunk when you decided to go with him to wherever you were going?"

Noah looked down at his beer, refusing to meet Jax's accusing eyes. He had heard the edge in his voice as he asked the question.

"He wasn't drunk. He was high." Which didn't make it any better, obviously, so why did he need to clarify? It wouldn't make Jax think any better of him.

"Were you ... using as well?"

"What?" Now it was Noah's turn to be shocked. "Is that what you think? That I fell apart so much after ... after you dumped me that I took up snorting and alcohol?"

*Well, this is going to shit right quick!* He found it easiest to be angry with Jax, because why would he think Noah had been doing drugs as well? He *knew* him. He *knew* he'd never even tried *weed*, for crying out loud!

"I didn't say that." Jax's response was so calm, it was almost bored. That pissed Noah off even more and he was about to get off the stool and walk out when Jax added, "And it doesn't answer my question. Are you gonna try and pretend that it's not a reasonable question to ask after years of no communication between us? You're the one who admitted to knowing he was impaired. I wouldn't have known if you hadn't told me, and this whole thread of conversation would not have happened."

*Reasonable as fuck.* "No, Professor Knox, I was not high. Nor was I drunk. I'd only had a couple of beers..." He stopped himself from reminding Jax that he was a lightweight when it came to alcohol because why go there? Enough with the TMI!

"So why did you willingly get into a car with this guy?"

"I didn't know he was impaired until it was too late to get out of the car. I don't even think *he* realized how bad he was. And then it was too late after that to get him to pull over. It was his car, anyway, so I'd need his permission to drive it."

Silence fell between them, and Noah drained the beer in his glass and ordered a second. Memories of that night ripped through him, and his hand shook as he poured from the second bottle that the bartender slid across the counter to him. Memories of the way Brad had begun to slur his words, the way he'd laughed maniacally as the car slid across the icy pavement before coming to a crashing halt against the guard rail, crowded in.

Noah had let himself be picked up by the handsome guy who had been coming onto him from the moment he'd cozied up to the bar a half hour before they left. The other guys had encouraged him to let loose ... they'd just come off a whirlwind six-month tour, and he needed to blow off steam. Instead, he had ruined the rest of his life. He couldn't even find it in himself to be angry with Brad, because on top of what he'd been using, someone had slipped *him* something earlier, but he'd not begun to feel the effects of the cocktail of drugs until it was too late for them.

What would Jax say if he knew the rest of the story of that night? That the cops had suspected Noah of being the one who had roofied Brad? That he hadn't been sent to the hospital until his story could be verified, and that Brad hadn't regained consciousness for almost a whole day? His friends had had to come down to the police station to corroborate his story, and the bartender had also been questioned. The humiliation of that whole night, in addition to the pain he'd suffered had been, and still was, more than he could bear.

"I just wanted a break. It had been more than a year since…" *No more TMI, remember?* "Anyway, I was ready to let loose a little, to have some fun after the tour ended. I should have known better, but it wasn't like he reeked of weed or anything, and he'd only had a couple of beers when he sat down next to me. There was no way to know."

"So why do you feel so guilty about it?"

Jax's question made Noah look him in the eye for the first time since they'd started the interrogation, as he was feeling it.

"I don't." But he was lying, and he knew it. As far as he was concerned, it was *his* fault for not being more observant, for being so needy for human touch, for intimacy, that he'd been about to break one of his cardinal rules … no sex with strangers. And that the stranger had come there with someone else who had roofied him before he found Noah was all kinds of sick, because it meant that he'd been headed to bed with a guy who picked up sex partners like clothes picked up lint.

"You do, Noah. But even if you could have made better choices back then, the accident was not your fault."

The fries were cold by this point, but Noah didn't care. He needed the carbs and the fat to help him process the alcohol because now that he was remembering, there was no way he could handle the grief without more mind-numbing drinks. Jax would see to it that he got home without mishap.

"I'm sorry that happened to you, Noah. And I hope you'll tell your dad."

Noah wouldn't have a choice when his father came up in a week, but he wasn't ready to face that reality just yet. Time to get the conversation onto a different track.

# Chapter 7

## *Noah*

*Who was he and what had he done with the real Noah?*

"So what have you been doing since we lost touch? I know you sometimes worked with orchestras during the summer." Noah knew that Jax had had a full life before they'd met and had maintained it after their relationship fell apart.

Jax nodded, not calling him out on the sudden and drastic subject change. "That's mostly what I did. A couple of them in London and Salzburg."

"So you're slumming this summer?" He took a big swallow and waited.

Jax laughed. "I'm taking a summer off because I'm moving. Have to find a place to live and get set up with the new routines. So, in another couple of weeks, I'm off to check out housing."

"Sounds like fun," Noah said sarcastically.

"You have no idea." Jax ignored his tone. "It's nice to just be able to relax for a change. Riverdale may not be a big city school, but they have a busy program and I'm going to have to keep up once I get started."

The thread of excitement in Jax's tone filled Noah with an unwilling envy. He wanted to be excited about something, as well. He wanted new adventures too, but nothing could ever make him feel the thrill of performance again.

"Lenny, hit me up again, please."

Noah set his jaw when Jax looked over at him, ready to defend his decision to drink a third beer. He was a grown man, and he could drink as much as he wanted. He didn't need anyone's permission, and especially not the man who ten years ago had given up the right to have any say in how he lived his life. He felt raw and exposed. Beer would help drown that feeling. Bracing himself, he waited for Jax to speak and then felt irrationally irritated when all the other man did was to ask for an order of wings.

Noah noted that he only ordered water this time. *Good for you, Mr. Control.* He let the snark out in his head, reluctant to start a fight even though he was beyond keyed up. This was how he'd been feeling that night, and Brad had stroked his ego with the flattering words that'd had him sliding off the stool at the bar and heading out the door to a vastly different future than the one he'd envisioned.

*That's not gonna happen tonight.* Jax wasn't hitting on him, and even if he wished he would, Noah knew he wasn't quite ready to forgive Jax for wrenching them apart. And until he could do that, he knew he wasn't ready to sleep with him. Such irony ... the man he'd been head over heels for, the man he still wanted, had less chance of getting into his pants than a stranger high on drugs had done. Who was he and what had he done with the real Noah?

The food came and he watched as Jax snagged a wing and tore into it, wiping the sauce off his lips with a napkin. They were plump and moist, even after he'd cleaned them off, and when Jax's pink tongue snuck out to catch an errant drop of the sauce, Noah's eyes remained glued to him. His heart rate sped up, and he felt hot under his tee. What would Jax's tongue feel like on his skin after all this time?

"Not gonna have any?"

He looked up to find Jax watching him, his eyes full of heat and recognition, and Noah blushed. He'd been caught ogling him. He picked up the drumstick part of a wing and bit into it without replying. The less he said going forward, the better for them both. Polishing off the meat, he swallowed deep from his beer. He was already buzzed, and he hoped eating something would help to soak up the alcohol he knew he would keep drinking so he could avoid the confusion of his thoughts and feelings.

"When does your dad come up?"

"Next week," Noah finally said around a mouthful of chicken. "He'll be happy to see you. He asked about you all the time until I graduated."

And after the breakup, that had been painful, but Noah had made sure his father never knew that anything was wrong between them, because then he would have had to explain that things had been right between them, as well. His father was nobody's fool, and he would have seen the hurt and figured out why. So Noah had told him just enough about Jax, things everyone in the music department knew, to keep him satisfied.

"I liked him too. He's a good man, and he raised a great son."

Noah emptied the beer in the glass and drained the rest of the bottle into it. He didn't want to talk about his father.

He didn't want to talk about the accident. He didn't want to talk about their past. Which left exactly nothing to talk about except, perhaps, the weather. And he wasn't interested in talking about the weather, either. However, he'd been letting Jax carry the conversation so far, and it was only fair for him to bear his part of the burden. And it *was* a burden, this awkward silence while Jax no doubt wondered what he had said to offend Noah or what he could say to defuse the tension.

"Are you looking to find a townhouse like the one you lived in before?"

Jax's townhouse had been a row house on two levels with beautiful bay windows and an arching front door on a quiet, tree-lined avenue where other comfortably middle-class families raised their children in relative safety. Noah had loved visiting—the few times he had done so—and had entertained the notion that he might one day be part of that community. Maybe this wasn't the best conversation to have, after all, but it was too late now to backpedal.

"No. I'm looking for a house with a full basement this time, and with a lawn and enough room for a dog."

"I have a dog." Why did he sound so slurred? It had only been three beers.

"Yes. Klinger. I remember you telling me about him and showing me pictures. He must be old now."

*He remembers my dog's name and how old he is? Fuck! I'm screwed.* "He's almost fifteen. Not quite as chipper as he used to be, but still a great pet."

"Do you think I should get a German Shepherd like him? Does he do well on his own all day?"

Jax seemed hellbent on talking about dogs now when all Noah could think of was how his lips looked wrapped around a wing bone, and how his Adam's apple bobbled deliciously when he swallowed more water. How was he supposed to concentrate on dog facts at a time like this?

"Depends on how much you know about dogs, I guess. If you like, we can go to the animal shelter and look at what's available and you can talk to them about what kind of dog you want."

Just what he didn't need ... more time alone with Jax. They could be friendly without being in each other's pockets all the time. But three beers made him loose-lipped and he'd just ordered another to cover his increasing nerves. He was sure he could feel Jax's disapproval, but he just snagged another piece of chicken and bit into it.

"When would you be able to go with me?"

"I'll text you." *Once I manage the hangover I'm sure I'll have in the morning.*

Someone approached the jukebox and dropped coins in. The soft strains of a love song poured out, and an older couple stood up to dance to the music, swaying without much movement in the same spot. The sight made Noah smile. The pub wasn't meant for dancing, but no one cared if people were so touched by the tunes that they made room to move.

"Do you still like to go dancing?"

Jax's question interrupted his musing. He thought about it for a second. "I haven't been out clubbing since the quartet's schedule started filling up. There's just not been time."

That was an excuse, and he knew it. The other guys in the group all had partners whom they went out with, and Noah had hated being the seventh wheel, always the one with no date. And even when he managed to find someone to go home with, it wasn't the same thing. He wanted more than hookups, and now, in his boozy clarity, he could admit to himself that he wanted someone he knew he would never have. Someone who was currently looking at him with something too close to pity in his eyes. Fuck that! He didn't need anyone's pity. There was nothing wrong with wanting something more than going to a club would give him.

"So you didn't have any fun while you worked? That also doesn't sound like you. How did you relax? You used to love going out with your friends and having a good time."

"Did *you* spend a lot of time tripping the light fantastic while you were working your way up the ladder of success, Prof?" He didn't bother to keep the sarcasm out of his tone, aware that he hadn't answered the question.

"I didn't give up enjoying myself completely when things got busier than normal. I had people to help me keep a balance. Sounds like your friends let the ball drop there."

Noah sighed. Jax didn't know the other guys in the quartet so he couldn't know how wrong he was, and Noah hated that he had put them in a bad light.

"It wasn't their fault. I just wasn't interested, after a while. They had people to be with, and I was … well, I didn't. It got old being the odd man out all the time, and hookups lost their appeal as well, after a while. It was just easier to avoid all that."

If Jax hadn't been feeling sorry for him before, there was nothing to stop him from doing that any longer. How pathetic was all that? The beer was not only making him overshare, but it was also making him look like a loser. *Poor me! I don't have a boyfriend!* He needed to leave before this pity party got any sappier. He ignored the dribble of beer that ran down his chin to his neck when he raised the bottle to his lips and emptied the contents down his throat. He was leaving now anyway, so it didn't matter if he got a little sloppy.

"Where are you going?" Jax asked him when he stood up.

"Little boy's room."

He waggled his fingers ridiculously and walked unsteadily toward the men's room. He barely made it to the urinal before he was emptying his overfull bladder, doing his best not to splash himself. Despite his current state, he was sober enough not to want to smell like piss when he got into Jax's beautiful muscle car. His head spun a little as he washed his hands. *'S what you get for overindulging. Suck it up!*

Back at the bar, Jax was having them box up the rest of the chicken and fries and paying the tab. Noah had wanted to contribute, but it was too late for that now. While Jax took his own men's room break, Lenny handed Noah the bag with the food and he headed toward the door, concentrating so he wouldn't stumble. He knew when Jax caught up with him, ushering him out of the now very crowded pub with a gentle hand at his back.

"You okay?"

Guess he hadn't done enough to disguise how unsteady he was after all. "Yeah, I'm fine," he lied anyway. If he didn't admit to it, he could continue to pretend he was just dead on his feet after a long day, right? He put the food on the console between the seats and strapped himself in. He didn't know when he dozed off, only that Jax was shaking him awake.

"Come on, let's get you inside."

Noah struggled to release himself from the seatbelt and gratefully accepted the hand that Jax lent him to get to his front door. After a bit of fumbling—was he drunker than he realized?—he managed to get it open, and this time couldn't help the stumble inside. Klinger came running out to greet him, nearly toppling him off his feet, and only Jax's swift save stopped him from face planting on the floor.

"Does he need to go out?" Jax asked.

"Yeah. I'll get to it in a second. Thanks for the ride home."

Jax walked past him. "Kitchen this way?" he asked, heading in the right direction.

Noah nodded, too fuzzy to note that Jax couldn't see the gesture. When he walked back out, he had Klinger's leash.

"I'll take him out. You go get ready for bed." He picked up the keys that Noah had dropped on the table in the hallway and whistled for Klinger who trotted over obediently, tail wagging at the thought of a last walk before bed.

"You don't have to…"

Jax interrupted his protest. "I know. Go on, you're in no shape to walk the dog. I'll be back soon."

He would just change into his pj's and wait for them to come back before he went to bed. He undressed, dropping his clothes where they fell—he would pick up after himself in the morning—and went in to brush his teeth, staring at his reflection in the bathroom mirror. His eyes were a little bit bloodshot, a sure sign that he'd had too much to drink. His first date in eons and he'd messed up. He just couldn't win for losing, could he?

Out of the bathroom, he sank onto the side of his bed, trying to wrap his brain around what he was supposed to be doing next. His eyelids drifted shut against the glare of the lamplight. He should get up and shut the lights off…

The next time he opened his eyes, Klinger was whining next to his bed, and the digital clock on the radio said it was almost eight in the morning. Shit! He'd overslept. He caught sight of the bottle of water, two painkillers on top of an index card on the bedside table. Doing as the note on the card instructed, he swallowed the pills quickly before the hangover headache took hold. Then he swung his legs off the bed and stood up gingerly, recalling how he'd had to think hard about not falling over to stay upright the night before ... on his drink date with Jax.

Damn! He was such a lightweight that four beers had knocked him off kilter. And he'd managed to embarrass himself in front of Jax. He hadn't heard him return with Klinger, and he had no recollection of making it all the way into bed, which meant that Jax had also put him to bed and tucked him in. He shook his head, making his way to the bathroom to relieve himself before slipping on his sweatpants and a t-shirt and taking Klinger out for his morning constitutional. The bright sunshine made the dull ache behind his eyelids a little sharper. He needed a new pair of sunglasses ASAP.

"Morning, Noah. Have a good one."

He responded to at least four such greetings with a "Thanks, you too!" on his way back to the house and prayed he didn't look wasted. His small town was notorious for minding your business and for keeping tabs on you so they could report back to the elders ... in this case, to his dad. He didn't want his old man to worry about him, nor did he want him to arrive with a head full of questions that Noah wasn't ready to answer.

Once Klinger was fed and watered, he took a shower, hoping to wash away the sickly feeling that four beers in quick succession and not nearly enough food had bequeathed him. He rolled his eyes as he considered how he had used the drinks as a way to avoid talking or thinking about all the uncomfortable topics that had come up in his conversation with Jax the night before. *Avoidance, thy name is Noah.* His cellphone vibrated on the counter where he'd left it on his way out the door earlier.

Two missed calls and a text message ... all from Jax. He woke the phone and read the message, which was what had just come in.

[Prof: Everything okay there?]

Noah bit his bottom lip as he composed, deleted, composed, deleted and composed a reply that would be cool, not embarrassed. He didn't think he could manage friendly right now. Maybe once the wave of shame receded, if Jax texted him again, he could try that.

[Noah: Everything is fine. I just came back in with Klinger.]

He looked apologetically at Klinger as though the animal would know he was being used to perpetrate a misdirection. *Sorry, buddy. Needs must.* And wasn't that the most pitiful thing he'd ever done, apologizing to his dog? He needed to get a grip.

[Prof: Good. I was about to come over to check up on you.]

*No, thank you.* He sent back a [Noah: No need], suddenly done with the conversation. He needed time to process his feelings in the light of day, without the influence of alcohol to make things more confusing. Then he set down the phone and started a load of laundry. He needed to clean, as well, because his next private lesson was at one sharp, and the house could stand to be vacuumed and dusted before then. He also needed to be clear-headed, so obsessing over what Jax was doing with his morning was a waste of valuable time.

Once the washing machine was going, he slapped together a quick pb&j sandwich, sucked down a cup of coffee and a small glass of orange juice, and wielded the vacuum. Dust motes floated in the sunbeam across the living room as he dusted and polished. His dad would be proud if he could see him now, house-husbanding like a boss. Would Jax want a man who could keep a tidy house?

*What the fuck, Noah?* Why did he even care what Jax wanted in a partner? They had left that behind ten years ago, a discussion that had never happened because he'd been too chicken to raise it. If Jax wanted kids, he'd let him know. And if he didn't tell him, that would be because it was never meant to be. They had followed different paths since they were last together, and his life was suddenly overshadowed by injury.

"Stop moping!" He spoke aloud into the silent house, needing the grounding of his own voice in his ears to quiet the thoughts that seemed to be running on a never-ending loop. Over all the other emotions clamoring to be felt, loneliness settled around him. He tried to shrug it off, losing himself to the cadence of the vacuum and the huffs of his own breath and Klinger's gentle snoring. But soon, it wasn't enough.

He took his cellphone into the bathroom with him and found one of his go-to soundtracks, letting George Michael, Bryan Adams, Adam Levine, and Sting distract him from thoughts of Jax. He had half an hour before his student arrived, so he sat at the piano planning out the sequence he'd be following. The boy was fairly advanced with potential, if he applied himself to practice. He sighed as he stood up from the piano to get a glass of water. Not every kid was like he had been, thirsty for the music that watered his soul. In fact, most of the boys he knew back then had found their fulfillment in one sport or another.

Promptly at one o'clock, his doorbell rang. Klinger barked and ran to the door, ready to welcome their guest. Time to get a move on. At least for the next hour, he wouldn't be alone.

# Chapter 8

## Jax

*How did a guy talk to his best friend about
his epically failed relationship?*

"That was great, Jim. You've definitely improved since the last time you cooked me anything."

Jax ducked the swat that Jim aimed at him with the dish towel, chuckling at his friend. It had been a simple meal, but Jim had followed his wife's directions to the letter and produced a really palatable feast. The boys had cleaned their plates and asked for seconds, and Annie had declared herself proud of her husband's efforts. Now she was taking a nap while they cleaned up.

He was grateful for the time he was spending with his found family in the absence of his blood relatives. At the very least, it kept him from dwelling too much on the events of the evening before, when Noah had managed to get a little drunk on too many beers. What else had he expected, really? Well, maybe not that the other man would get drunk, but he *had* hoped they could talk about what they wanted going forward. Despite his excitement at the prospect of his new job, he knew very few people in this part of the country and could use the support of a friend who understood the world he inhabited.

That someone could be Noah, if he could ever get past whatever awkwardness was making him avoid any conversation to do with them or with his accident. Friends didn't do that. His heart wrenched at the word … he wanted more than friendship with Noah, no matter what his brain said was reasonable. But until he knew what Noah wanted, he was better off going under the assumption that he wanted nothing else and certainly nothing more.

"So tell me about your boy." Jim's words crashed into his head, abruptly dragging him back into the kitchen. It was as though he had seen inside Jax's heart and peeled away the layers keeping his most private thoughts and feelings hidden from the world.

"He's not my boy." A deflection, and not a very good one, as Jim's next question made immediately clear.

"Semantics, as you used to like to tell me when I tried avoiding a subject with you. Are you really going to try to convince me that there isn't something between you two? I have eyes, bro, and I've been married long enough to be able to read the signs."

Jax turned startled eyes to his friend's face. "Signs? What signs?" Had he not hidden his interest well enough?

"The two of you were like hedgehogs at a ballroom dance, trying to participate while avoiding the spines. Not a whole lot of dancing happened."

Jax rolled his eyes at his friend's exaggeration. Even if the metaphor was apt, they *had* managed to hold a conversation and be civil to each other. As he recalled it, there had even been a shared laugh or two.

"I don't know what you're talking about," he said. Because really, he didn't.

"Jax, the tension rolling off the two of you when y'all couldn't avoid looking at each other was heavy. I felt like a third wheel half the time." Jim's smirk irritated Jax but he obviously didn't care, since he continued, "Do you think I took two eight-year-old boys for a two-hour boat ride for my health, dude? Did you really think I was being this great dad giving them what they wanted?"

This time, his laugh was boisterous. Jax considered chucking the glass that he was holding at his friend but thought better of it. Wouldn't want to piss off Annie who might throw him out on his ear, even if he and Jim *were* best friends.

"The last time we saw or spoke to each other was ten years ago. There was bound to be some awkwardness."

"So that's what you're going with? Okay, fine." Jim leaned against the counter. "I'll let you have awkwardness, but that brings us right back to my original question. What's up with you and the pretty hot Latin musician?"

'Pretty' and 'hot' were most assuredly two good words to describe Noah. But if Jax stopped to consider descriptors, he'd chub up in his jeans and that wasn't a sight Jim needed nor one that Jax was willing to give him.

"Nothing's *up* with us. We're just getting reacquainted, that's all. We lost touch after he graduated." No need to explain that they'd lost touch before he graduated, after Jax broke his heart.

"Were you close?"

Jax heaved a heavy sigh. There was no getting past this, was there? Jim had always been intuitive enough to recognize signs most other folks might miss and, like a well-trained bloodhound, he was able to sniff out the truth with ease. And when it came to Jax, he had honed those skills over time.

"Why the sigh, bro? You got something to hide?"

Jax shook his head, a reluctant smile curving his lips upward. "I'm not hiding anything, exactly."

Jim put away the last of the dishes and went to retrieve two beers from the refrigerator. Leading the way out to the back porch, he handed one of the beers to Jax and asked as he sat down, "Then what are you doing, exactly?"

How did a guy talk to his best friend about his epically failed relationship when that friend was in one that was working like a charm? Where did he even begin?

"Noah was a student in my performance class, and as part of his training, he had to have individual lessons. He was assigned to me for those, which meant we spent a lot of time together." He swallowed some beer. Why the hell was this so hard to talk about? "I was attracted to him from the beginning, but he hadn't turned twenty-one yet and I was in a position of authority over him. There should have been nothing between us. It was unethical and dangerous for both of us."

He took another mouthful of beer, searching for a way to continue.

"We'll come back to the last part of that in a second," Jim said. "But first, which of you made the first move?"

There was no hint of disapproval in his friend's tone, but neither was he salivating after salacious details. Jax appreciated that. Jim understood him and knew how difficult it was to bare his soul, to make himself vulnerable.

"He did at first, after a Halloween party for the students. Once I came to my senses after that make out session, I made sure it didn't happen again. I figured he'd get over his crush. Then the students performed at the first concert of the college year, and he'd played beautifully. Standing ovation and all. After the show, he called me over to introduce me to his dad. They invited me to dinner, and I said yes. That was probably not a smart thing to do, but I figured I was safe because his father was there."

He had blown off his colleagues who'd wanted to take him out for drinks, telling them he could have a drink with them anytime, but spending time with their upcoming star and his dad was important for the college's reputation. A satisfied parent could do a lot not only for *his* reputation as a professor, but also for the college as an institution. He had convinced them that this was an inexpensive way to build trust and hopefully draw attention to the college's efforts to improve on diversity and inclusion.

He'd known he was lying to himself and to his colleagues. He just wanted to be near the younger man, to bask in the beauty of his smile and his passion for music, to enjoy his quick-witted sense of humor and his sharp intelligence. He wanted to be closer than their student-teacher relationship allowed, especially after that Halloween kiss. If Noah's dad was giving him the only chance he'd likely ever have for that to happen again, he wasn't going to refuse it.

"So what happened?"

He'd gotten lost in his memories and forgotten he was telling Jim the story.

"Dinner was great. Noah is his father's son ... warm, friendly, open. Mr. Santiago was so proud of Noah; it was impossible to miss. He told me stories about how he discovered that his son preferred playing the piano and violin to playing baseball. How he scrimped and saved to send him to music lessons, how his teachers said he would go far and pushed him to enter the state's competitions. How he and Noah had pored over colleges, when he first started high school, to see which ones gave the best scholarships, and how he had spent all his down time pushing Noah to practice harder, to sharpen his skills, to decide which instrument he preferred and do the most work with that."

"Wow! What it must be to have a dad like that behind you!"

"You're right. By the time Noah was a junior in high school, he'd chosen the five schools he wanted to attend and had been working on his college essay for a while. He got into all five schools, including Curtis." At Jim's puzzled frown, he explained. "That's the most exclusive music conservatory in the country. It's really small and tuition-free."

"Hell! Why didn't he go there?"

"He didn't feel comfortable. The Latino student population was small in an already small school, and he didn't want to stick out. Our school was much larger, so it would have been easier for him to disappear, if he tanked. Apparently, he thought he might disappoint his dad, and he didn't want the trauma of doing that in the college version of a small town. Where everybody knows your name and everything about you, was how he put it."

Jim chuckled. "I'll bet he hated living in *this* small town then. Anyway, I'm still not hearing how things went from professional to personal with you."

"I drove them home ... his father back to the hotel where he was staying and Noah to his frat house. But on the way to his place, he asked me to pull over because he needed to talk to me." Jax huffed out a laugh. "I had no idea what he could want to talk about that he couldn't say in front of his dad, and it hadn't even occurred to me that he might still feel the same way about me that I felt about him."

"Jax, buddy, I hate to break it to you, but this just sounds like you were dumb as a box of rocks and didn't read the room. I'm assuming he told you again that he was attracted to you?"

"Yes. And he gave me some pretty explicit descriptions of what he wanted to do to and with me. But he knew it wouldn't be right, so could he please just have one more kiss to remember me by, and then he'd ask to switch tutors for his lessons. That way, I wouldn't have to see him at all except in orchestra practice."

Shock was insufficient to describe the emotion that Jax had felt when Noah had dropped his bombshell. And the thought of not seeing him again outside of a large group, of giving up the closeness they had been cultivating during his lessons, of relinquishing control of his performance to someone else had made Jax see red. Hell fucking no! Noah was his to train and his to have and he'd be damned if he let anyone else close to him like that.

"That was when it hit me how gone I was for this guy, so I said yes, but only to the kiss. I had only gotten to know him properly as more than my student over the previous three months, and I wanted more. So once we stopped making out like teenagers—though granted, he was way closer to the teen years than I was—I told him we would do whatever he really wanted." He glanced over at Jim, before adding sarcastically, "That was me being so mature that I was giving him a reason to change his mind. I knew if I didn't agree, he would rethink his decision, and I wanted him to be the one to choose me over any hesitation he was feeling."

Suddenly the club chair he was sitting on was too hot and he needed to get up and walk around. He put the beer down and went to stand by the railing for a beat before starting to pace. He should never have given Noah any opportunity to pursue him. He should have nipped that attraction in the bud. Woulda, coulda, shoulda ... if he'd been a better man, he would have done it then. The hurt that Noah would have felt would have been nothing to what Jax had inflicted on him when he broke things off six months later.

"So why exactly was it dangerous for the two of you?"

Jax sighed, running a hand across the back of his neck and turning to lean his hips against the railing so he was facing his friend.

"Noah got a full ride scholarship to the college, and he could lose it if there was even a hint of any impropriety. They could accuse me of rewarding him for servicing me and accuse him of soliciting me for higher scores. We could both have been dismissed from the college."

"But you took the chance anyway. What made you pull back? And how did he take it?"

"We were together at a concert and almost ran into some of my colleagues who would have realized at once that we were on a date if they'd seen the way we were together. I just couldn't keep doing it. So I broke things off, switched him to another professor whose hours were different from mine, and got on with my life. Needless to say, I broke his heart. I broke mine too. We managed never to see each other again unless it was at required concerts, and we avoided each other as much as we could even then too. I could tell he wasn't doing well physically, but he kept up his grades and graduated *summa cum laude*, the star of his class."

Jim got up and went to stand next to him. He felt the action like a warm hug, even though his friend wasn't touching him.

"How long, Jax?"

Jax understood what Jim was asking him and he hoped he could keep the pain out of his voice when he answered. "Eleven years."

"Damn! That's a long time, my friend. I'm taking it that your feelings haven't changed? I mean, based on all that heat that I saw, I'm guessing they haven't."

Jim was way too smart for Jax's liking, but it was still a kind of relief to let go of the burden of his feelings for a moment, to let someone else share in them, someone who could understand the weight that love could carry, the strain that it could bring to bear on a heart.

"It doesn't matter, does it?" A vise gripped his heart at those words, squeezing tightly, leaving only pain and regret.

"Why? Are you afraid he's not where you are after a decade? Because I'm here to tell you, you're probably wrong about that." Jim raised a hand to stop Jax before he could disagree. "You weren't watching the two of you. I was, and I know what I saw, buddy. That man is as hung up on you as you are on him. Yeah, there's some anger in there that I won't pretend to understand, but there's also longing. I could see it in those few moments when he let himself relax and look at you, when he felt safe that you wouldn't notice."

"It doesn't matter, Jim. He's dealing with some stuff that will make anything he might be feeling for me pale into insignificance. It's not my story to tell, but trust me, it's big enough that even if you're right, he's not in the right headspace to deal with me. And by the time he gets his act together, he'll probably see I'm not really who he needs anyway."

More pain swelled inside him, a tsunami of emotion rolling over his bruised heart. It had been a long time since he had allowed himself to think about Noah, and he had thought he'd be over the self-administered wound by this point. Rehashing the story with Jim had proven him wrong.

"Now why would you say a thing like that?" Jim wondered aloud. "What makes you think you're not who he needs?"

"Jim, I'm eleven years older than him." The protest was ashes in his mouth. "And a forty-something guy is a lot less of a catch than a thirty-something guy."

Jim burst out laughing, spewing beer everywhere. When he was finally able to get himself back under control, he turned amused eyes to Jax, a grin still prominent on his face, and said, "Boy, I can see I have my work cut out for me."

Jax eyed him suspiciously. "What are you talking about?"

"Well," he pointed the beer bottle at Jax. "First, we have to get rid of that negativity that you've got going on there, and then we're going to work on getting you two back together. Starting with dinner."

"Dinner?"

The word erupted as an inelegant and not even the slightest bit masculine squeak. Jax retrieved his beer, needing something to help him swallow the panic that flared at the idea of doing anything to get Noah back. He had buried all that ten years ago. He couldn't reopen old wounds, even if he thought there might be a sliver of a chance that things could go well. Because there was more than a sliver of a chance that they could go horribly wrong, and he wasn't going there. He couldn't bear that particular heartbreak a second time, and the last thing he wanted to do was hurt Noah by anything he did.

"Jim, I'd rather you not do anything at all okay? Let sleeping dogs lie and all that. We're fine, or we will be. It'll just take a bit to get comfortable around each other again."

Sharper words never crossed his lips, leaving their stinging marks in his throat. He swallowed the last of the beer, needing to soothe the ache and push the feelings back down where they belonged.

"What could be easier for a first date than dinner at our place with Annie and the kids, man?"

"Annie doesn't need to be on her feet making dinner for a houseful of guests. She's about ready to drop that baby and needs her rest."

Jax wasn't above using his friend's wife as an escape route. As far as he was concerned, Jim's suggestion just had bad idea written all over it.

Jim's laughter rang out again in the back yard. "You think you're slick, don't you? Who said anything about Annie cooking? We can make a great meal, and all she'll have to do is guide us from her lounger."

"I'd just rather not rush into anything, Jim, if you don't mind. I'd prefer for him to make the next move. I took him out for drinks last night. Now it's his turn to reciprocate. Why don't we see what he does before you go off half-cocked making wedding plans?"

He tried to inject some humor because he didn't want his friend to lose patience with him. Thankfully, Jim seemed to consider his response seriously before nodding. "Okay, fair enough. We'll wait, but not longer than a few days. You'll be gone before you know it, and nothing can begin if one of you doesn't make the next move."

Relief swept over him, slowing his heart rate, and Jax nodded. "Thanks."

Jim did put his arm around him in a one-armed hug this time. "Don't thank me yet, J. Wait until you've bagged him first."

His wink was a wicked tease, but it did its job. Jax chuckled and relaxed. He had a reprieve before he'd have to think of new excuses. In the meantime, he could laugh with his best friend.

# Chapter 9

## *Noah*

*Noah wasn't sure he knew how to
do this with Jax anymore.*

"Y ou did well today, Missy."
Noah smiled at Melissa Farley as she packed up her violin. She was a shy little thing, but her violin skills were stellar for someone her age. He could see her making it in the competitive world of music performance if she could get past her almost painful need to be invisible.

"Have you thought any more about the contest I suggested?"

Noah already knew the answer, but he felt it was important for him to keep pushing it because it would be a shame to lose the talent of this one child to baseless fear of failure or to timidity. The contest wouldn't be for another eight months, but he thought it best to introduce the idea earlier rather than later, so she'd have time to think it through. She would be such a gift to the world.

"My mom says I get to decide." Her voice was stubbornly quiet in the stillness of his living room. "I want to wait until my dad comes back."

Her father was in the military and was apparently a highly decorated soldier. Noah had never met him, but the way Missy talked about him, Noah figured out really quickly that she adored her father. Maybe he could get her dad to convince her that she could do anything, if he came home before the deadline for applying to the competition passed. He didn't even know if the man was due home or not, and he wasn't about to stir up a hornet's nest by asking.

"Okay."

He smiled as she went to stand by the window to look out for her mother. Once the lesson was over, she was always in a hurry to leave. After the mother and daughter left, Noah tidied up the area and went in search of dinner. His dad had texted him to say he'd be home in another couple of days, and though Noah couldn't wait to see him again, he dreaded having to tell him his news. He couldn't bear the thought of disappointing his father, who had stayed the course with him from the time his mom died when he was a baby. How had he managed for so long without a lover? Noah couldn't remember his dad ever being with anyone, though he realized that it wasn't something he would have thought about anyway unless it happened. Could Noah do that?

Jax sprang to his mind unerringly. He had lived without Noah for over a decade. Maybe it was something older guys could do? He sighed as he walked into the kitchen to rustle up something for dinner. He had lived without Jax for a long time as well, so he knew it was doable. Not acceptable at all, but doable.

Thinking about Jax made him realize that he hadn't made any effort to continue the plan to rekindle their friendship.

Getting a little sloshed the other night hadn't helped, he was sure. What must Jax think of him? A man over thirty who couldn't hold a few beers ... ridiculous! Jax already knew that, though, because Noah had gotten more than a little tipsy on the night before his twenty-first birthday when Jax had invited him over for a celebratory dinner. They'd decided that he should go to the frat party that his friends had planned for his birthday on the actual date. The less attention they called to themselves, the better.

Not that any of their caution had stopped Jax from calling a halt to their affair. Six months in, and one close call spelled the end of any need to hide. And after eleven years, Noah wasn't sure he knew how to do this with Jax anymore. He wasn't trying to seduce him, like he had been doing in college. All he wanted—this was his story, and he was sticking to it—was to regain a friendly footing with the man. If they were going to be in the same state, and close enough to drive to each other if they so chose, it was better to not be on the outs, right?

"What do you think, Klinger?"

He turned to look at his dog, who opened one eye, looked him over, then closed it again, ignoring him. Maybe he could have Jax over for dinner when his dad got home. That would be a nice surprise for his father, and Noah could hope it would give him things to think about other than when his son was going back on tour. The more he could do to delay breaking the bad news to his father, the happier he'd be.

So, dinner on Friday. Alvaro Santiago liked it when his son cooked, and Noah knew just what would make him happiest. His dad loved traditional Mexican food. As he checked his pantry to see what he would need to buy the next day when he went grocery shopping, memories of spending time with his dad in the kitchen brought a smile to his cheeks. Deciding that the easiest things would be foods they could eat with their fingers—the boys would love that—he made a list for ceviche, tacos, and guacamole, as well as chips for the dips, and ice cream for dessert.

He finally texted Jax when he was getting ready for bed. As before, it took him a minute to decide what to say.

[Noah: Hi. Can you find out if your friend and his family would like to come over for dinner on Friday? My dad's coming back that day, and I think he'd enjoy some company.]

An answer came immediately.

[Prof: Only Jim and his family are invited?]

*Fuck you, Prof!* Noah chuckled, despite himself. Why was Jax being all cute and teasing him right now? They didn't have that kind of relationship anymore. His foolish heart fluttered against his ribcage, but he ignored it, choosing to focus on how to answer. He could flirt too, if he could just think of the cool thing to say. *You're not a teenager anymore, for fuck's sake, No!* Internally berating himself, he replied.

[Noah: I wouldn't know them if it weren't for you, so what do you think?]

[Prof: I didn't want to assume. You know what they say about that, and I'm not trying to make an ass of myself.]

Somewhere in that response Noah could almost hear the unspoken fear of rejection. He got it. He had lived with rejection for over ten years. He could keep stringing this out, making Jax feel more anxiety before letting him off the hook, or he could act his age and clarify his meaning. He really needed to let go of the impulse to hurt Jax after all this time. It was pointless, especially if they were going to be friends going forward.

[Noah: Yes, you are definitely also invited.]

[Prof: Good to know. Not sure I would know what to do with myself all alone here on a Friday evening.]

Noah could think of something Jax could do all alone on any evening, not just Fridays. *And that right there is why you can't get a date these days, No!* Apparently reuniting with Jax had also reawakened every juvenile impulse he had managed to outgrow in that summer after their breakup, if he thought self-pleasure was any way for a grown man to spend an evening.

"Just me and my trusty left hand," he intoned aloud, self-mocking in a voice like the guy selling super glue on TV, gripping his half-hard cock through his sweats.

Pitiful! How lame was that, getting hard over thinking about jerking off to the idea of his ex-lover pleasuring himself alone in his room? He dragged his hand away, inhaling sharply to cool the fever he'd started with his randy thoughts. Time to end this conversation.

[Noah: I'll see you on Friday, then.]

[Prof: Can't wait, Noah! ;)]

Noah observed the wink at the end with greedy delight, his skin prickling with anticipatory excitement. He hadn't been this keyed up about anything apart from music in more years than he could count. Even the odd hookup had not had him feeling such a complicated cocktail of emotions … delight and dread, anticipation and anxiety, arousal and annoyance. What the hell was Jax doing to him? And how had he missed the memo that said this is how he'd be reacting after so many years apart?

Supermarket shopping the next day added another layer of stress to Noah's shoulders because it seemed like the rest of the population, or at least the ones he bumped into in the store, all now knew that Alvaro was on his way home and had something to say about it.

"I'll bet you've missed your old man, Noah. I know he misses you when you're not around."

That from Henry, the town's resident drunk, who was surprisingly sober for a change, and who loved Noah's dad unrepentantly. Noah didn't know all the details of Henry's story except that the man was gay, and his father refused to enlighten him. And he had never seen his father be anything but kind to Henry, for whom he also seemed to hold genuine affection.

"Remind Alvaro he owes me a twenty for the last game he lost before he went down south."

That from one of his card-playing buddies. Why he didn't just wait to give Alvaro the message himself was anybody's guess, and Noah wasn't going to bother trying to figure that out. He nodded and moved on, putting items into the cart as he practically sprinted around the store.

"Do you think your dad will be up for a game of pool soon, my boy?"

Now how would he know that? Noah shook his head. "I dunno, Mr. Johnson. You'll have to ask him when he gets here."

The cucumbers and avocados were next on his list, and they weren't exactly next to each other, which meant navigating through more unwanted conversational waters.

"Who's the hottie you were with at The Lake and Inn the other night, Noah Santiago?" Clara Haines never called anyone by just their first name. "Does your dad know him? How long is he here for?"

Noah almost crashed his cart into the display of different varieties of apples that he'd been about to walk by to get to the avocados.

"Excuse me?"

What the hell else was he supposed to say in response to that? Mind your own damn business? You don't need to know who he is, he's not available? He'll be gone before you get your hooks into him?

"I saw you and him at the pub the other night. He's a looker for sure. And he's got that whole sexy silver fox thing down pat."

Noah took a calming breath and counted to twenty while the woman currently delaying his shopping trip rattled on about what she would do with a colt like that. The old lady was at least seventy if she was a day, but she looked a lot younger, and based on the escapades she was rumored to be part of, she was an unapologetic cougar and then some. He tried not to chuckle at the thought of Jax having to fend off her amorous advances.

"He's a friend from my college days, Ms. Haines, and no, he's leaving soon."

She didn't have to know any more than that, though why he felt the need to protect Jax's identity wasn't something he was prepared to look into too keenly. It was silly to feel annoyed by the interest of an old woman in the sexy silver fox who used to be his, especially because he knew Jax didn't swing that way.

"Pity," she was saying. "I'll bet we could have a good time together. Big men like that are my kryptonite."

*Mine too.* Something else she didn't need to know. "Well, I'd best be getting along, Ms. Haines. It was nice talking to you."

"You take care of yourself, Noah Santiago. You look a little peaky for a young'un. Gotta keep your strength up, not to mention your looks, if you expect to snag a man."

Noah wasn't touching that comment with a ten-foot pole. He merely smiled politely and pushed past her to continue what was becoming an increasingly trying chore. He managed to make it to the checkout line before he was once again accosted, this time by a very pregnant woman.

"Hi. You must be Noah." She must have overheard his conversation with Clara Haines. "I'm Annie, Jim's wife. The boys haven't stopped talking about you, and Jax passed on your invitation to dinner tomorrow evening. It's nice to finally put a face to the name."

Noah shook hands and smiled at her. He wasn't exceptionally tall, but next to Annie, he was almost a giant. Beautiful, soulful brown eyes took him in as she switched the shopping basket from one hand to the other. Noah reached over without thinking twice and took it from her, placing it on the edge of the conveyer belt.

"It's nice to meet you too. Why don't you go ahead of me and then wait so I can help you with this?"

"Oh, that's so kind of you."

She stepped ahead of him and once she was through, he moved to help her put her bags to the side so his things could be bagged. Then he put hers on top of his bags on the cart and they walked out together.

"I hope you guys like Mexican food." He was screwed if they didn't, and why he hadn't thought to ask before he spent money shopping the menu was a mystery for the ages.

She grinned as he put her bags into her car. "Jim will be your best friend for life. It's his favorite. And the rest of us are easy. I'm sure it'll be fine." Extending her hand again, she said, "Thanks for the help. I'll see you tomorrow."

Noah waited until she had backed up and driven off before heading to his own vehicle. It was his dad's truck. He'd have to get his own soon, if he was going to be staying. The quartet was getting ready to fly out on their first tour of the year. He would call them before they left so he could wish the guest artist filling his spot good luck. But not today. He couldn't handle that just yet. He had to steady himself first so no one would hear the sadness he couldn't uproot from his spirit.

After two lessons and a thorough cleaning of his house, plus changing the bed linens on his dad's bed, he was ready for a shower and some shut-eye. He was going to pick up his father from the airport, and his flight was arriving just before noon. Noah needed forty-five minutes to get there, which meant he'd need to be up and out by ten thirty. With the way his eyes felt as he stripped for bed, he'd be asleep as soon as his head touched the pillow. Dreamless would be great too.

His cellphone vibrated on the nightstand. Who the hell is sending messages at … oh, wait, it was just nine forty-seven on a Thursday night. Maybe no other adult expected him to be crawling into bed so early. A heavy sigh accompanied his outstretched hand to where the phone vibrated again.

"Hold your horses," he grumbled and woke it without looking to see who was sending him a message. And then wished he had.

[Prof: What time's your dad arriving tomorrow?]

[Noah: 11:45 a.m. I'm heading out to get him at 10:30.]

[Prof: Annie told me she saw you in the grocery store today, and she wants to know what you need us to bring tomorrow for dinner.]

[Noah: Drinks for the kids. I picked up adult beverages but forgot soft drinks for them. Do you know what their favorite flavor of ice cream is?]

He'd somehow managed to forget not only child-friendly beverages, but he'd lost the opportunity to ask their mother what dessert they liked best. Apparently, he couldn't multi-task in the supermarket, and dealing with nosy neighbors while filling his cart had been more of a distraction than he'd thought.

[Prof: I'll ask Annie and we'll bring it tomorrow. That's it? Anything else?]

Why did Jax sound like he was hoping for more? What more could he want? Cheeks heating as he considered what else Jax might want from him, Noah sensibly ended the chat.

[Noah: Nothing else. Well, I'd better go. I have some last-minute things to do.]

Jax didn't have to know he was lying like the rug in the living room.

[Noah: I'll see you tomorrow at six.]

[Prof: Night, Noah.]

Any chance of dreamless sleep just went out the window. Talking to Jax, whether in the flesh or remotely, seemed to be all he needed to chub up a little in his shorts. Good thing he hadn't called, or Noah would have been fighting off the boner from hell instead. Turning onto his side, he valiantly ignored the feel of the silk against his half-hard flesh. *Sleep, Noah, not sex.*

The next morning, an accident on the highway delayed him long enough that when he finally got to the airport, his dad was already out and waiting for him. Noah took in the man who had been his whole world for his entire life. Alvaro Santiago was heavyset and shorter than Noah, but his hair had not a streak of gray and his eyes were clear and bright.

He was a handsome man, even if Noah did say so himself. Not for the first time, he wondered why he'd never married again. He had seen more than one woman eyeing up the older man, but his dad never gave any of them the time of day. He hurried over to hug him and let himself sink into the arms his father wrapped him in as they gently squeezed each other and exchanged kisses on each cheek. Nothing felt better than hugs from his dad. Well, except maybe hugs from Jax, but he wasn't going there.

"It is good to see you again, *mijo*."

Despite having lived in the States for more than half his life, Alvaro's speech was still lightly accented, and he peppered it with Spanish words and phrases more often than not. Noah had grown up bilingual, which had come in handy in high school and college.

"Good to see you too, *Papi*. You look well. I'll bet you left one or two unhappy ladies back in St. Pete."

Alvaro grinned and winked at his son, but only shrugged instead of answering that obvious fishing comment. Noah laughed. That was always his father's way. He gave nothing away that he didn't want to, and there was nothing anyone could do to change that. He took the suitcases that his dad was pulling and led the way back to the truck, loading them quickly before getting in next to his father.

"I have a surprise for you," he began, once they were on their way back. Better to get it out now and hopefully he could put off the harder conversation a little longer.

"Oh?" He felt his dad's eyes on him for a moment. "If it is a good surprise, then let's have it."

Noah wasn't sure what he'd think about having Jax over for dinner since they'd not spoken of him since he'd graduated ten years ago, but he knew it would be better than the news about his career being down the toilet. He swallowed the lump in his throat at the thought and concentrated on the here and now.

"Remember my college professor that you met and liked a lot? The one you always used to ask me about?"

Noah glanced over as he asked the question. Hs father thought for a second before he replied.

"Yes. Professor Knox was his name, no? Very handsome gentleman and so talented. What about him?"

Noah did his best to hide his shock at his father's description of Jax. How had he not known that his dad would notice Jax's good looks? He'd never once thought those kinds of observations crossed his father's mind. What the hell did it mean? Did it even matter? Those were questions for another day.

"He's here visiting with friends, and I've invited them over for dinner tonight, as a kind of welcome home for you."

He could hear the smile in his father's voice. "It will be good to see him again, *mijo*. He was very kind to you, and it was clear to me that he liked you."

Noah's skin heated at the same time that his heart stuttered. Say what now? What did his father know? Or was he just making a general kind of statement? He had never told Alvaro about his relationship with Jax, because it hadn't lasted long enough for him to broach the subject. Would he have been okay with his son dating a man so many years older than he was? Noah didn't know, and since it didn't matter now, he'd let it slide.

Making a noncommittal sound, he changed the subject, asking about his dad's family and friends in Florida. Alvaro's anecdotes and the news about Jax changing jobs kept the conversation off unwelcome topics for the remainder of the ride back home, where Klinger was overjoyed to see Alvaro.

Noah watched his father and his dog reunite with affection. His life had been one filled with the privilege of a loving parent who nurtured his soul and spirit as much as he cared for his mind and body, and Klinger had been one of the ways his dad had shown him love. He was an only child, and the dog had become his faithful companion.

"What would you like for lunch, *Papi?*"

"I'm not very hungry. Maybe just a grilled cheese sandwich done our way with a beer?"

"No problem. Let me just get your bags into your room first."

Once lunch was over, Alvaro went out to the back porch and lay dozing on the old leather easy chair with Klinger at his feet. Noah took a picture of them to send to the quartet members who all knew and loved his dad and Klinger. He'd send it just before he called them to wish them luck. Then he got out the things he needed to make dinner and had everything ready to go, including the beef and the fish for the tacos, with enough time left over after he set up the large picnic table and chairs under the trees in the backyard for him to shower and fret over what to wear before it was time to go down and finish prepping the food.

When the doorbell rang, his dad went to get it, and he heard excited children's voices first, then the calmer adult tones. He shook out the tension gathering in his hands as he plated the ceviche and finished cooking the meat and fish. *Calm down, No.* He couldn't allow himself to be nervous just because Jax was in his house. He was tough. He could do this.

"Need help with anything?"

Jax's voice shook him out of the anxious haze that had been trying to settle over him. Managing not to jump at the sound of his voice, Noah turned and said, "Sure. Can you help me put these things on the table?" He pointed through the kitchen window. "We're eating outside."

Jax nodded, picked up two of the platters, and took them out, returning just as Jim walked in to help. Soon everyone was seated under the spreading oak and maple trees, the boys opting to sit on the big blanket he'd put down as an afterthought.

"This is good, Noah," Jim said, holding up one of the fish tacos. "You can cook for me anytime."

Noah laughed. "I'm glad you like it. Annie did say it was your favorite food."

Once the meal was over, the boys wandered off to play with Klinger while their parents chatted with Alvaro, who was clearly enjoying the company. Jax was quiet for the most part, though he did chime in every now and again. But Noah could feel his watchful attention, even when he didn't appear to be looking at him. They hadn't had a moment alone together since the guests had arrived, and he didn't see any opportunity presenting itself. That might not be a bad thing since he was so tied up in knots at the thought of being alone with his former lover.

"So my son tells me you are going to be working in our state, Professor Knox." Alvaro spoke into a lull in the conversation.

"Please, sir, it's just Jax. And yes, it's an opportunity I didn't want to pass up."

"I imagine it will be a big change from what you're used to in the city." Alvaro eyed Jax with curiosity.

"It definitely will, sir, but I'm ready for a change."

"A young man such as yourself will do well with positive changes, yes? Will those changes only be professional?"

Oh no! His dad hadn't just gone on a fishing expedition into Jax's business, had he? *What the hell, Papi?* Noah glanced over at Jax, whose face showed no signs of annoyance. Instead, he seemed to be faintly amused, as though an older almost-stranger asking him such a personal question was an everyday occurrence. Jim also seemed highly amused by the question, if the smirk he was trying to hide behind his beer was any indication. Thankfully, Annie was watching her sons, so she missed the byplay.

How would Jax answer such a nosy-as-hell question? Noah remembered Clara Haines's comments to him in the supermarket the day before and wondered if this was an old people thing. Did they just feel free to say what they thought without any filter? Was it some kind of privilege of being older? Did they think they had paid their dues to propriety enough that they were allowed to be increasingly inappropriate and inquisitive as they aged?

*Dios mio!* How would Jax answer this?

# Chapter 10

## *Jax*

*Noah still had his heart, even if he
believed he had lost his chance.*

Jax's lips twitched with the effort not to laugh out loud at Mr. Santiago's question. The guys all knew what the old man was asking … where was his good little woman? No one seeing him assumed he was anything but straight, and he was used to being asked about his love life by older folk who had even a passing acquaintance with him. And while he didn't care what anyone would think if they discovered he was gay, he wasn't sure what Noah's father would think if he knew that Jax had been in a relationship with his son. Had Noah told him?

Now wasn't the time to go down that rabbit hole though, because the old man was clearly waiting for an answer. Parents must all be the same everywhere in the world. Jax could hear his mother's soft but firm tones as she quizzed him about his lack of a partner. *You're not getting any younger,*

*Jackson*—she always called him by his full first name when he was in trouble, or she was being serious—*and neither am I. Don't make me die without a grandchild.* As though he didn't have siblings!

"For the moment, yes, sir."

He didn't need to add anything else for the older man to get the message that he wasn't going to say more and that no, there was no one. He didn't mind inquisitive questions from people he knew and cared about, but that didn't mean he was going to answer their questions in any more detail than he wished. And in this case, since what he was hoping for might not happen, the last thing he wanted to do was embarrass Noah.

"Well, you are still a young man," the older man opined with a wise nod. "You have some time to settle down."

This time Jax didn't suppress the laughter and the others joined in, though Noah's was barely audible. His expression was more of a grimace as he glared at his father, heightening Jax's amusement even more. He caught Noah's eyes, saw the apology in them, and winked. The pretty blush that immediately colored his cheeks made Jax's dick stir, so he looked away to avoid trouble. Neither of them needed to become the center of anyone else's attention for the rest of the time they were there.

Noah began clearing away the dinner things and Jax helped, seeing it as the perfect chance to steal a few moments alone.

"Dinner was great, Noah," he began when they brought in the empty platters and took a fresh bag of ice out of the freezer to take back to the cooler. "Thanks again for the invitation."

"You're welcome. And thanks, I'm glad you liked the food." Noah turned away to add more lemonade to the jug and pulled a few more beers from the freezer. Turning to Jax, he added, "Can you bring the two kinds of ice cream and the box of cones, please?"

Jax knew what Noah was doing and he didn't like the way it darkened his mood, like rain clouds over the sun. Maybe he was still irritated with his dad?

"Hey," he reached out a hand to stop Noah from leaving. "It's okay. Your dad is fine. He just..."

"Doesn't have a filter?" Noah interrupted him. "I know. Must be an old people thing."

Jax chuckled. "Can we talk soon?"

Noah's eyes caught the evening light streaming in through the kitchen window, sparkling like diamonds. He seemed to be deciding what, if anything, to say, then closed his mouth and nodded, taking the things he had in his hand out to the others.

"Who wants ice cream?" he called out, knowing the boys would come running. When they stood next to him, he gave them exactly what they asked for. "Anyone else want some ice cream?"

His father asked for one scoop in a cone and then he took a seat, pouring himself some lemonade. Desultory chatter followed while they watched the boys play frisbee with the dog. The backyard wasn't really big enough for an outdoor party as well as playing with the dog, but Jax's soul eased into the joy of being outdoors in pleasant company.

"When are you leaving to take up your new position, Jax?"

"I'll be gone in three or four weeks, sir."

"Has my boy been showing you the sights?"

Jax could see Noah cringing and he hurried to answer. "We only just caught up, sir. We did spend some time at the festival last weekend."

That was enough of a distraction as they talked about how the event had changed over time. Then Annie declared herself ready to go.

"It was great to hang out with you guys," she said once her husband had helped her up. "The boys had a great time, and I'm sure they're going to want more play dates with Klinger." She reached out to shake hands with Mr. Santiago. "It was good to meet you, sir. Once this little munchkin is born," she rubbed her belly, "we'll have you all over before you head back down to Florida."

"I can live with that." Alvaro shook her hand gently, before turning to say something meant only for Jax in his ear.

Noah walked with them to the front door and watched as Jim helped his wife into the front seat of his truck. Jax held back and when Noah finally looked at him, he could feel a fine tension stretching between them like spider webs, fragile yet tensile.

"I had a good time, Noah, and even though your dad put you on the spot, you don't have to take me anywhere. I'll be fine."

Color bloomed in Noah's cheeks, raising a corresponding warmth in Jax's chest that he fought to keep from traveling any further south. He had forgotten how Noah's blushes telegraphed his embarrassment or arousal, yet they turned him on regardless of the reason. He wanted to capture the warmth between his palms, to deepen it with kisses that would build a fire between them.

"It's not a problem. I have lessons most days, though I'm often free in the mornings."

"I'm at your disposal, as long as you won't mind me bringing the boys along sometimes. Annie is about to pop, poor thing, and she needs all the rest she can get, but with two rambunctious eight-year-old boys, that'll be hard to do."

"We can do kid-friendly things if that's what you need."

Was that disappointment that Jax was seeing in Noah's eyes? Did he want them to have alone time? How would that even happen, since they both lived with other people in each house? And why would he want that anyway, since it was clear that he was conflicted about how to be with Jax?

"We can do whatever you like, Noah. I'm not fussy. If you'd prefer, we can wait until Jim gets home and then go where you want to show me."

Noah smiled. "Most of the places I'd like to show you aren't open after six. But we can always talk about that. You'd better go." He looked over Jax's shoulder. "They're waiting for you."

Jax wanted to stay. The need to talk to Noah, to get rid of all the ugly feelings, the anger and hurt, had been burning inside him all afternoon, but short of inviting him out and finding some place where they could be alone for that conversation, he had to let it go. For now.

"Okay. I'll text you."

"Yeah, okay."

Jax wanted to kiss him. Badly. He clenched his fists to stop from reaching for him and stepped away. Noah's gaze was a searing flame licking against his spine, lighting him up as he settled into the back seat of the truck with the boys.

"I had a great time, Jax." Annie's voice dragged him away from his thoughts. "Your friend is a sweetheart, and his dad is a hoot."

"Yeah, they're nice people."

"I like his dog," Jude piped up. "Can we go and play frisbee with him again?"

"We'll have to see, buddy. They may not be home a lot." Jim sounded a note of caution.

"Then we could walk him," Jake chimed in, making Jax laugh.

"We'll still need their permission. How about I ask my friend the next time I see him?"

He wouldn't pass up any excuse to contact Noah again. In fact, this was the perfect opportunity to send that text he'd promised, and the reason would be legitimate. Silently thanking his godsons for the in, he got his phone out and started to compose the text message.

[Prof: Hey! The boys want to know when they can come back over to play with Klinger. And oh, they also want to walk him, if that's okay with you.]

He sat on it, not hitting send until he had changed into his sweats and was on his way out for his evening run. Half an hour of distance was as much as he could manage, and at least he didn't look desperate for Noah's attention, even if he was. Sliding the phone into the side pocket, he set off for the running path where he'd first bumped into Noah, wishing he could bump into him again.

A lot had happened since that fateful reunion. He'd had to come to terms with the truth of his feelings for the younger man. They hadn't changed, dissipated, or lessened in any way. Noah still had his heart, even if Jax believed he had lost his chance. Anything to keep Noah in his life though, even if only as a friend, was enough to keep Jax trying to rebuild the bridges broken between them.

The phone vibrated against his thigh. Jax slowed to a stop, jogging in place off to the side of the path. There was a text message and a missed call. He stopped jogging so he could read the message first.

[Noah: Where are you? I tried calling but you didn't pick up. I'm not a fan of texting if I have a choice, remember?]

Jax did remember. He'd been surprised at how impatient Noah had been with communicating with him in that way. *What's the point of a phone,* he'd ask, *if you're not going to talk on it?* He looked around and saw a convenient bench up from the beach but off the jogging path and sat so he could call him.

"Jax?"

"Yeah. Sorry for not answering before. I'm out on a run."

Silences between them, no matter how small, were fraught with anxiety on Jax's side. Patience was a strict schoolmaster, forcing him to wait until Noah decided how he wanted to respond.

"On the same path as before?"

Jax understood what he was asking. "Yes. I'm sitting on one of the benches right now, but I think there's a little way left to go before the path ends."

"Where are you exactly? Can you see street names or any landmark?"

Jax looked around him. He could see the lighthouse from where he sat, and what, if he wasn't misremembering, was the Harbor Lights Marina. And across the road from where he sat was what looked like an RV park. There were multiple campers lined up in their spots facing the street, their lights illuminating the park.

"Wait for me. I'll meet you there."

Noah hung up before he could reply. Jax put the phone away again and did some stretches before sitting again and checking his emails. There were a couple of messages that he would need to respond to as soon as he got back to the house. He dumped the junk mail, flagged the ones he needed to answer at once, and marked everything else as read. Footsteps approaching made him look up in time to see Noah headed his way, hoodie covering his head, his runner's form lithe and supple.

Jax wanted to know how long Noah had been in the hospital after his accident, who had been with him while he recovered, and what he had decided to do going forward. He wanted to know what Noah had done to move on with his life after graduation. Had he become one of those twenty-somethings who sowed a lot of wild oats, hooking up with anyone who smiled at him? Had he been in a long-term relationship, or had Jax spoiled him for any other man with his actions?

"Hi. Thanks for waiting."

Noah sat down next to him on the bench, panting slightly. Jax let him breathe. Truth be told, he needed a moment to breathe himself, because Noah's scent, which had apparently been imprinted on his brain never to be deleted, slammed into him again. His body remembered how Noah smelled after a run, after a shower, when he was dressed up for a concert, when he was dressed down for a slow weekend in his room. The memories that each of those scents evoked were some of the most endearing in Jax's life.

"The boys can come over any time to play with Klinger. My dad usually only goes out in the evenings, except for the two days a week that he plays golf. I already asked him, and he's fine with having them walk Klinger with him on his non-golf days."

"Thanks, man. Annie and Jim will be glad for that, not to mention Jude and Jake."

"No problem."

Silence spread out between them again, separating rather than connecting them. What could he say to close the gap? Noah beat him to it.

"It was hard being without you those last two years of college. So hard. Everyone knew something was wrong, but there was no one I could talk to about it. That made me even angrier. You isolated me so that I didn't have anyone I could confide in. After the first semester, I had my routine down pat, so people stopped noticing. But inside I was raw. Even with all the accolades I received for performances and the like, and with the establishment of the string quartet, I was so lonely."

Jax saw Noah's hands fisted in his lap as though he was stopping himself from punching him. Understandable, but still better than disciplinary action against one or both of them and a career perhaps in shambles before it had begun on Noah's part.

"I'm so sorry, b…Noah." He caught himself before the endearment cleared his lips.

"Why didn't you just switch me to Professor Parks? We could have continued to be discreet, like we'd been doing before. You jumped to the most extreme measure and didn't even discuss it with me. You treated me like I was a kid who didn't know what was best for himself."

Hurt and anger bubbled in Noah's tone, and they scorched Jax deep inside where he'd buried his own hurt.

"I know you weren't a child, Noah. D'you think that was easier for me? Or that I didn't think about how I could have done things differently? Hindsight is 20/20. I can't tell you the number of times I picked up my phone to call you and didn't. What was I going to say that would make you trust me with your heart again? And how would that have made things better?"

This time the silence was weighed down by all the emotions that had been sparking between them since that first night on this path, since their first meeting in the parking lot outside the music building at the college. It spoke volumes about how much each had meant to the other and how deep the wounds had run.

"God, I couldn't even stand to hear your name mentioned." This confession was so quiet that Jax almost didn't hear it. "I hated you because you made me have to face the rejection alone, because it made me weak, because I knew I shouldn't be mad at you since I knew why you did it."

"A clean break, Noah." Jax had to reiterate what had been so obvious to him back then, even as the pain of hearing that Noah had hated him wrenched at his heartstrings. "That was the only way I could see to manage it without succumbing to my grief over losing you."

Noah looked up then, as though Jax's words had struck a chord with him. "You grieved?"

Jax stopped himself from touching Noah by a sheer act of will. He pushed his hands into the pockets of his sweatpants, pressing his fingers into his thighs hard enough to leave bruises.

"Every day for the eighteen months where I saw you on campus and went in the opposite direction, or when I heard you practicing and a knife-edge of pain gutted me. Every concert I attended where you performed. Every smile that wasn't for me, that I knew would never be for me again, was fresh cause for grief."

Turbulent new waves of heartbreak washed over him as he raked over the memories of those early years after the breakup.

"At graduation, when you walked across the stage and didn't look at me, it killed me, Noah. I was so proud of you, so happy for your success, and so desperate to share those high moments with you. I knew it was my own fault that you'd shut me out, but it didn't make the hurt any easier to bear."

"Why didn't you call me after graduation?"

The raw question scraped Jax's bruised heart. "Why would I call you when I was the one who broke things off? I assumed that if you were still interested, you would call *me*. I thought I was respecting your need to keep your distance. Why didn't *you* call me?"

A bitter laugh burst from Noah, surprising Jax. "Is that why after all these years, we're still mad at each other? Why we're still caught up in what ifs and whys? Because we didn't have the guts to call each other?" He heaved a heavy sigh. "I thought you and Jim and the boys were a family when I first saw you at the festival, did you know that? And it burned me to think you'd moved on so far without me as to have kids when I couldn't even find a guy to start something long-term with."

Jax let a small smile escape. "Guess we're both in the same boat then, huh?"

"How's that?" Noah held his gaze a moment, then looked away.

"I told you I don't have anyone, Noah. I haven't had anyone since you." Sobering words, to be sure, but true nonetheless.

"No one? No one at all? You haven't had a man since...?" He trailed off.

"No, Noah. I've been propositioned and there was even the one guy I told you about who wanted to start something, but I was never interested."

There seemed to be nothing else to say on the subject. He didn't think he could bear to hear about Noah's sexual escapades if he'd become a hookup kinda guy. It was enough to know that they were both single, both hurting, and both scared to open up again, especially to each other. Time to move on to some other topic.

"Have you figured out what you're going to do now that playing with the quartet is off the table? Is there any other capacity in which you can be with them, so you're not completely cut off from them?"

"I have a few ideas. Nothing concrete as yet, aside from giving private lessons. I'll have to see, won't I?" Noah's voice had turned sad again.

"Have you told you father as yet?" One last try.

"No."

Jax understood at once that that one-word response meant the subject was off-limits. What had he done to upset Noah now? He was too old to keep chasing after someone who couldn't decide what he wanted, and who would probably keep blaming him for his heartbreak no matter how unreasonable that was. Fresh pain welled in his chest. He swallowed it down and stood.

"Well, thanks for checking in with your dad. The kids will be over the moon. I'd better get going now. Call me when you've got a plan for an outing."

He turned, preparing to jog away, when Noah's grip on his bicep stopped him. He looked over his shoulder at him, impatient to be gone before his pain boiled over into hot tears. He hadn't wept for Noah in years, and he wasn't about to start again now.

"Is that all you have to say?" Noah's voice was wrecked, as though he was struggling to keep himself together.

Jax sighed. He didn't want to keep playing cat and mouse games. Either they would be friends or they wouldn't, but he was done trying to figure out what Noah was thinking.

"What do you want me to say, Noah? What am I missing?" He half turned, keeping his frustration from leaking into his voice. *Cool and calm, Jax.*

Noah dragged him all the way back around in a surprising show of strength and stepped into his personal space.

"Don't you care, even a little bit, about what we used to have together? About what we could have had before...?" He stopped, then spoke again, this time not hiding the pain. "Am I the only one who's been fighting against old feelings, Jax? Did I mean so little to you back then? Was I really just imagining it?"

*Dammit!* "Noah, I don't think we should start something else again now, a decade after we last saw each other, unless it's for the right reasons. Renewing a relationship just because we're allowed to now *isn't* the right reason."

"So you're prepared to just let it go? You're not gonna fight for more? You're just gonna leave me, again?"

*How the hell am I supposed to answer that?* "I won't do anything that you're not interested in doing, Noah. If you want us to be friends, I need to know that. If you want more, I need to know that too. I'm not a mind reader any more than you are, and I've already told you that I'm not going to make any assumptions. I'm too old for that."

Noah let go of his arm and turned away. Jax saw his shoulders lift, then fall before he turned back and said, "That doesn't sound like a ringing endorsement of a relationship between us, so I guess I've got my answer. Maybe you should ask Jim to help you find places to visit."

*What the fuck?* Jax's patience disappeared. He grabbed Noah by the wrist and did what he'd been wanting to do for a week. He pulled him close and took his lips in a kiss that he couldn't keep from being just this side of brutal, because it was pent up with frustration and desire and need. His blood sang with a fiery hunger that Noah's response echoed, their tongues searching for more than a simple kiss would give them. He didn't care that they were out in the open where anyone could see them. He suspected Noah didn't either. Zero to a hundred in seconds, the way it had always been between them.

Lightning still sizzled in Jax's veins, a fire banked, barely contained, the kiss a poor substitute for all that swirled in his heart to do with the man he held in his arms. Everything he wanted, every pleasure he desired, every beat of his heart still belonged to Noah, would forever belong to him. He had always known that, even when he denied it most vehemently. But his hunger, unsatisfied, left him starving now for things he could not have without a change. And change was a fearsome, ravenous beast. Jax dragged his lips away, hauling in a deep, centering breath before speaking.

"The last time I made a decision for the two of us, we didn't look back when we walked away. This time, when we walk away, I need you to know that the decision for what happens next is all yours."

He let him go then and stepped away. This time, Noah didn't stop him.

# Chapter 11

## *Noah*

*He had to choose which pain he was most
willing to endure for the prize he desired.*

"Why are you moping around like a lost puppy, *mijo*?
What's going on with you?"

Noah stood up to clear away the breakfast things, words churning in his mind but stalling on his tongue. There was so much happening with him that he didn't even have a handle on it himself, so how was he supposed to explain it to his dad? Maybe he should start with the easier issue? Easier ... if it weren't so painful, he would laugh at the word. He sighed instead.

"I won't be playing with the quartet any longer, *Papi*."

There ... he'd said the dreaded words. He waited for the pain to swamp him, but nothing happened. It hurt for sure, but not in the way it had been for the last six months. Apparently digging up his one and only real relationship had eclipsed even the loss of what he had thought would be his life's career. When his father said nothing in response, Noah turned to look at him properly.

"Come and sit down," Alvaro said after a minute. "The dishes can wait." He waited until Noah was seated across from him again before continuing. "I suppose this is because of the accident?"

Noah nodded. "Even with therapy and daily exercises, I will never have full range of motion in my hand again, and playing for long periods of time is very painful. I can't handle the long hours of practice or the grueling tour schedules anymore."

"Will you be unable to perform at all?" His father's eyes grew shadowed with sadness for him, but not pity, thank God.

"Not for a full concert, no. Maybe a solo piece, but even those would need to be fairly short. You remember when I was in middle and high school and played solo pieces? It would be like I was in high school again."

Alvaro reached for his hand across the table. "*Lo siento, mijo!* I know how much it pains your heart to say those words. You must grieve this loss as you would any other. And then, when you are ready, you must move on. You will know what to do when the time is right, when the heart is eased."

Noah squeezed his father's hand in appreciation for his solidarity. No questions, no recriminations, not even a concern for how he would make a living going forward. His father gave him what he needed in the moment, and he was more grateful than he knew how to say it.

"*Gracias, Papi.* And I'm sorry I didn't tell you as soon as I knew."

Shame swept through him as he realized that his father was never the one who would be in any way disappointed in him. It was his own disappointment with himself that had colored his decision to hide the news from his father. His own devastation and despair had pushed him into making a poor decision, and when he looked into his father's eyes as he apologized, he saw the disappointment in them as well. He had let him down, because he hadn't trusted him to have his back as he had done all his life.

"When did you begin to mistrust me, Noah? What did I do to earn it?"

Noah tried to pull his hand away, but Alvaro held on, strong despite his advanced years. He would need to confess the whole truth about this debacle. His father did not deserve to bear any guilt in the matter.

"You didn't, *Papi*. That was all on me. I should have told you, but I was embarrassed. I couldn't bear the thought of you thinking less of me because of my poor decision-making."

His father released his hand and sat back in his chair, his eyes assessing his son. "Were you driving the vehicle when the accident happened?"

"No, someone else was."

The one thing he would never share with his dad was that he'd only met the man an hour earlier, and that they'd been headed off to fuck each other when it happened.

"Yet it sounds like you are blaming yourself for what happened."

His father had never been slow on the uptake. "We shouldn't have gone out that late after leaving the bar. We weren't drunk, but..." He paused, searching for a good way to say what he had to say. "Someone had drugged him, but he didn't know, and it only began to take effect after we were in the car."

Alarm showed on Alvaro's face, but he said nothing for a moment, as though he needed the time to absorb the shock. Then he spoke. "So it was an accident because of a third person. You could not have known that, Noah, unless you were the one who drugged him. And since I know you didn't, you must let it go."

Another long pause, while Noah said nothing. What else was there to say? His father was right, after all.

"Now, tell me the rest."

Noah's eyes shot up to his father's face, his brow creasing in confusion. "The rest?"

Alvaro smiled as though he knew a secret. Noah's heart began a heavier rhythm in his chest.

"It is not just the bad news about your work that has you looking like an eagle with its wings clipped, *mijo*. There is something else weighing you down. I cannot help you if you hide things from me." His smile turned smug.

"I..."

What the hell was he to say? He had never told his father about him and Jax, and though the older man had asked him every year when he was going to introduce him to his man, Noah had always denied having anyone. And it had been true. He hadn't been in a long-term relationship with anyone after Jax, so he'd never brought a boyfriend home.

"Do you remember that Christmas concert that you played at the college in your junior year? You played two solo pieces and were the principal violin for the orchestra. Remember that night?"

Noah remembered it vividly. He had been overjoyed that his father had been able to make it, that he had seen him perform ... and that he'd been able to introduce him to Jax. He looked into his dad's eyes again and saw knowledge and understanding alongside his amusement. Did he know? How the hell *did* he know? Was he angry? He knew his dad could hide his emotions and reactions when he wanted to.

"Yes, I remember it. It was a great night," he answered truthfully, keeping his tone neutral. "Why?"

"It was really good to see your professor again after all these years."

The abrupt change of subject had Noah searching his father's face to try to understand what was going through his mind. Only a smile showed, kind and understanding, as well as amused.

"I thought you might like to see him again since he's in the neighborhood. But why did you ask if I remembered the concert?"

He wasn't going to let that go. He had to know what was on his father's mind before he panicked. His dad had known he was gay even before he'd come out to him, and his admission had been met with a hug and a demand for another beer. So he knew objectively that Alvaro wouldn't be surprised if he admitted to feelings for Jax. Noah just didn't know if he would approve.

"He seemed uneasy, though he tried to disguise it. And you were on edge as well. Why did you have them over if you weren't comfortable in their company?"

Fuck! This wasn't going to be an easier conversation than the last one because now they were talking about the elephant in the room ... Jackson Knox, former lover.

"I wasn't exactly uncomfortable," he began, words escaping his brain like rats from a sinking ship. "It's just ... it's been ten years since I graduated, and we haven't been in touch in all that time. It was just a bit awkward that's all."

Alvaro sat forward, placing his elbows on the table and clasping his hands under his chin, his eyes still trained on his son.

"That concert night was the last time I saw him, and after that, you never talked about him. I was surprised, because you seemed to get along with him so well before. And now you tell me you didn't keep in touch. Again, I have to ask, why?" He raised a forefinger to silence him before Noah could answer. "Just so you know, I think you have another confession to make, one that has been a long time coming."

Noah sighed. Should he quibble, or should he just come clean? His dad was like the FBI when he got wind of something, and even though he never played his hand until he had to, you always knew he had something up his sleeve. And you always knew he wouldn't give up until he got the answer to his question. It was just how he was.

"There's nothing to confess now, *Papi*," he began.

Strictly speaking, he wasn't lying. He and Jax weren't in a relationship. In fact, after last night, and despite that hot-as-hell kiss, they were probably really over for good, unless he could get his shit together and stop acting like a damn teenager. Jax had made it clear that the next move was his. He was just paralyzed by fear of the unknown. He'd never been in any relationship either before or after Jax, and he didn't know the moves. A cresting wave of panic, which his father's next comment did nothing to contain, threatened the calm he was trying to project.

"Ah, but what about before now?"

How had he missed the fact that his father had guessed that something was going on between him and Jax? They had never talked about Jax aside from when he and Noah had worked together. And after the breakup, they hadn't talked about him at all, though his dad asked about him every time Noah went home. And once he told him that Jax wasn't his tutor anymore, even those seemingly innocent questions had stopped. But had they really been innocent, or had his father been gently trying to get him to come clean?

What harm would there be in rehashing the story to the one man he had trusted his whole life? Alvaro was wise enough to know when to speak and when to be silent. He wouldn't offer unsolicited advice, but that didn't mean Noah shouldn't ask ... if only he could figure out the questions.

"Jax and I were together briefly before he broke things off between us."

"Did he take advantage of you because you were his student?"

Noah's horrified "No, *Papi*, no!" echoed around the kitchen. "It was consensual. He never did anything I didn't want him to do."

He stood up again and went back to the sink, suddenly needing to occupy his hands to stop them from shaking. Jax had had his whole heart and soul then, and now he realized he wanted that again. Each of them had made mistakes in the aftermath of that office visit where Jax ended things. Both were guilty of causing the other pain. Now Jax was waiting for him to say what he wanted, as he had always done in the past.

"Did you love him, Noah?"

His father's voice was right behind him. He hadn't heard the old man move, but he welcomed the warmth at his back and the hand on his shoulder when he nodded wordlessly. Alvaro squeezed him gently where he held him, then moved to make himself another cup of coffee. Noah washed the few dishes they had used, along with the pan and the utensils. By the time he was wiping down the counter, his father had a full mug of coffee, doctored with his usual fixings, and was heading back to the table.

He pulled a bottle of water from the refrigerator. He was keyed up enough without adding to it by having more caffeine.

"Sit down again and talk to me. It is hard to bear the burden of a lost love twice over, *mijo*."

He took a loud slurp of his coffee and then rested the mug on the table before speaking again. He had a faraway expression on his face, one that Noah had seen a lot less frequently in the last decade, but one he knew meant his father was remembering something poignant.

"I will tell you a story. Maybe it will help you to decide whether or not you want to take this second chance that the heavens have granted you, *si?*"

Alvaro had always been a romantic, although he had never married anyone after Noah's mother. He only knew that his mother was a beautiful woman who had died when he was still too young to know her well, and that his father had loved her.

"Your mama Isabella was a beautiful woman." Noah smiled, recognizing the words, welcoming them. "We met when she was leaving Florida. She was on the train from Miami to Washington, D.C. At that time, I was working in the cafe car. She came in to buy breakfast, and the coffee spilled as she was moving away. She looked so young, so lost, so alone. I couldn't leave my station, but I replaced her coffee, paid for it myself because I suspected that she didn't have money for more. And then I went in search of her on my break and found her sitting next to an old woman who wasn't pleased that I had come to ask after her."

"Who was the old woman?"

"Isabella's grandmother. She was taking her up to D.C. to live with her uncle because her parents had been killed trying to escape from Cuba."

Noah's heart clenched. He knew the horror stories about the Cuban refugees and had felt a keen sense of loss whenever he heard of another tragedy. And now he understood why ... a part of him lay beneath the Atlantic as well.

"To make a long story short, I was able to get my information to her when they got off the train in Washington. It usually switches engines there, and the bathrooms are cleaned and so on. I took a quick break so I could slip my number into her hand when her grandmother wasn't looking."

Alvaro's smile was wide and full of love. "Isabella was ... I couldn't resist her beauty. And I could feel her innocence. I worked that route for the rest of the year, hoping to see her, but she never rode the train again, at least not when I was working."

"And she never called?"

"Not for two years. I had just given up hope of ever seeing her again when she called. You have to understand, I was twelve years older than she was, and when we met that first time, she was a mere girl of twenty, though I didn't know that at the time. I would have waited for her forever if I had to, though, but only if she wanted it. When she was ready, we would be together. My work meant I wasn't at home often, so I couldn't be upset if she didn't want me."

"But she wanted you?" Noah found he was dying to hear the rest of the story, even though he knew how it ended.

"She did. And when she called, it was because she had been thrown out by her aunt who found out that she had a boyfriend."

"What?"

Alvaro laughed bitterly. "That boyfriend was me. Isabella used me to get away from them because her uncle started molesting her six months into her time there, and he didn't stop. It was then she called me to ask for my help. She was twenty-two, alone in a big city and I couldn't let what happened to her continue, especially as she wasn't very fluent in English. So, I married her."

Noah gaped at his father, shock reverberating through him. "So it was a marriage of convenience?"

"I suppose you could call it that. But I felt something more than lust for her. I wanted to protect her, and the best way I knew to do that was to make her mine, so she could remain here with me without worrying."

Noah was trying to do the math in his head. His father was seventy years old, which meant that he was thirty-eight when Noah was born. So they'd been married for six years before he came along.

"Why did you wait so long to start a family?"

"Six years isn't a long time when you have the kind of relationship that we had in the beginning. Isabella had to get to know me, to trust me with more than her physical safety. And she needed to get qualified to do more than clean office buildings and be an off-the-books nanny to rich people's bratty kids. We agreed that we'd wait to have kids until she had at least a high school diploma to start with. But then she decided she wanted to be a nurse, so we moved the timeline to include an associate's degree so she could begin that work as a licensed practical nurse."

Hearing about his mother after all this time settled something inside Noah that he hadn't even been aware had been waiting for that knowledge.

"She sounds like she was a really strong woman, *Papi*."

"She was." Pride colored his father's words, pride and an ineffable sadness that Noah could almost feel from across the table. "By the time she was twenty-four, she had a degree and two jobs. We wanted to buy a house, because by then she knew she could trust me with her heart. But to do that, we would need to leave Washington."

"That's how you ended up here?"

"Yes. We spent almost two years trying to find a place we would feel comfortable in, a place where I wouldn't worry about her when I wasn't with her." He paused, drinking more of his coffee. "It was not easy to be her husband without the comfort of her body in those first years. But I knew what I wanted with her was more than the pleasures of the flesh. And I knew when she saw me for who I was, she would reward me with her love."

The smile that lit up his face was almost blinding. Noah had never seen his father like this before. Is that what love did to a man? Did it make him shine like the sun? Did it make every painful memory still one to be treasured? Suddenly, he understood why his father was telling him the story he had kept to himself for all these years. He had to decide what he wanted from a partner and whether he was prepared for that person to be the man who had broken his heart once before. He had to choose which pain he was most willing to endure for the prize he desired.

"For two years, we were lovers, partners, friends, and when you were born two years later, we were also parents. And then your mama was killed by a drunk driver."

Noah's heart stuttered at those words. His father had never told him exactly how his mother had died, just that she had been gone since he was two years old. She had been so young when she died ... two years younger than his thirty-two years. He felt wounded, as though she had just been killed this instant. He supposed, for him, she had been. Why hadn't he asked before? He had taken her absence for granted and felt shame now at the thought of it.

His father was still speaking. "I have been tempted by a few special people since Isabella's death to fill the hole she left behind, but I couldn't. I did not have the strength or the will to take a second chance. And though my memories of her are bright and unforgettable, they do not warm me at night, and I have grown too used to living with the fear of losing again." Alvaro sat forward once more, his hands flat on the table between them. "Don't make my mistake, *mijo*. Don't be afraid of a second chance."

Noah reached out to touch his father's hands. "I am sorry for your loss, *Papi*, and for the pain you still bear. I am sorry that I never asked about my mother, that I let you bear this burden of grief alone."

"My grief was never yours to bear, my son." Alvaro squeezed Noah's hands, a sad smile on his face. "But there is always room for love. If you still love this professor of yours, you must make a way to get whatever it is you want with him before it is too late. He is getting older and more settled in his ways, and most likely more afraid to risk a change that may cause him pain. You have it within your power to stop him from ending up where I have been stranded these many years. You are still here, alive, and well. Do not let this second chance pass you by."

# Chapter 12



*Jax had told him that the next move was his,*
*so now he'd have to be tough enough to wait.*

"Good morning, Dr. Knox. Mary Morgan here. We spoke briefly about your housing needs two weeks ago. You left a message yesterday that you were ready to come up to look at some prospects."

"Yes, good morning, Ms. Morgan. Thanks for returning my call."

"I've lined up three homes for you to visit, but you should know that one of them is a townhouse condominium unit. I know that that's not your first choice, but it is close to the campus and is below your price point. Also, one of them is a rent-to-own property. I thought you might be interested in that one since it sits on a lake and your closest neighbor is a quarter mile away on your left. You'd have no neighbors on your right, though there is construction happening the same distance to the right."

Jax appreciated the agent's attention to his needs, so even though he was almost certain he wasn't going to choose the condominium, he decided he'd give it a fair shake.

"I'd like to see the condominium first and the rent-to-own property last, if that's convenient."

"Certainly. I can make those arrangements immediately. I'll call you back to let you know the date and time to meet me. We'll meet at the first site. I'll send you directions to that. I'll speak with you soon, Dr. Knox."

After she rang off, Jax sat back in the chair at the desk he was seated at and stared out the window at the boys, who were playing stickball in the backyard with their friends. Jim's lot was larger than most of the others on the street, and because it was also a corner lot, it had that extra give, so he often hosted some of the younger neighborhood boys on lazy summer days like this one.

Annie was doing a lot of going back and forth from her bedroom to the nursery. Jim said she was nesting, which made her sound like a bird to Jax, but he didn't comment. Jim had gone into the office today to get some much-needed paperwork done that could only be handled in person. He said he'd be late, which was fine with Jax. Anything to stop him from obsessing over that kiss that he'd planted on Noah three nights before was more than welcome.

What the hell had possessed him to do a thing like that? He wasn't a green boy; he was a grown-assed man in full control of his impulses. Except for that night apparently. And then to run away like a coward ... pitiful! He wouldn't be at all surprised if Noah never spoke to him again, even if his response had had Jax shaking in his running shoes and hardening painfully in his sweatpants. Just because Noah seemed to enjoy the kiss didn't mean that Jax should have crossed that line.

Sighing, he moved on to the next item on his To Do list ... responding to the head of the music department regarding his proposed schedule. Jax really didn't care who they gave him as students, as long as they didn't change any of the duties required of him as a distinguished professor. And he wanted his weekends free, except for performances. The book he'd just finished working on was with the editor, and the college already knew its contents. He was looking forward to becoming part of the performance team at the college, more than ready to accustom himself to the culture and to the academic climate in general.

He opened up his laptop and found the email, letting the professor know he'd be in town in a day or two if she cared to meet him in person to go over the details. Then he answered the friend whom he had left in Rochester to let him know that as soon as he had a place of his own, he was invited for a visit. Dan Vogel had befriended him from the first day of his tenure at the university, and that friendship was still going strong after fourteen years.

The only thing that Dan didn't know about Jax was that he'd had a student as a lover for six months. Happily single at sixty, Dan had often tried to set Jax up with what he called "suitable men" but they had all been staid and unimaginative. Thankfully, Dan had given it up after the issue with Jax's pushy wannabe boyfriend got to be unbearable.

Once the note was sent, he called his mother. "Hi, Mom."

"Jax!" His name was a joyful sound in her voice. "I'm so glad you called. I've been thinking about you. How are you, honey?"

"I'm good, Mom. How are you? I'm sorry I haven't called before."

"Well, you've called now and that's all that matters."

The warmth and delight in her voice told Jax she meant everything she'd said. Relief filled his chest with an answering warmth as she continued to speak.

"I'm doing okay, just waiting for your little brother to finish his breakfast so he can take me food shopping."

"How is Eli, and what's he doing in Florida?"

His younger brother Elijah had been walking a straight line since he'd been arrested twelve years earlier and had spent time in prison for aggravated assault. At thirty-eight, he was making a good living in construction, had managed to find a strong woman who loved him, and had twin baby girls whom he would die for.

"Remember that he broke his wrist a few weeks ago? Well, he's got at least another four weeks on disability, so he decided he'd bring the family down for a little vacation. It's so wonderful having my grandbabies here with me. But you know Eli … he can't sit still. The kids are out with their mothers, and Dale is on his way to work. He just got off a two-day break, so he'll be doing twelve-hour shifts the next three days."

Dale was his little sister's husband, a nurse at the Naval Hospital in Jacksonville where they lived.

"So, how is everything with the new job? Have you found a place to live yet? When are you going up?"

"I'm visiting with Jim and Annie," Jax told her. "Annie's about ready to pop out her little girl, and Jim's staying close to home, so I'm helping keep the boys occupied so she can rest."

"Aw, bless her! I'm so glad she's doing well with this baby. Give them my love, won't you?"

"Will do, Mom. And I'm going to be looking at some places in the next couple of days. Hopefully I'll find something I like so I can move my things from storage and be ready to start by the end of August."

"Will you be able to pop down for a visit before then?"

Jax wished he could, but he wouldn't promise something he wasn't sure he could follow through on. "I don't know, Mom. Depends on how soon the housing issue gets resolved. I'll let you know."

"Alright then." Jax heard a shuffling on his mother's end, then she said, "Well, say hi to your brother so we can go. And take care of yourself, please. Next time, I'll want to hear about you, not your job."

Jax said a few words to his brother, who wasn't much of a talker to begin with, before he hung up. He had understood the meaning behind his mother's last coded words. She was going to pry into his personal life ... again. He'd been forced to give her some version of the truth after he ended things with Noah because her sharp eyes had not missed the fact that he'd lost weight and was generally not his usual self. It was almost as though distance and time apart gave her a keener eye and ear where he was concerned whenever he was where she was. Since then, she hadn't stopped asking about his love life, insisting that there was still time to find the love of his life.

He knew he'd already found him though. Eleven years ago, things had been new and uncertain, and he had convinced himself that aside from the impropriety of their relationship because of the power dynamic involved, he was really too old for Noah and it was better for the two of them if he let him go so the younger man could find someone with whom he had more in common. It hadn't made the breakup easier, but at least it had made him feel less like a heel.

Now he would have to deal with the pain of that loss a second time, unless Noah chose him again. What were the odds of that happening though, especially after his hot-tempered ultimatum? There wasn't time to dwell on any of that now, because his phone chimed a message. The realtor had texted him back with an address and time for the next day.

He replied confirming the information and then sat back, feeling completely out of sorts. Things were going just as he planned. He would have enough to do these next two days at least to keep his mind off Noah. Pocketing his phone, he went in search of Annie. He'd promised to do some food shopping for her, and she had been making a list before she started in on the nursery. He found her there, smoothing the coverlet over the small mattress in the crib. The colors in the room were a soothing blue and gray, with pops of yellow and pink.

"I'm ready to go shopping now, Annie. Where's your list?"

She turned at the sound of his voice and smiled tiredly at him, pulling a slip of paper from the pocket of her dress.

"Thanks, Jax. Don't worry if you can't find everything. Sometimes my shopping list is more like a wish list."

They chuckled together, but before he left, Jax said, "You look like you need to be off your feet for a bit. Why don't you go put your feet up until I get back, hmm? I'd feel a whole lot better knowing you're not tiring yourself out while I'm not around to help if something happens."

She closed the gap between them and rested her palm against his cheek. "You're a real sweetheart. Some lucky guy is going to win big time when he catches you."

Jax grinned. "Nice try, but a compliment, no matter how sweet, is not a promise. Are you going to get off your feet until I get back?"

"I promise, Mother!" Her sardonic tone was not lost on him. "See, I'm going now."

She walked out of the nursery ahead of him and went through to the back porch, settling herself in the recliner next to a small table holding the Kindle e-reader she had plugged in and a tall, insulated bottle. She'd been prepared, as though she knew he would make that request of her.

"Satisfied?" She lifted her brows at him when she was settled.

"Very," he returned with a smirk, ignoring her sass. "I'll be as quick as I can."

He had to drive past Noah's home to get into town. There was a car on the driveway that he knew wasn't Noah's. Who was with him? What were they doing? Maybe it was one of his students' parents waiting for their child. He turned his eyes back to the road and willed his thoughts away from Noah. Jax had told him that the next move was his, so now he'd have to be tough enough to wait. Whether forever or just for a while was not up to him, and if the answer was not what he prayed for, he would pick up the pieces and keep moving. No matter what happened, he had known love.

The supermarket seemed unusually crowded for the middle of the week, and he was grateful that no one in this little town knew him so he could zip through the aisles taking care of business without any delays. Except of course, when he couldn't find the natural peanut butter that Annie had on the list. And though she had said he could leave whatever he couldn't find, he knew that the boys could make their own PB&J sandwiches, so finding it would be helpful to her. He decided to make one more attempt, slipping down to the last aisle where all the natural foods were shelved.

Just as he snagged the last jar of the item on the shelf, he felt a tickle in his spine and turned around. Noah stood directly behind him, watching him. How uncanny was it that he could still feel the other man in his orbit? They hadn't seen each other in more than a decade, and yet he was as attuned to him as he had ever been. He set the jar in the cart and turned to walk back so he could do the adult thing and say hello.

"Food shopping for Annie?"

Noah eschewed the common courtesies, a sure sign he was as flustered as Jax felt. Jax opted to answer the question as asked.

"Yeah. She's having a lie down and watching the boys play with their friends in the backyard."

Why was he babbling like an idiot? He clamped his jaws together and pushed past before adding, "I'd better get going now. Nice to see you again."

Embarrassment dogged him as he headed to the cashier. If he were a cartoon character, he'd be melting into a puddle of slimy humiliation right now. Maybe he could escape before he made more of a fool of himself. Noah's cart had only two or three items in it, suggesting that he'd just started his own shopping. So maybe Jax would get checked out and be able to leave before he was done. He chose to hope and when he was out in the bright sunshine of midday again, headed toward his car, he finally let his shoulders down and sighed.

"In a hurry?"

Noah's voice behind him was a shock he wasn't prepared for. "Not really. But I wanted to get back so I could see about finding some touristy thing to do this afternoon."

His only plan had been to maybe drive to the closest beach and spread out his beach towel with a book. But he wouldn't mention that in case Noah took it as an invitation. He wasn't looking for company, unless it came willingly without any suggestion from him.

"Any plans for the rest of the week?"

They had stopped in the middle of the parking lot, right in the middle of the roadway. Jax moved to the side behind a big Ford F350 before answering.

"I'm going up to the college tomorrow. I have a meeting in the music department and three houses to see with the realtor after that."

See? He had a life, and the next day's plans were proof positive of that fact. He wasn't waiting around for validation from Noah. He had a career he still loved and was about to embark on another adventure that would hopefully take him through middle age to retirement.

"I can hang out with you this afternoon, maybe show you a couple of sights if you like, and then you can choose between a hike and beach time."

Was this another olive branch? "And tomorrow?" What the hell? That was *not* what he had planned to say.

"I have two lessons in the morning and one in the afternoon. Sorry."

"It's fine. I will probably be too busy anyway, once I get up there. And house hunting is no fun."

"So is that a yes for this afternoon? I can swing by and pick you up." Definitely an olive branch.

Jax had been trying to read Noah's face while they talked, but aside from the way he avoided direct eye contact—he wondered what was so fascinating over his left shoulder—there was no giveaway emotion. He would allow hope a foot in the door, but no more. Maybe this was Noah's next move and since he had nothing better to do, and really wanted to be with him, he nodded.

"Sure. Give me an hour."

If this was their second date, he was not going to look less than his best for an afternoon in a museum and maybe hiking or swimming. Which was a preposterous thought, forcing him to stifle the laugh trying to escape.

"Say hi to everyone for me, please."

"Will do." Suddenly, leaving was difficult. "How's your dad?"

Noah looked at him at last, his eyes shining as though he knew what Jax was doing and found it highly entertaining.

"He's fine. He went golfing yesterday and is worn out, so he's resting for his poker game at the men's club tonight."

"Retirement goals," Jax said with a laugh. "Good for him."

Noah smiled. "Well, I'll see you in an hour."

Jax watched him for a long moment before heading to his own car. He ended up driving behind Noah and watched him pull into his driveway, tooting his horn as he drove past. And once he got back to Jim's place, he unpacked the groceries in record time and texted Jim to tell him he'd be out when he got home in an hour.

[Jim: Hot date? 😜]

[Jax: You could say that. I mean, it *is* a hot afternoon. 😀]

[Jim: 😃 Have fun, bro. 😉 🍆 I'll see you later.]

Jax laughed out loud as he packed his beach towel, sunscreen, and Kindle into the duffel he pulled from the closet. Annie was just waking up when he walked out of his room with the bag in his hand.

"Going out?"

She mumbled a "Sorry" when she yawned before he could answer. He chuckled and hugged her lightly.

"No problem. I'm glad you got a nap. Yeah, Noah's taking me to see a couple of sights now, and tomorrow I'll be house hunting. I unpacked all the groceries. Hope I put everything in the right spot."

She smiled widely at the mention of Noah. "I'm glad. I don't know what's between you two, but I could tell you were both interested. Jim's right. It's time you found someone for yourself."

Jax shook his head. "Alright, Miss Matchmaker, stop worrying about me. I'm fine. I'll see you later."

# Chapter 13

## Jax

*Focus on the now, Jax.*

Jax headed toward the front door just as a knock sounded on it. Annie gave him a thumbs up sign as he walked out to meet his not-quite-date. Noah's outfit—board shorts and a yellow t-shirt—was as relaxed his own, and the sight of those sharply defined calf muscles, overlaid with a thin layer of silky dark hair, spiked his blood pressure.

"Hi. Thanks for the invitation," he said, focusing his attention on civilities. He didn't need to let himself get lost in the things about Noah that cranked his engine.

"Not a problem," Noah answered with a smile. "I know you love museums…"

He paused and looked away, and Jax knew what he was thinking. They had visited a number of museums while they were together, both sharing an interest in the stories of humanity that those places stored. In fact, their first date had been to a museum.

"Yes, I do. So where are we going today?" *Focus on the now, Jax.*

"Well, there's a military museum that I've always wanted to visit. Depending on how long that visit takes, I thought we could also take in the railroad museum at the north end of the park. My dad took me there often when I was a kid and I loved it. After that, it's up to you what we do."

"Sounds good."

They headed out, Jax enjoying the ride in the pickup truck. The windows were down, and he stole glances of Noah as they rode along. His hair was longer than he used to wear it when he was younger, and it blew gently around his face as the air lifted it. His big hands on the steering wheel were strong and veined, his nails clean and blunt cut. He watched those hands grip the wheel, remembering how they had felt wrapped around his biceps as they kissed and around his cock the first time they touched each other intimately.

"Here we are. It's a nice day for this visit."

Noah's voice brought Jax out of his trance. Thank God the man hadn't been looking at him as he'd been ogling him, or he would have seen the flush on Jax's cheeks at the direction of his thoughts. Stepping out of the truck, he looked around and decided it was a good thing they had stopped at this museum first. There seemed to be a lot of exhibits in the wide field surrounding the building that apparently housed the rest of the holdings.

Though there was no entrance fee, Jax dropped a twenty-dollar bill into the donation jar at the front desk. He wandered around behind Noah, listening with half an ear as his guide gave him the history behind this military facility. They walked through the whole house before stepping back into the bright sunshine to walk around the field while Noah regaled him with the rest of the story about the barracks, the men who were stationed there, the battles they lost and won.

Back in the gift shop, Jax decided he'd purchase a set of coasters for Annie with a military theme, and a mug for Jim with a picture of the fort. He'd get gifts for the boys at the railroad museum. He didn't pay attention to what Noah picked up, aside from wondering if he was buying gifts for his father. Then they were back in the truck, heading toward the railroad museum.

"So what did you think?" Noah asked.

"That was a great visit. The stories are intriguing. We don't often think about the hardships that soldiers faced back then, but it definitely makes you think about what they're enduring these days even with all the progress we've made. They're without their families a lot of the time with no guarantee that they'll ever see them again when they're deployed."

"Yeah. I could never be in the military. Too many sacrifices to be made with sometimes questionable rewards."

Jax understood his reluctance. He admired his own brothers who were deployed and who saw their duty to their country as the highest imperative. But they also chose to remain single because the family life of an enlisted man presented challenges they were not prepared to work through. He understood how lonely a life that was.

They drove on in silence, Jax making sure to keep his eyes off Noah's hands. The railroad museum sat in a pleasant glade, once again a mostly outdoor facility. The shade of the large trees around the outdoor exhibits, coupled with the breeze from the lake, eased the intensity of the summer heat, and the air-conditioned interior of the gift shop was a further welcome respite. Jax bought each of the boys an old-fashioned engineer's cap and a whistle, and without letting on what he was doing, he picked up an insulated water bottle with the words "Still Plays With Trains" and a single train car emblazoned on it for Noah.

"So have you had enough walking around? We can head to the beach. I know one that's not as popular as some of the others. It's one of the ones only us locals use."

"I had been planning to go sit on a beach somewhere before you suggested the museums, so that's fine with me."

The beach wasn't too far away and as promised, it was almost empty of people. Noah led Jax to an outcropping of rocks by a dune and they set up their picnic spot. Noah had brought a large umbrella in faded orange which he planted in the sand, so they'd be shaded from the sun.

"This is cozy."

Jax settled his back against one of the rocks and watched as Noah set up a collapsible chair and sank into it. The stone was hot against his spine, but he didn't mind since it helped to relax his tight muscles and he could focus on the heat behind him instead of the man beside him currently pulling two beers from the cooler he had placed on the blanket.

"Whenever you're ready we can go for a swim. I checked the water quality report today, and it's safe for swimming."

Jax had never given any thought to the water quality before when he went swimming, so he was glad he had Noah with him today. He wondered why there needed to be a report but didn't want to spoil the relaxed feeling by initiating conversation about something he could find out from a Google search. He'd rather sit here and watch as Noah stripped his t-shirt off and exposed his flat stomach and lightly furred chest. The hair on his arms also drew Jax's eyes to him and he realized with a start that he apparently had some kind of hair fetish where Noah was concerned.

He had never paid attention to any other man as lightly furred as Noah was, and in fact, couldn't remember ever having even been at all attracted to a hairy man before. But something about the way the hair on Noah's body lay sleek and soft-looking on his skin, how its darker color contrasted with his fair complexion, made Jax want to stroke him the way he would a cat, to bask in the sensual feel of it against his palm. He remembered how it had felt when Noah's chest was pressed to his, or when an arm or a leg brushed against his bare skin and now, he wanted that feeling again.

He really shouldn't encourage such thoughts when he didn't know where they would be going forward. He sipped the beer that Noah had handed him, distracting himself. The liquid was still ice cold, and he savored the sharp relief it gave him as it slid down his throat.

"Do you come here often?" *Why did that sound like a pick-up line?*

"Not often, no. I only come here when I have company."

Noah's full lips, wrapped around the edge of the can, distracted Jax from the uncomfortable feeling of jealousy that swept over him at the thought of Noah with some other man on this beach. Instead, saliva pooled in his mouth at their wet, glistening plumpness. It was a good thing he wasn't sitting close enough to snatch a taste of them for himself. He stifled a moan and swallowed more beer to cool the rising feelings inside him. He turned his eyes out to where foamy whitecaps barreled onto the shore. Maybe wading before the swim would accustom his body to the temperature of the lake while he put some distance between himself and Noah.

Jax stood up, resting the beer can on top of the rock he'd been leaning against, and pulled his outer garments off, revealing the slim swim trunks he'd worn beneath his cargo shorts. They were plain black and hugged his ass quite satisfactorily. He hadn't seen any need to replace the pair over the years, since his only swimming these days was in a pool at the gym, and no one cared what he looked like there.

"Wait up. If you're ready to go for a swim now, I'll come with you."

Jax held back a sigh. Foiled again! It had probably been stupid to think he could avoid the guy who had invited him out for the afternoon. *Suck it up, Knox!* He stepped out onto the hot sand and turned his gaze to the water, needing at least the space of a few moments to gather his control back around him. Noah's hand on his lower back quickly stripped him of the precious tendrils he'd just regained as he gasped in reaction to the touch. Noah kept his hand there as he spoke.

"You okay?"

Jax nodded, unable to respond for the moment, and stepped away from the tantalizing touch. They were there to swim. Noah hadn't asked for more, even if the imprint of his hand against Jax's spine was a burning reminder of everything he had given up and now wanted again desperately. He kept walking, hoping Noah would follow him yet dreading the moment when he must face him. Would he see hurt in those deep brown eyes at his denying the contact between them? He wasn't rejecting him, but Noah might be forgiven for thinking his actions meant just that.

He stopped and turned, swallowing the cowardice that'd had him running away for a minute.

"Hey." He paused, unsure of what to say that wouldn't make an awkward situation worse. "Thank you for this. I'm having a good time."

Noah's eyes were shadowed. "Are you? Because if you can't even stand for me to touch you, maybe we don't need to spend any more time together, you know? Why beat a dead horse?"

Damn! Jax deserved the disbelief, the anger that radiated off Noah as he spat the questions at him.

"Noah, babe..." Fuck, that was not what he...

Noah's lips on his stopped not just his words but his brain function. All he could do was feel the angry press of lips, the teeth nipping at his bottom lip, the insistent tongue that demanded an entry into his mouth. They were not touching anywhere except their lips. Jax let him in, placing a hand on the line of Noah's jaw to keep their mouths locked together. A spicy sweetness burst in his chest as Noah's mouth owned him, dominating the kiss with sharp, aching thrusts and commanding sweeps of his tongue.

How had he lived for all this time without the flavor of these kisses? How had he endured the pain of longing, the wound of an absence that he had caused? Finally unable to withhold any part of himself, he released Noah's jaw and wrapped his arms around him, bringing him into the warm expanse of his chest and holding on for dear life. That they were standing in the middle of a sandy beach where the world and his wife could see them meant nothing in the moment. Only the man in his arms, whose hands gripped his ass cheeks dragging their groins together, mattered.

"Noah!" His name was a wish and a prayer on Jax's tongue when they pulled away to breathe.

"Sorry." Noah tried to step away, but Jax held him firmly in place, not wanting any space between them more than they needed to breathe.

"Sorry?" His heart drummed a panicked tattoo against his ribcage. "Are you...?"

"No! No!" Noah's answering panic swelled around them, echoed in the rush of the spent waves on the shore. "The last time you called me 'babe' was almost twelve years ago. For years after we broke up, I couldn't hear that word without falling apart."

Jax pulled him back into a hug, resting his cheek on Noah's temple. "Thank God!" He held him there for another moment before releasing him and looking pointedly down at Noah's cock. "I think maybe we need that swim now, don't you? I'd rather not be arrested for public indecency."

Color rode up Noah's cheeks even as he laughed and pushed past Jax. "Last one in makes dinner tonight," he yelled as he ran into the surf, still laughing wildly.

The joy in that sound reverberated in Jax's heart, setting off a corresponding chorus in his own chest that threatened to burst from his lips in wild elation. Instead, he chased after Noah, already trying to figure out what he could do for dinner that would give them more time alone before they each had to return to their own occupied houses. The bracing water temperature on his feet and legs, accompanied by Noah splashing his abdomen and back when he turned to avoid it, was just the distraction he needed from thoughts of himself alone with the man who was still laughing happily just out of his reach.

Noah disappeared from view and Jax looked around, wondering where he'd gotten to. The water wasn't deep enough where they were to be a threat to someone who could swim, but the waves made seeing him difficult. He kept wading out before he threw himself into the surf, exhilarated by the piercing joy he felt for the first time since he and Noah last had been together. He rolled over, prepared to float when a hand dragging him down made him flap his arms to try to keep from going under. Noah slipped away before he could retaliate, and Jax laughed when he surfaced and found the younger man a few feet away grinning widely.

"Payback's a bitch, babe."

He spoke the word deliberately this time, watching as Noah's eyes widened and his nostrils flared. He swam away before Noah could respond, needing the last word, needing the upper hand if only for the moment. He wasn't foolish enough to think he held all the cards in this game they were playing, but he did know he wanted them both to win in the end.

When the sunset began to paint the evening sky in lavender and peach shot through with the last flecks of gold and gray, Noah finally came sauntering back to where Jax had been for the last half hour watching him frolic in the lake. His body gleamed as he leaned over to pull a towel from his bag to dry himself. Then he sat on the blanket, the towel draped over his shoulders, and pulled another beer from the cooler.

"My dad won't be home before ten tonight, unless the game goes longer. Wanna come home with me? You can make dinner with whatever's in the house, since I won the race." A cheeky grin split his cheeks as he glanced Jax's way.

"You mean the race you cheated in?" Jax kept his voice even to mask the way his heart beat faster at the thought of being alone with Noah in his home. "I'd like that, but I don't have a change of clothes and I'd like to shower, if that's okay with you."

Showering in Noah's bathroom with him in the house would be a challenge, but he was man enough to face it head-on. He was sure if he didn't make an offer, Noah wouldn't make another advance. That kiss on the beach had been a turning point on their path back to each other, but he wouldn't expect more than whatever he got. And he wouldn't push ... they both still needed to be sure of what they wanted going forward.

"I'm sure I can find something for you to wear," Noah was saying. "What time are you leaving in the morning?"

"My meeting at the college is at ten, so I'll need to leave no later than six-thirty. It's a three-hour drive and since I don't know the way or the traffic patterns, I'd rather be early than late."

"Okay. We have a little time then. Let's pack up."

The ride back to Noah's house was made in comfortable silence. Unlike earlier, Jax was not thrumming with unnamed tension, though his mind buzzed with anticipatory thoughts that he kept trying to quash. They were just going to have dinner. Well, maybe make out a bit as well, but that was all he could hope for right now. Nothing else seemed feasible, and he wouldn't get carried away with needful wishing.

"Bathroom's through there," Noah told him after he'd led him to their guest room. "Fresh towels and washrags are in the cupboard, and new toothbrushes are in the bottom drawer of the vanity. I'll put something for you to wear on the bed."

"Thanks. Do you have the fixings for spaghetti with red sauce and sausages?" He was supposed to be cooking for them, and he'd do well to remember that.

"Yeah. I'll get everything ready for you." Noah's eyes took him in as he turned from putting his bag on the chair.

"What?" The look in his eyes made Jax want to close the distance between them and take his mouth again.

"Nothing. Enjoy your shower." His eyes lingered on Jax's lips for a moment, as though he was having the same thoughts, before he turned and left the room.

Ignoring his cock proved to be the ultimate challenge of the evening as Jax washed his hair and showered. He resisted the urge to stroke himself to a quick orgasm as he soaped his body, wishing Noah was with him in the narrow shower stall. He tried to lose himself in the pleasing masculine scent of the shampoo and shower gel that Noah used. He'd smell like Noah when he walked into the kitchen. The thought of that kind of intimate connection plumped his already aching dick, and he squeezed the base to calm himself before wrapping the bath towel around his hips and exiting the steamy room.

The shorts and t-shirt that Noah left on the bed for him were a little snug, but he didn't mind. They were soft and well-worn, the color of the midnight sky with a sprinkling of stars and a new moon on the t-shirt. He noticed that his clothes were missing when he went to his duffel, and he could hear what sounded like a washing machine going. He could wear his own clothes home, or he could go commando and wear Noah's back to Jim's, where no doubt his friend would be up waiting for him. He chuckled softly to himself as he remembered Jim's last text message with the hopeful eggplant emoji.

*Cut it out, Knox!* He inhaled slowly before walking out to the kitchen where he found Noah making a salad, dancing to some music playing on the cellphone next to where he was working on the counter. His ass in the board shorts was begging to be squeezed. Jax groaned and walked over to where he danced, unaware of his audience. *I'm just letting him know I'm done so he can go shower now.* He ignored the snarky voice in his head calling him a liar when he reached out to touch Noah.

"Oh, hey!" Noah smiled over his shoulder at him, putting down the knife he'd been wielding and stopping the music. "My dad likes a salad with his meal, so I thought I'd make enough that he can have some tomorrow with the leftovers."

"That's fine. Shower's yours now."

"Thanks. I'll be back in a bit." He stepped away from the counter, away from Jax, and the sense of loss was immediate.

Jax reached for him almost blindly, almost unaware that he'd done so until Noah stood in his personal space looking into his eyes with heat and curiosity. Jax still could not find the words to say what he wanted, so he took a leaf from Noah's book and showed him instead. This kiss was hungry, demanding, almost desperate. Noah slid his hands into Jax's hair, pulling his head down and moaning as they kissed. Time stood still as they explored each other's mouths, reacquainting themselves with the way they had enjoyed kissing each other before. A nip here, a suck there, butterfly pecks on eyelids and the tips of noses, a scrape of teeth over a jutting chin, before they returned to the soul-stirring kisses that spoke with tongues of their renewed attraction.

Jax dragged his mouth away at last, reluctant to put any distance between them but needing to slow things down so he could cook, and Noah could clean up.

"We don't have all night, sweetheart. Go shower."

Noah's lingering gaze kept his body humming while he prepared their meal. The sausages were in the pan when Noah came back into the kitchen.

"Mmm! Something smells good."

Jax turned away from the pan for a moment, taking Noah in as he sauntered over to the cupboard, pulling plates and glasses out. His jeans shorts and band t-shirt were skintight, leaving little to Jax's overheated imagination. He didn't have much to imagine though, because while Noah had buffed up a bit, he was still the same gorgeous Latino with the same come-fuck-me eyes and kiss-me-now lips that he'd been over a decade ago.

"You look good," he said, suddenly unwilling to hide his reaction.

Part of being open was sharing emotional responses. It was the kind of intimacy that he'd always craved, that he'd missed from the moment he'd sent Noah away. None of the very few hookups he'd had since then had given him any of the warmth flowing in his veins now at the mere sight of the man he loved, had always loved, *would* always love. It felt right to accept that completely here, in Noah's space.

"Thanks." Noah's surprisingly shy smile lit him up like the Fourth of July.

# Chapter 14

## *Noah*

*Who needed air when there was Jax?*

Jax's clothes were dry, and after he finished his shower, Noah had placed them on the guest bed on his way to the kitchen. His hands shook slightly as he handled his lover's clothes. He knew they weren't back to that quite yet, but Jax had been his only true lover and it was easier to think of him in those terms, even if his mind was telling his foolish heart to take things slowly. He'd been so hard in the shower that he'd rubbed out a quick one, biting his tongue to stop himself from calling out Jax's name as he'd shot spunk against the shower wall.

What the fuck was he going to do with the man until he left? He'd been thinking with his second head when he'd made the invitation, and though he'd immediately realized it wasn't a smart move, he didn't have the willpower to recall it or step away from what his heart wanted. Besides, it would have been such a slap in the face, and he didn't want to give Jax any more mixed messages.

Delicious smells were coming from the kitchen. Jax had always been able to make ordinary ingredients shine. He would make the comfort food sing with the flavors and spicy sausages that he would add to the jarred red sauce. Composing himself to face the man who still held his heart in his hands, he stepped into the kitchen.

"Mmm! Something smells good."

He sniffed the air appreciatively, his eyes roaming over the man wearing his clothes, filling them out in the sexiest way possible, before returning unerringly to his lips. They were begging for another kiss, but Jax was cooking, and Noah could wait. He *would* wait. The anticipation would make the kiss all the sweeter when he took it.

Jax's eyes left a searing brand everywhere they landed on him, rendering him speechless for a moment, nerves and desire wracking him.

"You look good," Jax finally said, catching him off guard.

He remembered how it had felt to have this man regard him with affection, with lust, with love, and the weight of that memory filled this moment so fully that it took Noah's breath away. He smiled, feeling unaccountably shy … what the hell?

"Thanks."

He couldn't find any other words to voice the emotions churning inside him. He got plates, glasses, and cutlery and set the table, deciding that they'd have some of his dad's best red wine with dinner. If Jax wanted a beer afterwards, he'd get it for him.

"You can put the salad out now."

Jax's voice broke through his thoughts, and he turned to do as he was bid. "Is balsamic vinaigrette still your favorite salad dressing?" He hoped it was since that was all he had aside from his father's ranch dressing.

"It is." Jax looked up from serving up the pasta and meat dish. "You remember that."

Why wouldn't he? He had fallen in love with it once he'd tried it that first time at Jax's house, and he'd never looked back.

"Yeah." Another monosyllable was all he could muster.

They sat down to eat and Jax poured the wine into the glasses before raising his own in a toast.

"To second chances."

He kept his eyes trained on Noah, the hunger and warmth in them soaking into him as he raised his own to echo the words.

"To second chances." There was no way he was letting this chance go by.

Noah took a big gulp before digging in. As he expected, the food was mouthwatering, comforting, and hitting the spot deliciously.

"I've never forgotten how good you are in the kitchen," he mumbled around a mouthful of pasta. "Among other things."

He froze as soon as he said those last words, a single noodle hanging comically halfway from his lips like an aborted *Lady and the Tramp* moment. Why the hell had he gone there? It was one thing to flirt, but that was next level suggestive, as though he *wanted* Jax to think about the other thing he was good at that they probably weren't ready for just yet.

*It's been over a decade, No! You gotta ease up on the innuendo a li'l bit, let the man get used to you and your demanding ways again before you go off half-cocked.* The last thought made him choke as he stifled a hysterical giggle. He was half-cocked alright. He adjusted his ass in the chair to relieve the growing ache in his dick and kept his eyes studiously on his food, not daring to look up in case he found recognition and amusement at his expense in Jax's dark eyes.

"I seem to recall you being not half bad at a few things yourself," was Jax's nonchalant comment.

At least it *would* be nonchalant had it not been for the fast beating of the vein in his neck. *Holy shit!* He was letting go of more of the worries that he was going too fast with each bit of evidence that Jax was just as much on board with the pace as he was. He ate quietly for another half a minute, trying to find the best way to answer that would keep the sexual tension buzzing between them.

"I don't know, Prof." It felt so right to call him that again. "It's been a while since I had to use my violin-tuning skills," he deadpanned, then grinned when Jax choked on a laugh.

"Some skills are really easy to get back," Jax said once he'd swallowed some wine to clear his throat. "You know what they say ... practice makes perfect."

"True, but you know some things take more practice than others to get just right."

Jax lifted a brow, chewing the mouthful of food he'd just taken. "Oh yeah? Like what, for instance?"

Noah drained the wine in his glass and poured himself a second cup of courage. "Well, it depends on what we're dealing with." He sipped from the second pour, then sighed. "I mean, I don't think I'll ever be as good a cook as you are, no matter how much I practice. Some things are just a gift that people have."

"And some things are intuitive, like love." Jax's response was as serious as Noah had ever remembered him being. "Some people just know how to show love without having to be given lessons."

Noah's breath hitched. Jax had told him that the first time they'd made love, when he'd been tied up in knots and worrying about whether he'd disappoint his older, more experienced lover, because he was a virgin with a deep hunger to know everything and try everything at least once. The pride he'd felt at being able to bring Jax pleasure had been overwhelming then. He held Jax's gaze now, letting himself relax completely in the certainty of being accepted this time.

"A wise man once told me that," he said, keeping his eyes on Jax. "And I thought I understood it then."

"And now?"

"Now I'm ready to embrace it fully."

No more pussyfooting around. He was still the same person he had been the first time he'd dared Jax to kiss him. The Halloween party that the music department hosted for its students every year was a well-known event on campus, and the other professors who had come along to help wrangle a wild bunch of twenty-somethings had made it a fun yet safe place to be. Noah's Uber had been the last to arrive, so he'd had a perfect reason to remain behind when his classmates had departed.

A smile touched his lips as he recalled their first kiss. The Uber had been a minute away, and Jax had walked with him to the front door, ready to open it and step out into the cold night with him to await its arrival when Noah had set his palm on the older man's hard chest. Jax's heart had been racing, confirmation, so far as Noah was concerned, that this man wanted him as much as he did, that the looks he had intercepted were ones of interest, and that the flirtatious conversations that he'd initiated were not unwelcome.

He had studiously avoided all contact with Jax for the whole time that the party had been going on, spending time with the other professors and his friends, barely managing not to ignore him so as not to raise any brows. He'd been polite yet distant ... until the moment he'd reached up to cup Jax's cheek with his other hand and whispered, "I've tried really hard to tell myself that what I'm about to do is inappropriate, that you'll hate it, and me, that I am taking a huge risk and should rethink it. But now, feeling your heart beating like this under my fingers, I think I can take a chance, don't you, Prof?"

"Noah..." Jax's voice had been pained as he'd gently taken hold of Noah's wrists and had tried to put more space between them.

"If you really don't want to kiss me like I've been wanting to kiss you since the first day I met you, I'll leave, and I'll never approach you again, sir."

Jax had tensed at the word, making Noah wonder if he liked it, if it turned him on to be called "sir."

"Noah, no matter how I feel, we should not engage like this."

"Is that a yes or a no, sir?"

He'd said it again, teasing Jax, and had watched as he closed his eyes and swallowed. Noah had eased closer, moving his other hand up to cup the other cheek and pressing a soft kiss to Jax's jaw, first one side, then the other. The man had trembled beneath his touch, but he hadn't moved, instead transferring his own hands to Noah's waist.

"Yes or no, Prof?" Noah had whispered again, this time letting his lips touch Jax's.

The groan that had accompanied that chaste kiss was all the warning he'd got before Jax was opening him up, demanding entry to his mouth and access to his tongue, and they'd been tongue fucking each other as the Uber drew up to the curb. That had been over far too quickly for Noah's liking, but he'd won that first skirmish, and the battle for Jax's heart had been on.

Now, all these years later, he was back there again, demanding to be given what he wanted, getting the man he loved to see that what they could have together was worth every chance they were willing to take. And this time, Jax had no reason to refuse him, no reason to reject his advances.

"Noah?"

He blinked, coming back to the moment. "Sorry, what?"

Jax eyed him suspiciously. "Where'd you just zone out to?"

Noah sipped some more wine. He was older now, a bit more experienced, and he could be patient. "I was just remembering."

He could also tease, because he knew how that could ratchet up the desire that was now riding the air between them. He watched Jax eat another mouthful of food before speaking, and he grinned. The game was on. More warmth flooded his chest at the memory of the times they'd tried to see which one would break first in the flirting and seduction games they played. There'd been a lot of laughter but there'd also been a lot of making out and a lot of lovemaking.

Jax's response shocked him. It had never been like this before. "Do you really want to live in the past, Noah, or do you want to step into a smarter future? Like I told you before, I won't do anything you're not up for. But I'm beyond ready to end the games. Aren't you?"

Well, damn! "Yeah." He was speechless beyond that one word.

Jax stood up, pushing his chair back so hard it toppled over, shaking Noah to his very foundation. "Come here!"

The growly command stoked the fire already burning in Noah's body as he moved to obey, going to stand in front of Jax and holding the other man's heated gaze.

"The first time we kissed, back when you were an eager twenty-something, I let you drive me insane before I broke and took what we both wanted."

He lifted a hand to trace the line of Noah's jaw, to stroke over his plump lips, to push a thumb between them. Noah licked it, making Jax hiss, but he didn't remove it. Instead, he pushed it deeper.

"Suck it."

Noah gasped, and Jax took advantage, sliding his thumb all the way in. Noah sucked, moaning as he did so.

"It was the best kiss of my life up to that point," Jax continued, as though what Noah was doing was nothing.

Noah sucked harder, then reached up to hold Jax's wrist so he could guide Jax's index finger in when he popped his thumb out. He held his eyes as he made the switch, reveling in the way Jax swallowed but kept his eyes open, groaning in response to the seduction.

"Now you're trying to do it again." Jax's voice was rough with restrained lust as he held still while Noah kept up his sensual assault.

"You mean I'm not succeeding in driving you insane again?" He flicked his eyes up to look at Jax, a small, knowing smile curving his lips before he slipped his free hand between their bodies to grasp the hard evidence of Jax's growing desire. "This doesn't give that impression, Prof."

Jax chuckled. "You know exactly what you do to me. You've always known."

That, at least, was true. He stroked the hard length beneath his palm slowly, in time to the sucking motion of his tongue on Jax's digit. Even he was not immune to the utter sensuality of his actions, and when Jax dragged his finger out of Noah's mouth, lingering for a long moment on his bottom lip so he could drag it down to expose his teeth, Noah groaned.

"I need you to know that every hurt you felt, I felt as well, Noah."

Jax breathed the words into his ear, more than an apology, more than regret. They resonated with truth in his very bones. He inhaled against the remembered anguish and Jax pulled him impossibly close and held him while they both let go at last of the hurt they caused each other in the past. Noah had no idea how long they stood there, offering comfort to each other, his hand trapped between their bodies above a rock-hard erection, but he received the healing vibe flowing from Jax, welcomed the desire that arced between them, embraced the love.

"I'm only human, Noah, and imperfect. But I promise I'll never break us apart again. Are you with me?"

Jax had moved away enough so he could look into Noah's eyes as he waited for his reply. Noah nodded, so Jax wouldn't worry that he wasn't all in. Then he took another moment to gather himself so he could speak the words he knew Jax needed to hear.

"I forgive you, Jax. I know you only wanted what was best for me. The part of me that wasn't falling apart back then loved you so much for making the hard choice. You know me ... I wouldn't have made it. I would have done anything to keep what we had. But now, hindsight being what it is, I know it made me stronger, braver, better." He smiled into Jax's eyes. "I know this may sound maudlin and silly, but it made me a man, the man you needed, even if we had to wait a decade to get back to each other."

Jax was on him before he could say anything else, demanding entry to his mouth and branding him with his tongue. The kiss was everything he could have prayed for if he'd had the time to say the words. Noah relaxed and let him have his way, giving him back kiss for hungry kiss, unsurprised when Jax backed him up against the island and pushed into him so hard he felt the edge of the countertop against his spine.

"Unh!" he groaned in mixed pain and pleasure.

"What time is your dad getting home?" Jax eased off him without losing contact with his body.

"He doesn't usually make it back before ten. We have time."

"Show me where."

No need to ask what Jax meant. His hunger beat against Noah's lips as they kissed furiously again, everything forgotten but their need for each other. He grabbed his hand and pulled him along to his bedroom, barely managing to shut the door before he was pulling at Jax's shirt, trying to get it off him. The fumbling to undress would have struck him as more hilarious if he'd had enough functioning brain cells left over to consider how they must look, stumbling around to get their pants and boxers off.

When they fell in a heap on his bed, though, they both burst out laughing, the pure joy of their amusement cleansing the last of the hurt they'd both been carrying around. Then Jax rolled over on top of him, and amusement turned to desire, morphed into lust and raging need as he ground his hips into Noah's, stealing his breath with deep, ravenous kisses. The skin-on-skin contact kept Noah on the ragged edge of cumming with nothing touching him but his lover's steely cock.

"Hot as ever," Jax panted against his mouth when he released it to catch at the air. "Condoms? Lube?"

Noah dragged his eyes open. "Over there." He turned his head in the direction of his nightstand.

Jax's laugh was soft, sexy. "Easy, baby. Relax! I've got you."

Oh yes, he did! There was nowhere else that Noah wanted to be but right where he was, wrapped up in bliss. And they hadn't even made love as yet. He reached up, pulling Jax's mouth back to his. Who needed air when there was Jax? He rolled his hips up, needing a closer connection, and Jax rewarded him with an answering plunge before sliding to the side so he could stroke Noah's weeping cock.

"Fuck!" The expletive slipped past his tight lips, a wish and a prayer.

"Yes!" And there was his answer.

Jax slid away for a moment to get the supplies, then returned to lie beside him. Pulling Noah onto his side to face him, he took his lips again while he pulled his leg over his hip, opening him to his now questing finger. Noah hissed, waiting for a burn that never came. Jax went unerringly to the one point guaranteed to send Noah screaming into orbit and pegged it over and over, not wasting time in getting to where he wanted Noah to be.

Two fingers, then three, Jax remained unrelenting in his assault on Noah's prostate.

"Jax, I'm gonna blow before you get inside me."

Noah hated the whine in his voice, but he hadn't waited for over a decade to lose his shit before the main event. He needed the fullness of his lover's cock, the warmth and strength of it inside him. He didn't want to waste his first orgasm with Jax after all this time without them bound together in the most intimate embrace.

Jax eased out of him, leaning down to kiss him again before reaching for the condom.

"Cover me."

Ah! He remembered that Noah liked to suit him up, that rolling the condom over his erection always turned him on. As if he could be any more turned on! He took the foil packet from Jax with trembling fingers and ripped it open with his teeth, flinging the empty package away and reaching for Jax, who had turned fully onto his back. His dick stood tall as a flagpole, the pearl of precum beading at the tip distracting Noah into licking his lips and swallowing, forgetting what he was supposed to be doing. Jax chuckled, rousing him from his stupor, and he grinned sheepishly.

His lover's gasp when Noah licked the precum from his cock was immensely gratifying, and as he slid the condom down as slowly as he could manage, tamping down his urgency, he reveled in the tension radiating off Jax's body as his lover visibly restrained himself. Noah could imagine what he was feeling ... the need for contact was driving *him* wild, as well.

"Payback is a bitch, baby," Jax grunted when Noah's fingers at last rested on the tops of his thighs.

"I can take anything you can dish," Noah groaned as he slid over Jax's thighs and positioned himself above the straining muscle.

"All I hear is words." Jax held his dick ready for Noah to impale himself on it, his face a grimace of concentrated pleasure the lower Noah sank onto him. "Fuuuuck!" The expletive rolled over his lips as he squeezed his eyes shut against the pleasure swamping them both.

Noah took him all in, settling his ass cheeks against Jax's thighs with a contented sigh. He was desperate to move, to feel that hard dick shuttling in and out of his channel, but he also wanted to linger, to savor the moment, to bask in the heat and hunger of it.

"Move!" Jax's demanding growl sent trickles of flame up Noah's spine.

He moved.

"It's been too long, babe. You feel so good."

Jax's voice was strained, his movement jerky as he thrust up into Noah pliant body. Every hard lunge rattled loose something deeply buried inside him. He cried out over and over, needing the grounding that Jax's arms under his armpits and over his shoulders gave him and he let his lover plow into him, rolling them over when the lust burned out of control and taking him like a man possessed.

"I'll never hurt you again, Noah," Jax promised him just before he stiffened above him and roared out his release.

Noah's own silent scream as he came right behind Jax shot heat all over his body and tears flooded his eyes. He'd only ever come without touching himself when he was with Jax. None of the hookups he'd had had between then and now had ever been able to bring him off without jacking him. The memory hit him like a freight train going at full speed, bringing back with it all the beauty and heartache of their earlier times together. God, how he loved this man! And how stupid he'd been to think he'd ever be able to erase him from his heart!

Had it ever been *this* intense before, even with Jax? Noah didn't think so. He let Jax cuddle him, their bodies coming back down slowly, breaths mingling when Jax pulled his face away from his neck so they could look into each other's eyes. The tears that streaked his cheeks made Jax frown, and Noah just shook his head and smiled, smoothing away the worry lines.

"It's okay. I'm fine. Honestly. Just..." The enormity of the emotions swelling inside him almost stole his breath for a moment, but he steadied himself and continued. "It's never been like this before. Not even with you. Back then, it was intense, but I was young and impatient. I guess I've grown up, huh?"

"Yeah, you have." Jax leaned up to capture his lips in a sweet, tender kiss. "But *I've* changed too. It was always about more than the physical between us, and I knew it then. But now ... now, it's more still. We've gone through so much, given up so much, to get to where we are, that it only makes it better."

Noah couldn't argue with logic. Nor did he want to. All he wanted to do was bask in the intimacy surrounding them as they lay on his bed. He sighed sleepily, and Jax chuckled.

"I did forget one thing," he remarked, stroking the damp hair off Noah's forehead.

"Mmhmm? What's that?" Noah could barely keep his eyes open.

"Lovemaking always wore you out."

# Chapter 15

## *Jax*

*Having Noah in his arms again had been,*
*hands down, the best feeling in ten years.*

A soft knock roused Jax, who was instantly awake, his arms wrapped tightly around his lover. Noah snored gently beside him. He smiled, even as the knock sounded again. He shook his lover.

"Babe, someone's knocking on your door. I think it's your dad."

Noah's eyes snapped open, a look of panic passing over his face. "Shit!"

He scrambled out of bed and shoved his legs into his shorts, calling out as he did, "Sorry, *Papi*, one sec."

"It's alright, *mijo*. I just wanted to say goodnight. I didn't mean to wake you."

Noah opened the door anyway, while Jax tried for invisibility in the shadowed bed. "I guess I was a little tired. How was poker? Did you win anything?"

The amusement in his father's answer told Jax that he didn't mind that he'd lost. "I promised the guys we'd do a cookout this weekend, if you're interested," he added. "You should invite your professor. I think he might enjoy himself."

Did he know that Jax was there? How would he know that? And should he be embarrassed that his lover's father was standing on the other side of his son's open bedroom door while Jax lay naked in his bed? He waited for it to hit, but nothing happened. He was too on board with Noah to care much what anyone, including his father, thought about the matter. They were both consenting adults, and he was no longer in a position of power over the younger man.

"I'll see what he says," Noah mumbled in response, hiding his face from his dad again.

Jax had to swallow the laugh that rose in his throat at the rueful tone of Noah's reply. He tried not to listen to the rest of the brief exchange, and when Noah closed the door and turned to him in the moonlit room, Jax could barely make out the chagrined expression on his face. He rose from the bed, loping over to where Noah stood indecisively and pulled him into his arms.

"D'you think he knows I'm here?" he whispered against his earlobe. "And do you care?"

Noah's needy kiss was answer enough ... he didn't care too much. Jax returned it passionately, letting the moment stretch between them like a promise before he pulled away reluctantly.

"Even if doesn't he know though, I don't think it's a good idea for me to stay here."

He stepped away as Noah flicked the switch by the door and light flooded the room, pricking his eyes sharply. He looked around for his clothes, and Noah fetched him a robe from his closet.

"Here, put this on. Your clothes are in the guest bedroom. I'll meet you in the kitchen."

Jax changed quickly, wondering if Alvaro could hear him. He took his duffel and hurried back out to the kitchen where Noah was sipping a soda.

"One for the road?"

He held out an unopened can to Jax, who took it gratefully. Dutch courage ... just in case Alvaro came back out before he left. He leaned against the counter, watching Noah sip his own drink, the tension stretching like a taut wire between them. He knew he needed to leave so he could get enough rest for the next day, but being with Noah wasn't something he wanted to end either.

"I hope you find a nice place to live." Noah broke the silence. "Are you looking at anything special?"

"The realtor has two houses and a condo for me to look at. One of the houses is on a lake. I'm looking forward to seeing that one."

"I wish I could see it with you."

Jax heard the longing in Noah's voice and the echo of his own desire to share the experience with him in the non-committal grunt he gave in response. It would have been nice to have him along. If they were going to be together, the house would eventually be Noah's as well, wouldn't it? Tension eased back into his limbs at the thought. Was he getting ahead of himself? Even if Noah was on board with rekindling their love affair, that didn't mean he would want to live together, to...

The word hovering on the edge of his thoughts, waiting to drop into his mind and lodge there, was one he had never allowed himself to think about before. Marriage was a huge deal, not something he'd ever enter into lightly, and not something he felt confident that Noah would want. No matter what he might think, Noah was still ten years his junior with a lot of life left ahead of him, even if he never played another concert. He had more options than he might realize, and tying himself to one man might not be in his vision of his future.

"Jax?"

Noah's voice broke him out of the increasingly unhappy trend of his thoughts.

"Sorry ... just zoned out for a bit."

He had no other truths he was prepared to offer. He had to get a hold of himself, to remember that so far all they'd done was make love once. That did not constitute a basis for considerations of wedding vows and together forever. He needed to exercise some of the restraint he had been able to marshal back when they were first together, when Noah tried his last string of patience before he seduced him completely.

"Ready to go? I'll drive you."

"You don't..."

"What's with you and resisting all the time?" Noah asked, sounding a tad irritated. "Why can't you just say yes without a fight?"

"Yes."

Jax swallowed the laugh that rose in his throat and went with it. Whatever Noah wanted, Noah would get, even if it was just his agreement to a ride to where he was staying two streets over. He found an odd comfort in Noah's impatience with his pussyfooting around, even after what they'd just been doing in his bed. Maybe, with time, he could consider ever afters.

While Noah let Klinger out for his last potty break before bed, Jax finished his drink and then they headed out. Despite the heat of the summer day, the car was refreshingly cool at this time of night, and the soft breeze blowing in off the lake was a sweet kiss of approval on his decision to say yes to the ride home. It wouldn't take but a couple of minutes, but that was two extra minutes he'd have with the man sitting easily at his side, his free hand resting loosely on his thigh.

They didn't speak, but the air between them was full of unspoken hopes and dreams, of fantasies and desires ... at least on Jax's side. What would it be like to get home, after a long day, to Noah in his bed? How would it feel to wake in his arms? If he wasn't living with his dad, would Jax have had *that* wish fulfilled? There had been no plan for sleepovers or even for sex, but if one could happen, who was to say both couldn't? And sleepovers meant something, didn't they? So if they woke up together some morning in the future, maybe Jax could take it as a sign that Noah was thinking about something more than committed lovers. That maybe Noah was thinking life partners, like he was.

"I had a great time today," Noah said when he put the car in Park outside the Bell house. "And an even better time tonight." His voice grew husky.

Jax cleared his throat so he could be heard. "Me too." He looked over at his lover and smiled. "Thanks for inviting me out. The next date is on me, okay?"

Noah grinned. "Next date, huh? I'm in. When are we gonna get to it?"

"As soon as I get back, I'll call you."

Jax relaxed into his own grin, then leaned in as Noah did. The kiss started tender, full of hope and promise and a banked passion that Jax wished he could let loose. Noah fed him his tongue, and Jax let him have his way, sighing into the kiss as it swelled and shifted into something more than they needed to be doing in the front seat of a truck with a console between them.

"I'll call you tomorrow, okay?" Jax dragged his lips away to speak.

"Can't wait."

Noah's whispered response was lost in another quick and dirty kiss, and then Jax pulled away and got out of the truck. He lifted his hand in a farewell salute before going in and making his way quietly to his room. His body still hummed with need, and a myriad of thoughts whirled through his mind about where he and Noah went from this point. Sleep was long in coming, and when he rose at five to get ready, taking a hurried shower, he felt exhausted as though he hadn't slept at all.

By the time he got out to the kitchen to make himself coffee to go, Jim was already there. He took one look at Jax and chuckled.

"Long night, my friend?"

Jax sighed resignedly but didn't answer, knowing his best friend wasn't going to let him leave without at least that one sly dig. He got out the largest to-go mug and filled it with the wake-up brew.

"I don't know what time I'm getting back today, but it'll likely be well past dinner time, because the last house showing is late in the day. I'll eat on the road. Call me if you need anything before then, okay?"

Jim nodded, handing over something wrapped in foil. "Annie says to tell you to make sure you eat before you go into your meeting. A rumbling belly isn't a good sound on a new hire. You don't want them thinking you're desperate for this job because you're starving."

Jax rolled his eyes at his friend, but his grin made it clear he was just as amused as Jim was.

"I'm sure Annie didn't say most of that," he retorted. "You're just being an ass."

"Dude!" Jim feigned horror. "At least I care!" Then he laughed before adding, "Get going. Traffic is weird sometimes on the highway, and if there's an accident..."

"Yeah, I know. That's why I'm giving myself the extra time. I'll just potter around if I'm early until it's time for the meeting."

"See you later, man. Drive safe."

The sun was well above the horizon when he drove off, but the cool breeze off the lake meant he could drive with the windows down for a while. He switched the radio to an all-music channel and then let his mind wander back to the night before. Having Noah in his arms again had been hands down the best feeling. It was as though they'd never been apart. All the feelings of home that he used to have when they held each other before had returned, warming him, wrapping him in comfort.

And the sex ... damn. He had known that he'd be missing out when he'd sent Noah away, but the depth of the connection they'd had last night had brought home to him just how *much* he had given up, how *much* he had lost. And unless Noah called a halt this time or said he wasn't interested in more than friends-with-benefits, Jax would pursue this to the end he desired with everything in him.

He just needed to be sure of Noah.

The ride took just under three hours, and he was at the college a half hour before his appointment with Dr. Mann, the head of the music department. He hoped this part of the day would go quickly, because he was quite excited about viewing the houses and apartment that the realtor had found for him. He really didn't want that to be a prolonged process, because the sooner he moved into his own place, the sooner he could begin to learn his new community and make a plan to move forward with Noah.

His phone rang as he was finishing the sandwich he hadn't eaten until he parked. He smiled when he saw who was calling.

"Hey, morning!"

"Morning, Prof! Are you there yet?"

Jax laughed. "Been here about ten minutes. Just finishing my breakfast sandwich."

"What time's the meeting?"

"Ten. I'm going to head out and walk around a bit before I go in, just to see what the campus is like when it's not overrun by students."

Noah chuckled. "You make them sound like pests."

"Well, sometimes they can be," Jax agreed with a laugh. "How's your day going?"

"I'm just making breakfast for me and my dad, and then the first of my two students is coming for lessons. I'll be done by noon." He paused, then seemed to gather his courage and went on. "That's why I was calling actually."

Jax frowned, confused. "Why?"

"How late is your last appointment?"

Noah sounded so tentative that Jax wondered what he was thinking.

"Three-thirty. Why?" he asked again.

"How would you like a bit of company? My afternoon student cancelled so I can be up there by that time. We could see the last place together." He paused again, then added, "If that's okay with you?"

Jax hated how hesitant he sounded. "I'd like that." A lot, in fact, but he'd keep that to himself for the time being.

"Okay. Text me the address, and I'll meet you there."

The morning went by quickly after that. Jax's meeting with Dr. Mann went very smoothly, and she even had some advice about the places he was going to look at for housing.

Based on her recommendation, he figured he would probably not take the townhouse because of what she said about the neighborhood. But she loved the location of the house by the lake and seemed pretty certain he would like it, even if the house itself didn't suit him.

"I hope there'll be others available, if that one doesn't suit," she said as they shook hands by her office door. "I'm so looking forward to working with you, Dr. Knox. And good luck with the house hunting."

Dr. Mann's face was wreathed in smiles. She was a gorgeous woman, and though he had never met her before, he imagined that she had only grown more beautiful with age, and he didn't just mean her physical appearance. Her sweet spirit still warmed him as he drove off to his first realtor appointment. She would be a joy to work with.

Mary Morgan was waiting for him when he arrived at the first location. The house sat in the middle of a half-acre lot of land, surrounded by neatly trimmed lawns and a flowering hedge at the front and sides. It was a cheerful, bright blue ranch with white shutters. He took the tour because he'd agreed to it, but he knew before they were through that he wouldn't be making an offer on it. The decor was dated and there were clear signs that age and slipshod maintenance on the inside had not been kind to it.

"We can cross this one off, Ms. Morgan. Let's go see the townhouse."

Although he had half made up his mind to go with his new boss's recommendation, he decided to give it a fair shake. But even as they got closer to it, Jax could see that the neighborhoods were decreasing in appeal, and when the realtor's car finally stopped ahead of his, he looked around and shook his head. He didn't even want to see the inside of it. The street was clean enough, and there were no obvious signs of neglect, but the townhouse was part of a complex made up of eight or ten sets of row houses and once he was out of the car, he didn't like the vibe.

He looked around to see what redeeming qualities might make him change his mind, but aside from a few mature trees lining the street that his townhouse was on, there were no amenities that would make it worth his while to live among so many people. One or two cars were parked at the curb, and he already knew he wasn't going to enjoy moving his vehicle from side to side on street cleaning days or fighting for parking with his neighbors at other times.

He could see why this was below his price point. It was probably part of the university's contract to provide housing for grad students, and he had no desire to live where they did, especially not if he planned to have Noah in his life. His private life was his business. He walked over to where the realtor stood waiting for him, shaking his head as he went.

"Sorry, I don't think this is a fit for me. Thanks for trying to find me affordable housing, but I know you can do better than this."

Ms. Morgan smiled ruefully at him. "I figured you might not like it, but I had to give it a try. I've known professionals who lived in this complex for years without complaint, but it isn't for everyone."

"I really appreciate your efforts on my behalf. Let's hope this afternoon's viewing goes better."

"I'm sure you'll love that one, Dr. Knox," she enthused. "But if you don't, I've lined up a couple of others for tomorrow, if you can stay over."

Jax smiled. He liked the woman's enthusiasm for her work, and he could see that she knew what she was doing, so he'd trust her to line up the best that she could find. This townhouse mishap was probably a fluke, brought on by her desire to spare him some change.

"We'll see," he said noncommittally.

His head was already with Noah, who would be leaving to get to him in time for the third house visit. He'd take a drive around town and get some lunch before heading to the last one.

"I'll see you at three-thirty, then."

He gave her a thumbs-up and watched her drive away before checking to see where the closest diner was located. He'd have a late lunch before his last showing for the day and maybe get Noah a snack to tide him over until dinner time. And if he decided to stay over to see more houses, he'd take his man out to eat.

He grinned at the idea that crossed his mind as he followed the GPS directions back to town. He might even decide to view a couple of other houses so he could spend a night alone with Noah with no interruptions. The more he thought about it, the better the idea seemed. He'd need a change of underwear and a shirt, and so would Noah.

Maybe a bit of shopping before lunch? He could live with that.

# Chapter 16

## *Noah*

*"It was hell being apart from you, Jax.*
*I won't be able to bear it again."*

"I'll call you when I get there, *Papi*."

Noah smiled at his dad, who still treated him like he was eighteen going on his first road trip every time he left the house to drive farther than an hour away.

"And please wish your *profesor* good house hunting."

"Si, *Papi*."

He waved as he drove off, letting the music on the radio cool his fever. He'd been half hard all morning after talking to Jax, and despite his best efforts, he couldn't keep the zing of excitement from streaming through his veins at the idea of spending time alone with him. He'd even packed a small duffel for an overnight stay ... assuming he could get Jax to agree. Was he moving too fast? Maybe, but he was so done waiting. They had a decade of love to make up for, and he wasn't prepared to waste any more time.

The question of what he'd do with the rest of his life, aside from laying siege to Jax's heart, was something he was still avoiding thinking about. He didn't mind giving private lessons, but he couldn't spend the rest of his days in what felt like mindless work. He needed a challenge. Maybe he could go back to school? But what would he do?

The British-accented GPS speaker directed him onto the highway while he was still mulling over the answers to those questions. He didn't want to attach himself to Jax while he was still broken, without purpose or direction. He needed to be an equal partner in whatever they built together, which meant he had to choose a path ... which meant he had to get off his ass, stop feeling sorry for himself, and get back in the game. Having to leave the quartet would hurt—it already did—but he was more than his ability to play the violin. He just had to figure out what his Plan B would become.

There wasn't much he could do about his newfound outlook while he was driving, so he let himself sink into the music being piped through the speakers. Orchestral music always soothed something untamed and elemental in him. By the time he was pulling up to the address that Jax had sent him, he was almost Zen-like in his chill. Yes, this was how he wanted to be around Jax ... calm, cool, confident, collected.

He turned between the elegant lamps resting atop the tall stone columns that bracketed the driveway and followed it for a few hundred yards to a reasonably-sized yet comfortable-looking two-story house surrounded on the sides and in front by lush lawns and gardens and dotted with tall trees. In the back, he could glimpse the glint of sunshine on the water and as he watched, a boat sped by with a skier in its wake. The ghost of happy laughter drifted to his ears.

He stayed in the car. Jax's car was not the one parked in front of the shallow steps leading to the front door, so he'd wait for his lover to turn up before exiting his truck. He wound down the window and let the heat and sounds of summer drift into the cab. Birds chirped cheerfully and butterflies flitted by in graceful aerial dances. The growl of an engine caught his attention, and he watched in his rearview mirror as Jax pulled in behind him and got out of his car.

Noah's heart rate kicked up at the sight of his man striding toward him. He got out of the truck just as Jax reached him, and they embraced as though they hadn't just seen each other the night before.

"Hey! Thanks for coming." Jax leaned in and pressed his lips to Noah's.

"Thanks for agreeing."

Before either of them could lean in for another taste, the sound of a door opening had them pulling apart. Noah looked over to the front door from which a woman was emerging with a clipboard in her hand.

"Come on. Let's go see what's up."

Noah followed Jax up the steps to where the woman stood with a welcoming smile on her face.

"Mary Morgan, meet Noah Santiago. Noah, Mary's the realtor who's helping me find some place to lay my head when I move up here."

They shook hands, and Ms. Morgan turned briskly. "Let's begin out here since we're already standing on one of the best features of this house." She turned and spread one arm. "This is a wraparound porch. And as you'll see in a few, there's even a porch swing in the back."

The swing was painted an innocent white, but the cushions adorning it were flaming red and gold, immediately brightening up the entire space.

"Wow! Those cushions sure make this space pop," Jax commented. "Do you know how old this feature is?"

"The swing was built at the same time as the house was, but the cushions have very recently been replaced. And as you can see, there's room for any other furniture you might wish to put out around the house. The firepit got regular use, and the outdoor kitchen was recently updated."

Noah's head spun. How would Jax afford to rent this place? He knew the man had been working for a long time, and he knew that he was a frugal man, but this house was shaping up to be a major expense, and they hadn't even gone inside! His eyes wandered down to the lake, which was quite large and dotted with homes on both sides.

"Let's go in now. I think you'll love the inside even more."

Noah let his mind wander as they trailed after the realtor. The kitchen was huge, a chef's kitchen apparently, which prompted Jax to ask who had owned the house before.

"They were an older couple whose oldest son is a chef. He gifted them this kitchen when he opened his second restaurant."

"This is a great location, and the outside is very beautiful. Why would they want to sell this?"

Noah wanted to know the same thing as they walked through to the family room.

"The husband had a heart attack, and their children persuaded him that a move to a smaller place in a warmer climate would be best for his health. For now, they're only willing to rent it, but if the right person comes along with an offer they can live with, they'll sell it outright."

"You said it was a rent-to-own deal," Jax reminded her while Noah admired the bright colors in the airy living room.

"If they like the renter, they will start a conversation."

"Why wouldn't their kids want to live here, or at the very least keep it as a vacation home?"

The house was gorgeous, inside and out. Large windows let in a lot of light, and the almost old-world charm of the furnishings that remained, as well as the elegance of the spaces they were passing through, made it feel like a shame to let it slip away from the family. Noah's thoughts went to his dad's little bungalow and though it was nowhere near as large or expensive as this place, he couldn't imagine giving it up altogether. Once his father had decided that he'd winter in Florida, they had agreed to rent it out for the months that he wouldn't be in residence as a way to augment his retirement income.

"I did make a similar suggestion to them, and they've said they'll consider it."

Ms. Morgan led the way from the comfortable den with the widescreen television mounted on the wall, to the equally-sized office where he pictured Jax's lovingly polished oak desk taking pride of place by the window, through the living room with the piano next to the fireplace, up the stairs via a short hallway to the second floor where the bedrooms were located.

"Except for the master bedroom suite in the attic—though the owners used it as a guest suite since they were no longer able to manage the additional stairs—all the sleeping quarters are on this floor."

She led them into each bedroom and passed by the hall bathroom shared by two of them. There was a sitting room up here as well, with the steps leading up to the attic tucked into the corner.

"I'll let you go up to the master suite on your own." Ms. Morgan's smile was rueful. "My knees can't handle any more stairs for the time being. I'll be in the kitchen when you come down."

The roof had been lifted to make more headroom and the entire space was like a studio apartment, though there was no kitchen. Noah's mind went to places he really ought to avoid if he didn't want to appear downstairs with a boner. The alcove overlooking the back porch and the lake would hold a full sofa as well as a side table and small coffee table. There was a fireplace across from it, above which a wide-screen television hung. French doors led out to a balcony with room for two armchairs and a table between. A small wood-burning stove sat in one corner.

"Wow! This is the life." Noah didn't try to hide his admiration for the setup.

"Indeed it is, if you can afford it."

Jax's words sounded a note of caution, making Noah wonder if he was already thinking to refuse it. Despite his own misgivings earlier, he didn't want his lover to give up the house. They could live here together and share the expenses... *Whoa! Hold your horses there, Noah.* He couldn't afford his own eagerness for more to cloud his judgment when it came to Jax. Yes, he was ready to move on, but until Jax said the words to let him know where exactly they were headed, he'd be best served by reining in his wild imagination.

Sure, it'd be fabulous to live in this gorgeous old house with Jax, to be domestic and romantic together in the kitchen and on this seductive little balcony, but Jax had to share that dream before it could become a reality. And until he could figure out how to raise the subject, Noah wouldn't go any further along that thought pathway.

Instead, he followed Jax back into the bedroom and imagined Jax's bed taking pride of place in it. The California king-sized bed had been a dream to roll around in in the much smaller bedroom that it had occupied. In this lush space, it'd be perfect for lounging late in the morning and playing hard at night.

His cock stirred at the thought, and Noah tightened all his muscles for a moment before turning to look into the bathroom. He didn't see anything though, because he had to close his eyes against the rush of lust that he had set off by thinking about Jax's bed.

"You okay?"

Jax's voice shook him to the marrow of his bones, and he hoped his lover didn't see the shudder that ran through him at the sound of his voice.

"Yeah, I'm fine. Just taking it all in."

"With your eyes closed?"

Noah looked up at Jax, who had walked back toward him, amusement and knowledge sparkling in his eyes.

"I was just ... imagining, is all. This is a really cool bathroom." He glanced around briefly so he could answer any question that Jax might throw at him with some measure of credibility.

"Uh huh." Jax was clearly unconvinced, but he didn't pursue it. Instead, he turned away, heading back to the door and the little landing outside the master suite. "So what do you think?" he asked when Noah made it back onto the landing with him.

"It's a great house, Jax, but can you afford it? And why would you want such a huge house to live in all alone?"

Noah knew he wasn't being subtle, but he wanted to know what Jax was thinking. Was he looking for a family home, because if so, this was perfect, even if it was also likely to be very pricey. But what if he just wanted a large bachelor pad? This was too much. He could find smaller luxurious spaces if he didn't have forever plans with anyone in mind.

"Maybe I won't be alone," Jax murmured in response, then turned and walked down the stairs all the way to the first floor.

The realtor made any further conversation impossible, but Noah didn't mind, since he was at a loss for how to continue it. He followed them down to the finished basement where the laundry room was and a lot of extra storage space. Back on the first floor, he listened half-heartedly as she answered the questions Jax asked, and they drifted away to talk price. Giving them full privacy, he walked out to the front porch and sat on the top step. The sun was at the back of the house and on the shaded front steps the air was comfortably warm.

Noah sat sideways with his back against the railing and closed his eyes. Birds chirped, a lone woodpecker was busy at its labor, and if he wasn't mistaken, was that an owl? He looked up, trying to find where the huge bird might be, but could see nothing.

"I'll see you at nine tomorrow morning, then."

Jax's voice broke into his drowsing, and Noah stood up hurriedly and went the rest of the way down to where their vehicles were parked. After a moment, Jax joined him.

"Ready for dinner?"

Noah nodded. "Sure. Where are we going?"

"I saw a restaurant in a sweet little spot when I was driving up here earlier. It's right by the river."

"Lead on, Prof."

The drive to The River King took twenty minutes, and the parking lot was fairly full when they got there. Fortunately, they managed to find parking next to each other in the back of the lot and were soon seated at a table for two on the wide back porch. The sun still lent its brightness to the late afternoon, painting the sky in rich gold. They placed their drink orders before Jax spoke again.

"So what do you think of the town?"

"I didn't see much of it, but what I saw was pretty neat. There's a music shop on one of the streets I took to get here."

Jax grinned at him. "Trust you to notice that!"

"I'm a musician ... it's what we do." Noah's grin matched his.

"I like what little I've seen of it, but I really want to explore a bit more before I go."

"Makes sense, I guess. I mean, you are gonna be living here for a while at least, so it's best to know what you're getting into."

"I've booked a room for the night because I'd like to see the other two places the realtor has lined up for me. They are also single-family homes, but smaller than the one we just saw. We can go drive around and get a feel for the town after dinner."

Jax's eyes gleamed for a moment as he regarded Noah. What was he thinking so hard about?

"What?" Noah had to know.

"Can you spend the night? It would be nice to have you along for the other two house visits."

Jax wanted another sleepover, and Noah was all about that. "Yeah. I brought some extra clothes on the off chance that you'd need me to stay."

"Good."

That one word set fire to Noah's imagination. What were all the ways that he could make Jax feel good, that Jax could make him feel good? Images rose up before his mind's eyes of him and Jax taking and giving each other pleasure ... in his big bed, on that balcony, down by the edge of the lake.

Who knew he had an exhibitionist streak in him? The idea that someone might see them gave him a small thrill. Would Jax be up for some open-air lovemaking?

"Enjoy your meals, gentlemen!"

*Snap out of it, Noah! Pay attention.* He smiled his thanks to the server who was setting his food down and waited until Jax was served before he began to eat. Although he loved the food he'd ordered, he had no real idea of how anything truly tasted. He registered light, flavorful, butter in the potatoes, and the steak was cooked to just the right level of doneness to suit him. Even the vegetables were crunchy the way he preferred them, but his whole focus was on the man sitting across from him enjoying his salmon dinner.

"Not hungry anymore? We can bag it up for later."

"Yeah, sure."

Jax eyed him suspiciously. "What's wrong?"

"Nothing!" Noah's denial was immediate. "Just wool-gathering is all. Nothing important." He gathered his wits and continued, to forestall any further questions from Jax. "When do you plan to move up permanently?"

"Classes begin the last Monday of August, so I'll need to be up here at least sometime in the week before. But what I'd really like is to get the housing sorted so that I can move in as soon as the furniture arrives."

"So the latest will be in another week or two, then? Unless the housing situation falls through?"

"Yes." Noah could feel Jax's eyes on him as he tried to figure out what was going on.

"I'll be happy to help you move and get settled in." He couldn't be any clearer if he tried. Would Jax get the message hidden beneath the words?

"I'm not proud. I'll take all offers to help me unload my life again." A slow, seductive smile crept over his face when he added, "I can guarantee you'll be suitably rewarded."

Noah cocked a brow, raising the beer he'd ordered to his lips. "Oh? What's a suitable reward for a moving man?"

Jax slid a forkful of food into his mouth, chewed and swallowed, clearly giving his answer some thought.

"What do you think about a massage?"

"With a happy ending?" Noah teased.

Desire flashed in Jax's eyes as he answered, "If that's what you want."

"That's what I want." No sense in pretending.

"Consider it done."

Noah had never had a massage with a happy ending. In fact, he had never had a massage of any kind until therapy after the accident. But he did know what Jax's hands felt like on him, and the thought of having them on his body again was doing a number on his already stimulated libido.

"Would you gentlemen like dessert?" The server stood quietly at their table, a smile on her face.

"No, thanks, we're good. I *would* like a box to take home the leftovers though, please."

Jax didn't want dessert either, and he had no leftovers. Anticipation sizzled in Noah's veins as they left the restaurant. He was more than ready for some alone time with Jax, and the drive around town, slipping in and out of pretty side streets, and wandering for a while in the beautiful town park with its gorgeous, flowered paths and magnificent statuary was like extended and very seductive foreplay. The sun had dipped below the horizon by the time they got back to Jax's room, leaving the sky a vague, ghostly gray shadowed by the black of oncoming night, with purple highlights for extra richness.

He was still unprepared, though, when Jax pushed him up against the door the second it closed behind them and demanded his tongue. They kissed like two starving hounds finally let loose on the leftovers that had been thrown at them. Growls and groans were the backup lyrics to their lust, moans and sighs adding the perfect notes of desire.

"Strip!" Jax's voice was heavy with need when he released Noah's lips. "And then get on the bed."

*Don't need to tell me twice.* Noah was naked in record time, walking on hands and knees up the bed and lying on his back to watch his lover undress. Jax pulled his clothes off haphazardly before searching through his toiletry bag for lube and condoms. He was on the bed before Noah had time to fully appreciate the curve of his ass or the thick length that his hole was already hungry to engulf.

Jax kissed him again, dragging his emotions to the surface where he could not hide from them.

"Fuck, Jax, I..." How was he to explain how he was feeling? "I really wanted to keep being angry with you, you know?"

Jax chuckled as he slid the latex over his straining rod. "And I really thought you would never forgive me." He snicked open the bottle of lube and squirted a little down his shaft, spreading it quickly before adding more so he could slide a finger inside Noah's waiting body.

"And yet, here we are," Noah panted out as Jax's first finger penetrated him and sank in to the root.

"Damn, babe! You're so hot. Mmm."

Noah hissed as Jax sent a second finger in and all talking ceased as his lover prepared him to receive the gift of his cock. He was a shaking mess of emotion by the time Jax had three fingers in his ass, whimpering with a mixture of need and hunger and a bite of pain that disappeared when Jax hit his prostate.

"Fuck!"

"No coming till I'm inside you, babe," Jax ordered. "Then you can do what you like."

Noah raised his hips when Jax slid his cock in to replace his fingers and his body swallowed the steely length eagerly. Using his heels, he dragged Jax all the way inside him, needing only a moment to grow accustomed to the feel of the heavy weight. Then he was riding his lover's dick like a champion, pushing up to close the distance and refusing to let anything come between them but air.

"Don't want this to end," Jax whispered between his own gulps of air. "Wanna be in you forever."

His sentiments exactly, but Noah could only nod his agreement as he followed his lover's lead and sped up his thrusts, grunting with every one of Jax's plunges into his hole. They rode each other hard, sweat beading on Jax's forehead before rolling down his cheek to his chin. Another bead slid down to the corner of his lip and Noah leaned up to suck it off, the action making Jax's dick push even deeper into his body.

"I'm gonna come, Jax!" he cried out when he felt the warning of his release shoot up his spine.

"Come then," Jax growled, never parting from his body as he chased his own fulfillment. "Come, baby!" he commanded again through gritted teeth.

"Shiiiiit!"

Noah's whole body caved as his orgasm raced through him, spurt after spurt of semen shooting from his jerking cock onto his belly and Jax's, up to his chin, onto Jax's beard. And even when the tight grip eased and his body loosened, the last of his come still dribbled from his tip as Jax plunged into his body twice more before shouting out his own climax.

Noah welcomed Jax's full weight on him when his lover collapsed on top of him, both men panting heavily as they came down from the high. He wrapped his arms around Jax, feeling the sticky mess of spend and sweat between them and not caring too much. They'd finally made love the way he had dreamed of since the day they'd parted, even when he had let anger and bitterness color his emotions.

"You okay?" Jax whispered tenderly in his ear, leaving a fleeting kiss on his earlobe before raising himself up on his elbows to look at him.

"Good as gold," he whispered back. "I needed that," he confessed. "I needed you."

"No more than I needed you, babe."

A deep, claiming kiss followed their declarations, leaving them as breathless as they'd been when they climaxed. The love that had lain dormant for so long, that had begun to reawaken over the last couple of weeks, swelled up and overflowed in Noah's veins, washing away the hurt and anger of the last ten years, replacing them with a warm serenity and absolute completion.

"It was hell being apart from you, Jax. I won't be able to bear it again."

Jax pulled out slowly, disposing of the condom before rolling Noah on top of him and wrapping his arms around him, dragging him as close as he could be and tucking Noah's head into the hollow of his shoulder. They stayed connected like that, not moving, not speaking, just breathing each other in. Then he spoke tenderly into Noah's ear.

"It wasn't easy for me either, Noah. But I'll never push you away go again, babe. I promise."

# Chapter 17

## Jax

*Jax would willingly give Noah whatever he wanted.*

*I*f *you've never slept with the one you love in your arms, you're missing out.* That thought flitted through Jax's mind as he lay awake the next morning, feeling his lover's deep breathing against him. With Noah's back to him, Jax's arm was thrown over his waist and across his belly. He resisted the urge to stroke the smooth flesh beneath his palm. He wouldn't wake him. It was a delight just to hold him close, to listen to the soft, almost inaudible snuffles that interrupted his breathing, to feel the warmth and strength of him.

Things had moved along much more quickly than he could have imagined that they would, if he had been thinking about reconnecting with Noah. A month ago—hell, two weeks ago—the furthest thing from his mind had been finding the love of his life and being forgiven and accepted back. The nighttime run that had had them bumping into each other must certainly have been fate. There could be no other explanation for why, out of all the towns in upstate New York, Jax would meet Noah again in this one. He wasn't a believer in the supernatural, but he would swear by it in this instance. Some greater power was on his side—on *their* side—and he would be forever grateful.

"You're thinking so hard, you're making my head hurt."

Noah's teasing, accompanied by a breathy chuckle, pulled Jax back into the bed and the man he held.

"Morning, brat!" he said, ignoring Noah's comment and leaning in to kiss his cheek. "Did you sleep well?"

Noah turned so he was facing Jax before answering. "I did, thank you. I thought I was going to need to put some space between us because I can't sleep if I'm hot, but somehow you managed not to overheat me at all."

Jax raised a brow. "At all? I guess I need to up my game, then."

Noah's delighted laugh pleased him. "You've got great game, Prof. If you up it anymore, you may incinerate me."

This camaraderie, this intimacy ... *this* was what Jax had always wanted, what he had been missing, what he meant to treasure for the rest of their lives, if Noah would let him. He pulled him completely into his arms and breathed him in, sighing when Noah wrapped his own arms around him and stuck a thigh between his legs.

"Mmm," he rumbled above Noah's head. "I could get used to this."

Noah yawned loudly and slanted a sheepish smile his way. "Sorry. What time do you have to be at your first appointment?"

"Nine." He glanced over at the digital clock on the side table. "Which means we need to get moving, babe." He pulled away for a moment to add, "I'm going to assume that you didn't postpone any lessons to be with me today."

He tried to inject a serious note without coming off like Noah's keeper. He wasn't his father, nor did he want to take on that role, but he wouldn't be happy if Noah put his business, his means of making a living, below time spent with Jax, no matter how flattering he found the idea to be. Without the quartet, Noah's life was in a bit of flux, and he needed to think carefully about his future.

Jax wanted to be there for him when he chose to confront the decisions he needed to make. He would do his best to be merely the guide on the side and not offer any advice unless he was specifically asked for it.

"No lessons today. The boy who was supposed to have come called to cancel this week's session."

"Good. Let's shower and get ready to go."

The two houses they visited did not suit Jax, but he had suspected that they wouldn't because they weren't the one he really wanted.

"How long do I have to make an offer on the lake house?" he asked the realtor as they stood outside a small ranch house on a quiet, tree-lined street.

"I believe the owners have said the first reasonable offer they receive they will accept. And I know they've already turned down two offers this week."

"Can we sit down and put together a plan? I'd like to make an offer sooner rather than later."

"Of course, Dr. Knox. I'll meet you back at the office this afternoon at three. I have two appointments with other clients first."

Jax agreed, then took Noah back to his truck. "Will you wait with me, or do you need to get back earlier?"

"I'll wait. My dad knows where I am and what I'm doing. He says hi, by the way."

They spent the rest of the morning exploring another nearby state park and after a leisurely lunch, strolled hand-in-hand from one end of the boardwalk to the other before returning to the realtor's office. Jax reluctantly accepted Noah's refusal to sit in on the meeting. He understood that it was his decision alone, and since he hadn't specifically invited Noah to move in with him, there was no real reason for him to be included in the discussion.

"I think this is a fair offer, Dr. Knox," Mary said later after they had ironed out a few talking points and filled out a lot of paperwork. "And I can tell you that your offer is by far superior to the previous two. So while I would caution you not to get your hopes up, I don't see them refusing this one. In the meantime, in case they do, would you like me to keep looking for other properties?"

"Yes, thank you. I appreciate it. When will I know? And how soon will I be able to move in if they accept the offer?"

"The owners got back to me within a day on the last two offers, so I imagine it'll be about the same for you. As to when you can move in, I'm sure you'll be able to settle that with them as soon as the decision is made. I would assume you'll be free to move in as soon as the paperwork and legalities are taken care of, though, and they're already on board with that."

Jax shook her hand and took his leave, meeting Noah in the outer office.

"Well, it's time to get back. If all goes well, I'll be moving in pretty quickly. I know Jim and Annie won't mind me staying an extra week or two with them, especially since Annie is ready to have that baby now."

It would be a treat to be present to welcome the new Bell baby into the world, and if it was a girl, he'd be doubly happy for them since he knew that was what they hoped for.

"How about you come over for dinner, so Annie doesn't have to cook for you today? You can go home after that."

Jax smiled, a slow, knowing smile. He recognized what Noah was doing, and he approved. He didn't want them to be apart either, even if he knew they had no choice.

"Sounds like a plan. Let me just text Annie and tell her I'll be home after dinner."

Jax followed Noah back to his home, not even caring that the drive took over four hours because of an accident on the highway. Just knowing where he was going, not just in the moment on SR 69, but for the foreseeable future in his life, was a precious gift he hadn't understood he needed as much as he did. When the time was right, he'd be with Noah permanently, and that was where he was supposed to have been heading all along. They still had to say more than they had already confessed to, but that conversation could wait for another day. He preferred to have the housing situation resolved so when he made his move, he had more to offer his man than words.

Alvaro was sitting on the front porch when Jax pulled in behind Noah. He parked and got out of the car, going to join Noah in front of his father.

"*¡Hola, Papi! ¿Cómo te va?*"

Alvaro smiled at his son. "I'm fine, *mijo*. Welcome back." Then he looked behind at Jax. "It is good to see you again, *Profesor*. I hear that you were house hunting."

"I was, sir, and I think I may have found the place I want to live in for the foreseeable future."

Alvaro stood up and gestured for them to follow him into the house. "I waited for you because Noah told me you were coming to dinner. We can talk more as we eat."

After they washed up, they dug into spicy Indian food while Jax talked about the houses he'd seen and the one he wanted for himself.

"That sounds like a prime location. But what will you do with such a large house?"

"It'll be great for when family and friends come to visit, but ultimately, I'm looking to start a family, sir, and I'd prefer to be prepared for the day I begin to build one."

Jax swept his eyes over to Noah as he spoke, doing his best to telegraph his meaning to his lover.

"Hmm. I'm sure you have someone in mind to start over with."

Jax repressed the chuckle at Alvaro's non-subtle fishing expedition. He was pleased that he could confirm the older man's assumption.

"Yes, sir, I do. I just need to get all my ducks in a row before I say anything to him."

He could feel Noah's eyes on him, but he kept his attention on his father, curious to see how he would respond to that comment. He suspected that Alvaro knew who he had in mind, though how he'd have figured that out with only the little information he had was anybody's guess. Alvaro set his fork down and picked up his glass, taking a sip of his drink before speaking again.

"You see the elements of your life as a row of ducklings, *Profesor*?" Amusement colored his words and his cheek creased with it.

"There are a few parts to it, sir, so that is an apt comparison."

Alvaro's smile bloomed. "Well, I will wish you the best of luck keeping them in line."

After dinner, when Noah stood next to him by his car, Jax waited for what he could feel Noah had to say. He had no idea what it might be, but he could hope it would be something he'd want to hear.

"I know you're going to be busy, but when will I see you again?"

"When do you want to see me again?"

Noah's chuckle warmed him. "Tomorrow. I have two sessions in the morning, but my afternoon is free."

"Whatever you need, whenever you need it."

Still stunned at this happy turn of fate, Jax would willingly give Noah whatever he wanted. A quiet joy had been building in him since they made love that first time in Noah's bed, and the hope that rode shotgun with it was filling the spaces he'd thought would remain forever empty when he'd turned Noah away over a decade earlier.

"There's a regatta the next town over that we can catch if we leave as soon as my second class ends at noon."

"I'll make us a picnic lunch, then." Jax hoped Jim would be home for Annie. He knew his friend would approve of this and want him to go with it.

"Sounds good."

"I'll pick you up at twelve thirty," Jax continued. "Will your dad expect you home for dinner or can we go out that after?"

Noah laughed. "He's been giving me some very broad hints about getting out of the house and being with my friends." He rolled his eyes. "As if I have any friends left here. He means you, but he thinks he's being subtle."

Jax eyed him questioningly. "So he knows about us."

Now it was Noah's turn to send a questioning glance his way. "Is that a problem?"

Jax shook his head immediately, understanding the answer to his statement was yes. "Not at all. I just didn't know when you would tell him."

"I had no choice really, because he'd apparently known all along and was just waiting for me to confess," Noah said wryly. "I don't know why I thought I could hide anything from him."

Jax chuckled. "Parents are like that. My dad could sniff out a lie like a dog can sniff out bacon." He loved the hearty laugh that Noah gave. "I'll see you tomorrow. Sweet dreams."

Leaning in, he dropped a quick peck on his lips before getting into his car and driving away, glancing back through the rearview mirror to see Noah watching him. The feelings warming him were almost overwhelming, but he tamped them down. He had a lot to do over the next two weeks, and people he needed to talk to, once he and Noah did. He whistled as he parked the car and took his duffle out.

The house was quiet when he got in. "Anyone home?"

Silence was his only response. He dropped his bag in his room and went to see where everyone was. No one was around and when he looked, Jim's truck wasn't in the garage. He pulled out his cell and noticed the message he'd missed. It had been sent half an hour ago.

[Jim: Annie's in surgery. The boys are with the neighbors. Can you get them for me? I'll call in an hour.]

Jax hurried next door where the twins were watching television but jumped up as soon as they saw him. He turned to the young woman who was holding a baby on her hip.

"Thanks so much, Carrie. I know Jim and Annie appreciate you stepping in to help. I'll take these two off your hands now."

Carrie smiled shyly at him. "It's no problem, Dr. Knox. Jake and Jude are sweethearts, and they helped me with Timmy here when he was kicking up a fuss earlier." She turned to the two of them with an even wider smile. "You're gonna be such great big brothers," she praised them. "Are you guys excited to meet your little brother or sister?"

"I hope it's a sister," Jake said, not answering her question.

"Me too. I hope she comes home soon," Jude added.

Clearly, they weren't unhappy with the thought of a new baby. Jax herded them toward the door.

"Come on, you two. Let's get you home and into bed. You're gonna need your sleep when the little one comes home, and your mom's gonna need your help."

Jim called as he was tucking them into bed. He shut the light off in their room and went into the kitchen to take the call.

"Hey, Jim, what's going on?"

"They did an emergency C-section. The baby was breech and not doing so well."

Jim's worry leaked into his voice. Jax wasn't sure what to say that wouldn't be just a meaningless platitude. He had to try, though.

"Congratulations, man! I'm really happy for you. But why are you talking to me instead of being in there with Annie?"

"Her mom's with her," his friend said. "I stayed until the baby was born and saw that she was okay." His breath hitched, but he paused as if to gather himself and then went on. "She's so beautiful, Jax. I mean, the prettiest little thing you ever did see. But it took her a minute to holler like they wanted her to." He chuckled a little. "Poor Annie's exhausted, though. She fell asleep almost as soon as they put the baby on her chest."

"I'm sure the baby will be fine, man. They both will be, and Annie's gonna need you when she wakes up. You ready for that?"

"Yeah. Worried, but ready."

And by the sound of his voice, determined to do whatever would make Annie and his new daughter comfortable and happy. That was better than imagining worst-case scenarios, as far as Jax was concerned.

"You know I'll do whatever I can to help." He reassured his friend whom he was sure needed to hear the words, even though Jim already knew for a fact that Jax had his back.

"Yeah, I know. Thanks, man." He paused, clearing his throat. "So how did the house hunting go?"

Jax smiled. A change of subject wasn't a bad thing. It was certainly a great way to distract Jim from his worries.

"I found a place and made an offer." He told Jim about the house and his plans for himself and Noah.

"So when are you gonna ask him to move in?"

"We have to talk about all that first," Jax said. "I don't want to assume that he wants to go as far as I do…"

"But you bought that huge house with him in mind, didn't you?" Jim interrupted. "Why drop all that dough on a place you'll rattle around in on your own if he's just into friends with benefits?"

"I can still adopt kids on my own and have the family I want. It'll probably be harder if I'm single, but if I get a surrogate to bear my child, no one can refuse me parental rights because I'm single, can they?"

"You've really thought about this, haven't you?"

"Last night, while Noah was sleeping, it was all I could think about." He sighed. "And yeah, the thought of not having him in my life as a co-parent, to have to do it all on my own, is pretty daunting. But I'm not getting any younger, and I'd like to enjoy my kids while I'm still fairly young and healthy."

"I don't think you have to worry about him," Jim declared. "The way he's been around you, I'm sure when you propose, he won't say no."

The thought of proposing to Noah had been the other thing that had filled his thoughts. It would have to be something inventive and fresh, like the man he wanted in his life forever. That would take some planning, but he couldn't focus on that now. He had other things to do, including contacting the storage company about ending his contract and finding a reasonably priced moving company so that as soon as he got the go-ahead, he could move his things up to his new home. Then there was the planning he needed to do for his first semester in the new college. And he had to watch out for Jake and Jude so that Jim and Annie could have a few days' grace where their only concern was Annie and the baby.

After he hung up from the call, he went into the kitchen to see what groceries he might need to buy so the Bells wouldn't have to worry too much about that for a bit. Making a quick list, he decided that he'd take the boys out for breakfast in the morning, then take them grocery shopping and after that, Jim and Annie might be ready to introduce them to their new baby sister. He'd forgotten to ask what her name was, but he'd find out when they got to the hospital. Satisfied with his plans, he went to bed. His phone pinged with a new message as he shut the light off on the bedside table. It was Noah.

[Noah: Just wanted to say goodnight.]

Dammit! He hadn't told Noah about the Bells' good news, and he'd forgotten all about their plans for the next day. He didn't want to break their date, but he had to be the godfather the boys needed right now. Biting his bottom lip, he answered the text.

[Jax: I'm so sorry I forgot to tell you. Jim and Annie had a baby girl. She had to be delivered by Caesarian because the baby was in distress, but they're both on the mend now. I'm with the boys.]

He sent that, then sighed as he wrote the rest. This was *not* how he'd planned to start the next phase of their relationship.

[Jax: Jim will need me for at least the next day while he and Annie's mom sort out arrangements for them. I don't think I can meet you tomorrow afternoon. Raincheck?]

While he'd been writing, Noah had been as well, and their notes crossed each other on the way. Jax smiled when he read Noah's message.

[Noah: That's great news! Please give them our congratulations and best wishes. Is there anything you need me to do for you?]

This man was a treasure and Jax felt the glow of gratitude warm him as he thanked heaven that he'd found him again and that Noah had forgiven him. He only hoped his man was with him all the way to marriage and family and happily ever after. Another message popped up as he was basking in warm thoughts.

[Noah: Have they met their little sister yet?]

[Jax: No. I'm taking them tomorrow after we go grocery shopping. I'll call you from the hospital to let you know what the plans are.]

[Noah: Sounds good.]

There was a pause—what writers might call a pregnant pause—and Jax felt the weight of whatever Noah was trying to decide whether he should say or not. He knew what *he* wanted to say, but he would make his declarations of love when the time was right. Which, he thought with a wry smile, was code for *when I'm not running scared*. Was this how it was for people in love? Was saying the words supposed to be this daunting?

# Chapter 18

## *Jax*

*He was so happy, his joy was likely to
spill right out of him in bursts of light.*

His phone rang. Apparently, Noah wanted to say whatever it was he had in mind instead of merely typing the words. Jax swallowed and answered.

"Hey."

"Jax, I..." Noah paused, obviously choosing his words with care. "I want you to know that I understand why you did what you did, and I appreciate you for caring about me enough to do it. It hurt, I can't deny that, and I was furious for a long while after. But time and distance have taught me that sometimes we can't have the things we know are ours without some kind of struggle. And anyway, I needed to grow up, to toughen up so I'd be worthy of you."

"Noah..." Jax began, but his lover cut him off.

"No, let me finish. I won't get this out otherwise, and I'm not gonna be a chickenshit anymore." Jax heard an audible swallow before he continued. "I just want you to know that I love you for loving me all those years ago. I've never stopped loving you, even when I was so hurt and angry."

He stopped speaking then, and Jax's heart beat a wild tattoo in his chest at how neatly the decision to declare his love had been taken out of his hands. There was no way he could keep his feelings to himself any longer. Noah had been brave enough to open his heart completely. It was his turn to man up.

"I love you too, Noah. I never stopped … I couldn't. I always knew that you were the one for me, even after you graduated, and I never saw you again. That's really why I couldn't start anything new with anyone … no one else measured up. Thank you for forgiving me, sweetheart. We wouldn't be here if you hadn't."

"Call me tomorrow as soon as you know what Jim and Annie will need from you. I need things from you, too," he added, his tone going sultry. "But I understand that you have other people who need you more right now. I can be patient and wait."

Jax chuckled softly. "I'll call you the minute I know more. Goodnight, Noah. Sweet dreams."

"Night, Prof!"

Wrangling two little boys early in the morning was more stressful than Jax had realized. How did Annie and Jim do this every day?

"Have you showered?" he asked Jude, who appeared in the kitchen first, looking like he'd slept in his clothes.

"Jake is in there," the boy said nonchalantly.

"Did you at least brush your teeth?" he asked, going over to lead him back to the bathroom where the shower was still going.

"He won't let me in!" There was a definite whine in his voice now.

Hmm ... since when does an eight-year-old boy lock the bathroom door when he's in it? Was that a thing these days? Jax didn't have time to think on it.

"Jake, open this door now, and get out of the bathroom, buddy. Your brother needs to come in, and we need to leave soon."

He waited, Jude slouching against the wall with his arms folded across his chest. Jax held onto his patience when it took the other boy another minute to shut off the shower and fifteen more seconds to unlock the door.

"Get in there and hurry up," he told Jude, opening the door and stepping back from the cloud of steam that billowed out. "And don't forget to brush your teeth," he added more loudly for both of them to hear as the child went inside.

He drained the coffee he'd been sipping when Jude appeared, cleaned up the kitchen, and was waiting less patiently in the living room when the boys finally emerged, dressed in jeans and ratty, old t-shirts.

"Come with me," he said, turning them both and steering them by their shoulders back into their bedroom. "Find a better shirt to wear. You're going to meet your new baby sister today, and your grandma will be there as well. You don't want to show up looking like hobos, do you?"

"What's a hobo, Uncle Jax?" Jude asked, rummaging through the top drawer of his chest of drawers.

"A person who doesn't have an iron because he doesn't have a fixed address," Jax answered at once. "Now hurry up!"

They managed to find more acceptable-looking shirts, and soon they were on their way to the diner. Jax let them order what they wanted, cautioning them that they had to eat everything on their plates, or they'd not get dessert after dinner. He chuckled when they ordered pancakes and bacon and ate everything, draining their glasses of chocolate milk, as well.

In the supermarket afterwards, he picked up more eggs, bacon and sausages, bread, crackers and cheese, some fruit, the boys' favorite cereal and milk, as well as hamburger patties, hot dogs, and buns.

"We're gonna take these home and then go visit your mom, okay?"

The boys nodded, no doubt too pleased to be getting extra time in his car to care where they went. He got them to help him put the things away and then drove to the hospital, parking as close as he could and sending Jim a text message to find out where they were.

[Jim: Maternity ward's on the third floor.]

Once they were in the elevator, he texted Noah.

[Jax: Good morning. I'm at the hospital, going up to see the Bells and their new baby. I'll call you later.]

He smiled at the big red heart, the wink, and the wide grin emojis that were Noah's response to his message as the elevator doors opened, letting them out on the third floor. Signs pointed them to the maternity area of the floor, and he caught sight of Jim as he rounded the corner. His friend looked wiped out, but the sparkle in his eyes said he was ecstatic, despite his exhaustion.

Jax reached in for a hug. "Congratulations again, Jim! I'm really happy for you."

Jim patted his back before releasing him. "Thanks, man. I'm tired and all I did was hang out and watch Annie and the baby sleep."

"What's my new niece's name?"

"Joanna Marie Bell," Jake announced proudly before his father could answer. "Me and Jude helped pick the name for a boy and a girl."

A smug smile lit up his face, even as his twin chimed in, "If it was a boy, his name would be Jamison Andrew Bell."

Jax chuckled. "Well, it's a good thing you're all ready with the names, there, kiddo, because I'm sure your mama is dying to see the two of you and to introduce you to Joanna."

"We wanna call her Jojo," Jake added importantly, puffing out his chest. "That will be easier for her to say."

Jax met Jim's eyes above their heads and grinned. Big brother duties had commenced. Just then, Mrs. Blake, Annie's mom, stepped into the hallway, her face lighting up when she saw her grandsons.

"Grandma!" Both boys headed over to hug her, while Jim shushed them and shook his head.

"Come on. Let's get you in before mayhem starts."

Chuckling, Jax followed him into the private hospital room. Jim had many things planned for Annie, Jax knew, to say thanks for trying again between their losses and now, and he applauded his friend for going all out for the love of his life. The way he would do for Noah when the time came.

Annie's eyes were closed when they walked in, but they popped open when Jim went to stand next to her, as though she was attuned to his very presence. The loving glance they shared made him feel like a third wheel on a fancy date, and he turned and stepped away to let them have a moment to just breathe each other in. Then Annie's voice sounded in the quiet room.

"Jax, thanks for looking after the boys for me. Come and meet your new godchild."

The tiny human being cradled in her mother's arms was napping, red-faced and completely adorable with her flat baby nose, tiny eyes, and scrunched up fingers, fisted inside the socks they were presently wearing. Annie beckoned him closer and added, "Want to hold her?"

Yes, yes he did! He leaned in and took the sleeping infant from her arms, cradling the tender head against his bicep and swaying gently, humming into her ear as he planted a kiss on the top of her head.

"She's too precious, Annie," he whispered.

"Thanks, Jax." Her smile was proud and full of love for the child she'd been carrying for nine months.

Jax only had a brief moment with Joanna before her grandmother and brothers walked in, and he had to relinquish his hold on her so they could touch her as she lay once again in her mother's arms.

Not wanting to take up any more of their family time, he said, "I need to get going. I have a few things to do to prepare for the closing if the owners agree to my price. And I have to start getting ready for work. I'll be at home later. Do you need me to do anything?"

"No. We're set now Mama B's here," Jim said. "We can't thank you enough for looking after the boys last night. I know they can be a handful sometimes."

"They were fine, and I don't mind." Jax smiled at his friend and then turned to Mrs. Blake. "Do you need me to order dinner for you later, Mrs. B? I assume Jim's going to be staying here with Annie?"

"No, thank you, Jackson," she never called him Jax, no matter how often he begged her to, "we'll be fine. We'll see you later, son."

"Okay. Be good, you two," he said, pointing to the boys.

"Yes, Uncle Jax."

Back in his car, he called Noah, who picked up on the first ring. "Hey. How's everyone?"

"Mother and baby are well, and father, brothers and grandma are thrilled. I just left them."

"So, what now?"

"I need to find a lawyer to help me with the paperwork. I've researched it, and it seems it's in my best interest to have someone go over stuff with me who *isn't* the realtor, especially because it's a rent-to-own situation that the owners and I are kinda speeding up. Don't suppose you know anyone?"

"Not a lawyer, no, but I can ask my dad. He may know someone who knows someone. Come over for lunch and we can talk more before we go out."

"I'll be there around 12:30 … is that okay?"

"That's perfect. I'll let my dad know to expect his favorite professor for lunch. Give him something to look forward to."

Jax chuckled. "He needs to go out more if *I'm* his standard for something to look forward to."

"Mind what you say about his favorite professor," Noah retorted with a snort. "My dad's got good taste, and I inherited it."

*Look at my life!* The thought warmed Jax as he ended the call. He had never for a moment thought he'd find Noah again, let alone be forgiven for breaking them wide open and being taken back into his heart. This was the stuff of fairytales, or romance novels where the happily-ever-after was guaranteed. How was this his life? What had he done to deserve this second chance? Whatever it was, he was beyond grateful.

While he'd been on the phone, a message had come through from his new boss. Dr. Mann wanted to know if he would be available for the annual music department retreat. He read it with a smile.

[Dr. Mann: It's a time for us to welcome new members to our team, welcome back the old ones, and plan for the year together. It's more about bonding than work, but some work does get done.]

He liked the sound of that. He knew once the year began there would be little time for them to do much in the way of cementing camaraderie, what with all the work they'd have to do with students. But team building was important in a profession where rivalries could tear departments apart. He was grateful he had landed in a place where comradeship was as valued as professionalism.

[Prof: I'll be happy to join you, Dr. Mann. Just let me know where and when.]

He had an hour to spare before he was due at Noah's place, and not having anything else to do at the moment, he took himself off to the art gallery a stone's throw away from the pier and lost himself in the beauty of the works by local artists. One painting of a violin caught his eye, and he immediately thought of Noah. Without giving himself a chance to think twice about it, he bought the piece and had it gift-wrapped. He'd decide when to give it to him eventually, but for now, he'd take it home and store it in his room.

Lunch was moist, delicious cheeseburgers and home fries, washed down with lemonade. Alvaro was in his element, telling stories from his years as a conductor with Amtrak. Jax enjoyed how the old man's love for his job shone through every word, even when he was recounting sad stories of derailments and job actions. His struggles to move up in the ranks as a person of color were retold with pain but no anger.

"It must be great to have nothing pressing to do these days, sir," he commented.

"It was sometimes a challenge in the beginning." Alvaro's response surprised him.

"How so, sir?" he asked.

"I have always been a working man." Alvaro's accent thickened as he spoke. "To be without a purpose was a difficult adjustment for me, so I had to change the way I thought about what it means to be of use. Work had been my only motivation before I retired. Only when I understood that play can be a goal on its own did it become easier for me."

"When *Papi* told me he was going to retire in Florida so he could play golf with his buddies, you could have knocked me over with a feather," Noah interjected with a grin. "I'd never seen him so much as watch a golf game on TV."

Alvaro chuckled. "Do you see how golf is played? The players walk, or they ride in a golf cart if they're tired or it's far away to the next hole. They line up their shot, hit the ball ... next! They don't spend a lot of energy. Well, *I* don't." He clapped his hands together sharply once. "And because I am not Tiger Woods," he paused to chuckle gleefully. "I don't have to perform for any audience at all. It is just me and *mis amigos* having a good time with each other out on God's green Earth. That, *Profesor*, is my new purpose ... to learn something different, to enjoy my friendships, and to breathe in fresh air and enjoy the sunshine."

Jax liked the older man's joyful attitude. "Do you miss work sometimes, though?"

Alvaro's smile softened. "Oh, I miss it every day, but the feeling only lasts as long as I give it room to do so."

"And how long is that, *Papi*?"

Alvaro's eyes twinkled with amusement. "Until I have my first cup of coffee in my favorite mug sitting in my favorite chair, here or back in Florida."

Noah laughed. "I hear that. Not having to get up at the butt crack of dawn, or work until the wee hours and having quality coffee instead of whatever drivel you can find must be nice."

After lunch, as they were about to leave for their date, Alvaro said, "By the way, *Profesor*, I did not forget your request. I have a number that you can call to speak with someone about your legal needs." He handed Jax an index card with a name and number. "The lawyer is my oldest friend's son-in-law. He's a good man. You tell him I sent you his way, and he won't charge you an arm and a leg."

He winked and Jax laughed with him. "Thank you, Alvaro. I'll call him today."

He made the call as Noah drove to the regatta. Matt Stabler didn't pick up, but Jax left him a message anyway, making sure to refer to Alvaro in it. Then he put the phone away and turned to Noah.

"Aren't we going to miss most of the regatta?"

"Maybe the first half, but it'll still be fun to watch the rest. And we can have dinner there, so we don't have to rush back." He glanced at Jax before adding, "Unless you made plans with the Bells?"

"No plans. I'll call to check on them later and just let Jim know I'll be home late."

A short pause later, Noah changed the subject. "What are *you* gonna do when you retire, Prof?"

Jax chuckled. "Not that I'm anywhere close to that yet, but I don't really know. I've never given it much thought." He stopped to think a moment, then added, "There's one thing I do know, though." He waited for the inevitable question, and Noah didn't disappoint him.

"And what's that?"

"I know I want to spend those years with you." He looked over at his lover as he spoke, observing the flush that had pinkened his skin. Could he be any clearer?

After another weighty pause, Noah said, "Ah! So, you know *who* you want to do, just not *what*, huh?"

His deadpan tone and facial expression matched perfectly. Jax burst out laughing, and after a second, Noah joined him, the sounds of their amusement filling the cab of the truck.

"Asshole!" Jax answered, still giggling like a schoolboy.

"Sucker!" Noah retorted.

They both burst into laughter again. Jax's heart swelled with warmth and contentment. For the first time in a very long time, he was happy. God, he was so happy, his joy was likely to spill right out of him in bursts of light and heat. He felt giddy with the feeling.

His cellphone pinged a new message notification and he looked down to see that it was from Dr. Mann. He read it aloud when he saw what she'd said.

"Hey, listen to this."

"Who's it from?" Noah asked.

"My new boss. It's about the team building retreat. I asked her where and when it will be." He cleared his throat to repeat the message. "It'll be at Mayfair House, the university's guest house on the lake on the weekend before the semester begins."

"When's that?" Noah asked, glancing at him.

"Semester begins August 29. So that's August 26 to 28."

"That's two weeks from now," Noah supplied.

Jax nodded and continued reading. "Check in will be on Friday afternoon at four and checkout will be Sunday at noon. Please RSVP immediately so I can give accurate numbers to the guest services concierge. And feel free to bring a plus one, though he or she will need to fend for themselves while we're working."

Noah gasped. "Is she serious?"

Jax understood his shock. He hadn't expected that, either. In none of the places that he had worked before had there been any attempt to build a team in quite the way that Dr. Mann and her colleagues planned. Part of him was excited at the prospect of getting to know his peers outside of the stresses of their jobs, and part of him was apprehensive at the thought of coming out, yet again, especially if he took Noah along. And he found he wanted—no, needed—to take Noah along, to prove to him that he was committed to them sharing a future together publicly.

"As a heart attack, apparently," he answered his lover's question. Then he turned to look at him. "Are you interested in joining me?"

He might want Noah with him, but Noah might still want to remain withdrawn from the world, and no doubt some, if not most, of the music faculty would immediately recognize him. Was he ready for a return to the kind of lime-light he'd been avoiding since his accident? Did Jax have the right to ask that of him?

# Chapter 19

## *Noah*

*Honestly, he wasn't bitter … any longer.*

They ate at a little restaurant right on the boardwalk after the regatta ended, both tired and now full of good food. Noah hadn't been able to stop thinking about Jax's invitation to join him at his department retreat. He'd asked about what the agenda was like, but Jax didn't know, although he'd sent a message to ask his boss. She hadn't gotten back to him yet, but Noah didn't mind. He had other things to consider, more important than what Jax and his colleagues would be doing for a team-building weekend at the end of the month.

He had a lot to think about, like whether or not he wanted to come out of hiding, because yes, that was what he'd been doing for these last six months. True, he'd also been in physical therapy, but there was no reason to not keep up with his social media or to ghost his friends, whom he hardly spoke to because he was embarrassed and bitter that they'd been busy preparing for the tour he wouldn't be going on.

And then there was the relationship with Jax. Was he ready to be quite so public with his love life? Neither he nor Jax was unknown in the music world, and while Jax had not played the concert circuit nearly as often as he had, he was an established and distinguished musician in his own right. What would people say about the sudden appearance of a plus one at his side, after an entire career with no one? How would they explain what they had without raking over the past?

No doubt there would be those wanting to make assumptions about their relationship before Jax broke them apart while Noah was a junior in college. And though their speculations would most likely be true, did he want to bring that kind of notoriety to Jax now, at the start of his new job? Was it fair to him to expect that? Not that he did, because Jax might only be asking if Noah wanted to go with him out of courtesy. If he refused, they were both spared a load of stress and fuss.

He declined another beer and waited while Jax paid the bill. He hadn't been able to dissuade him, though they would need to talk about sharing expenses going forward. He wasn't destitute, and it wasn't right that Jax should be the one paying all the time.

"Penny for them?" Jax murmured as they stepped out into the cooling night air.

"What?" He was totally distracted and hadn't heard Jax's question.

"What are you thinking so hard about? I'm asking you to share the thoughts."

Noah registered the faint frown of concern on Jax's brow and the note of worry in his voice and hurried to explain.

"I was just thinking about all the issues that this invitation opens up for both of us."

Jax stopped him when they got to his truck, backing him up against the driver side door. "Issues such as?"

"Well," Noah began, swallowing hard. "What if my showing up with you raises questions about our relationship back when I was still your student? Do we want to go there? Are we ready to face the possibility of it finally coming out that we were an item for a while back then? How will that affect your reputation here now, in this new place? Can you afford to be seen as the older guy who preys on his students? What if they make assumptions about why you left your last post?"

He could hear himself getting worked up as the thoughts raced through his mind. The last thing he wanted was to hurt Jax's career in any way. Just because he was lost professionally and didn't see any real hope for participating in the thing he loved in the way he wanted to, it didn't mean he didn't care about his lover's prospects. Jax was a distinguished professor of music in a prestigious school, with a solid academic and performance record and many awards to his name. A scandal now, just when he was starting over somewhere else, would be a black mark against him.

Jax smiled at him. "I love that you're worried about me. And those are definitely some important considerations. I'm happy with whatever you decide to do, Noah. We're in this together, one way or the other."

Their lips met as if they'd been having a separate conversation from their owners and had agreed that they needed to taste each other. Noah let Jax take the kiss deeper, releasing the tension that had been building in his shoulders. Everything would be fine. He would make the best decision for the two of them because he knew that he had Jax's full support. When his lover ended the kiss, Noah smiled, shaking his head.

"What?" Jax asked curiously.

"I'm just thinking about the irony," Noah replied. "All those years ago, it was *you* putting on the brakes, keeping our relationship out of the public eye. This time, I guess it's my turn."

Jax pulled away to look him in the eye. "So is that a no to the invitation?"

Noah nodded. "It is. We've just found each other again, and you've just landed this new job. I think adding me to that mix won't help you, and I'm not sure I'm ready to have a spotlight on me yet. It's for the best if you go by yourself." He held Jax's gaze, needing him to understand. "I'm not rejecting you, okay? I'm protecting you. Just like you did for me back then."

"It's not exactly the same, though, is it?" Jax sighed. "I broke your heart when I let you go. But you're not breaking mine now."

Noah pouted, pretending to be hurt. "So, you're saying you're not even a *little* bit disappointed that you won't be able to show me off to your fancy academic colleagues?"

"Shut up, you!" Jax read through his act and laughed, leaning in to kiss him again. "I'll parade you around like arm candy if that's what you want."

Noah's face couldn't contain the grin that split it. "Arm candy, huh? And here I was hoping to be your boy toy."

Jax grabbed him by the cheeks and plundered his mouth, the kiss morphed quickly into something that Noah was sure would get them arrested for public indecency if they didn't call a halt to it at once. He pulled away, panting.

"Now, now, Prof, none of that. We need to take this someplace else. What kind of example is this to be setting for the young'uns?"

Jax raised his head and looked around the parking lot as if he expected to find that they had an audience. Then he looked back at Noah, an amused expression on his face.

"Thankfully, it's just you, me, and God out here right now, and I don't regret a thing I've done." Stepping back, he added, "But you're right. What I want to do to you is illegal in public. Not that we've any place else to play. The Bells are all home now, as is your dad."

Real regret colored his final words, and Noah understood. They wouldn't be alone together any time soon unless they went away together somewhere. They'd just have to cool their jets and be patient. He knew once Jax moved, he'd be able to spend a little more time with him. His summer tutoring was coming to an end, and until he decided what he wanted to do with the rest of his life, he was a free man. Well, as free as his disappointment at not being able to play would allow.

"Maybe we can steal away before you have to go up for work. Where will you stay until the house goes through?"

"I believe Dr. Mann said the college has a guest apartment on campus where visitors stay if they're not in the president's home. She said I could bunk there for a bit. Or I could just rent an Airbnb until then."

The idea of spending time alone with Jax cementing their renewed relationship was very appealing to Noah. He'd wait a few more days to see if Jax's house plans came through before endorsing the Airbnb idea. He didn't want to seem too eager, especially since he wouldn't be the one spending money on temporary housing.

"I'll call you tomorrow when I know what Jim and Annie need from me now," Jax said when Noah stopped outside the Bell home. "I can't imagine it will be much now that Annie's mom is here, but I don't want to assume."

"No problem. Talk tomorrow."

He met Jax halfway and they kissed softly as though they'd agreed not to inflame each other. After Jax closed the front door, Noah drove back home, wishing Jax could have come with him. He didn't think his dad would mind if Jax spent the night, but he wasn't completely sure about that, and he knew that *he* wouldn't be comfortable making love with his dad so close.

Classes kept him occupied most of the next two days, while Jax helped out with the boys so their grandmother could catch her stride and help her daughter heal. He stopped by briefly on the third morning after Annie and baby Joanna returned home, taking the flan he'd made for them as a gift.

"I hope you'll like this," he told Annie when her mother invited him into the living room where she was resting with the baby. "And it's extra delicious when it's warm."

"Thanks, Noah. I'm sure we'll love it."

Jax walked in just then, making Noah's heart clench with quiet joy at the sight of him in faded jeans and an old t-shirt, his hair mussed like he'd been running his hand through it.

"Morning, Prof," he said, winking at Jax.

He wanted to kiss Jax's smile right off his face, but Annie's mom was rolling Play-Doh with her grandsons, and Annie was watching the two of them with amused attention.

"Morning, Noah."

The stare-off between them, telegraphing hunger and desire, ended when Jax asked if anyone wanted coffee or anything to drink.

"No, I have to go. Running errands for my dad today. I'll see you all around soon. Please say hi to Jim for me."

"I'll walk you out," Jax offered, fooling no one, since the front door was just on the other side of the wall around the corner.

"Miss me?" he whispered when they reached the door.

"You have no idea." Jax leaned in and dropped a quick kiss on his lips. "I'm taking you out later. Be ready by six."

Noah's cock stirred at Jax's commanding tone. Who knew he'd like bossy Jax? "Yes, sir," he answered, saluting and making Jax laugh.

"Get outta here before I do something we shouldn't expose growing boys to," Jax growled at him and swatted his ass as he passed through the door he'd just opened.

Noah was still laughing when he got to the pharmacy to pick up his dad's prescriptions. By the end of September, Alvaro would return to Florida and Noah would need to decide whether or not he would close up the house for the season or do what his dad had been doing since he retired and rent it to people who wanted the winter experience in upstate New York.

He had to decide what to do with the rest of his life. He could potentially stay at home and grow his private music lesson business, but he knew that that wouldn't be enough to satisfy his need as a performer. Just because he couldn't play professionally any longer didn't mean the need to share his passion had died. He needed to think through his choices, and maybe talking with Jax about them would help him figure out what he wanted to do next.

Also, he needed to reach out to his boys this time, instead of waiting for them to do it, to let them know he was fine, and get their input on how he could contribute to the group he had helped to start. That was actually a great idea, and he hurried through the rest of his errands so he could get back home to make the call. Alvaro was dozing in the living room when he got home, so Noah moved quietly to put everything away, then went out to the back patio to make his call. Teagan DeVere, the cellist for the quartet, picked up on the first ring.

"Blimey! If it isn't Noah Santiago himself. To what do I owe the pleasure?"

Teagan's dry tone, coupled with his strong English accent, made Noah grin. "Don't even start, Tag. You have my number. You could have called, too."

Teagan chuckled. "After the reception that Joel and Blair got, I thought it best to avoid being cut off at the knees, as well."

"It wasn't that bad, bro," Noah protested weakly, knowing it was probably the truth.

"You didn't hear *them* tell it," Teagan said. "We decided it was best to wait you out. So, are you finally ready to talk to us now? You know we're a couple of months out from the tour, and there are a few gigs that we've signed up for to keep in practice and earn us some extra spending money when we get there."

"I know. You all have been busy between rehearsals." Honestly, he wasn't bitter … any longer.

"So, do you want to come down, or shall we come up? I assume you want a meeting?"

"I do."

Noah thought about what to say next. Should he have them come up? If they came before Jax left, he'd have to introduce him to them. Was he ready for that? He and Teagan had been in the same year in college, when his friend had introduced his older brother Tristan to him. They had become friends of a sort, and even Tristan had noticed the change in his demeanor after the breakup, though he'd accepted Noah's explanation of exhaustion at face value and hadn't dug any deeper.

"Why don't you talk to the guys about that and get back to me? I'll agree to whatever you decide."

That was probably for the best. At some point, he'd need to come clean about everything with his friends, after he apologized profusely for being almost a ghost around them after he left the hospital.

"We need to talk about where we go from here, once you come back from the tour. I need a brainstorming session about choices I and the group need to make. It can wait until you figure out whether *I'm* coming to you or you're coming to me."

"I'll let you know, bro. Either way, we'll most likely want to FaceTime with you in the meantime, if only to make sure you're not lying about being okay."

"Sod off, as you Brits would say!"

Noah laughed at Teagan's amused reply: "*Pendejo!* Tried and true English vulgarity before dinner. Spot on!"

Now it was Noah's turn to laugh when Teagan used one of the few Spanish cuss words that Noah had taught the group while they were on tour in Central America.

"Good accent," he complimented his friend.

"I'm a natural," Teagan replied, and they both burst out laughing. Then his friend sobered and added, "I'll call you back tomorrow to let you know what the lads say, okay?"

"Sounds good, my friend. Talk soon."

At six, Jax arrived and greeted Alvaro cheerfully when he answered the door. "Good evening, sir. It's good to see you again."

"Good evening. How is the new little Bell?" Alvaro asked.

"She's doing well, sir. Her grandma is there to help out now, and I know Jim is relieved because it means Annie will have help when I'm gone and he's back to full time at work."

Noah walked up behind his dad just then and winked. Jax smiled back, and Alvaro turned to stare at his son for a moment. Noah, lost in Jax's smile, barely heard his father's words.

"Enjoy your evening with your *cariño, mijo!*" Before Noah could respond, Alvaro turned back to Jax. "Have a very pleasant evening, *Profesor!*"

"What did your father call me just now?" Jax asked as he pulled away from the curb.

Noah wasn't surprised that Jax had overheard the exchange, because his father had made no attempt to lower his voice. He didn't succeed in keeping the blush from his cheeks as he answered.

"*Cariño* means honey or sweetheart." He hurried on before Jax could answer. "So, where are we going?"

Jax chuckled. "Your dad's a treat. We're going to that new place I discovered when I got here the first couple of days. It serves home cooking with a side of live music. I thought you might enjoy the music."

Noah's heart opened so wide that all the love he felt for Jax poured out of him in a rush of feeling. He would have to find a way to show him how much he loved having his needs be focused on, how he loved being wooed and seduced with thoughtfulness. The restaurant almost had the vibe of a supper club. It was small and intimate, the decor understated but elegant, with tones of gold and black throughout, the wall sconces adding subtle lighting to the space.

Once they were seated and their drinks ordered, Noah spoke. He might as well start the conversation with Jax, so that he'd have done it at least once before his meeting with the boys.

"I've been thinking about what comes next for me and the quartet," he began. "My time as a steady performer with them or with anyone is over, clearly."

He stopped to breathe away the pain that coursed through him at those words. He had not said them aloud since the accident, and it amazed him that they had so much power to wound his spirit. But he wasn't going back to those dark months in the beginning when he could see no light anywhere, even on the brightest days. Now, he was ready to discover what the light he thought he saw might mean for him going forward.

"I don't want to make being a music tutor my life's work. It's not enough for what I need. And I'd have to do a lot more of it to make a sustainable living that wouldn't require me to dip into my savings. What do you think are my other options?"

Jax rested his clasped hands on the table. "Do you still want a role in the group? Or are you considering doing something else on your own?"

"I would love to remain a part of the organization, even if not as a performer, but that's something we'd need to discuss. I don't see whatever I do with them as being financially sustaining in the way performing was, either. I'd need to supplement my income in some other way."

"Hmm. Do you enjoy the teaching at all? Do you think you are any good at it? What part of it isn't for you?"

These were not questions that Noah would have thought to ask himself, and he could see how Jax was using them to help him figure out exactly what his niche was so he could work in it. He was glad he'd gotten over the hurt enough to talk about his choices.

"I haven't heard any complaints," he said, needing not to sound like an arrogant prick. "But I also know through the grapevine, aka my dad, that the parents like how I'm getting their kids to play better and to be more invested in the music. So, I guess that means I do okay. What I don't like is the level. The kids I'm tutoring are all elementary and middle school students. They don't challenge me. I don't have to think to teach them."

A thought occurred to him as he spoke, one he had never entertained before. "What if I taught piano alone, instead of mixing it with violin lessons? It would require even less active showing, and it would be more of a challenge because it's not my primary instrument."

"You could," Jax agreed, then waited while the server placed their drinks in front of them, promising that dinner would arrive shortly. Then he continued. "But if part of the challenge is the age of your students, then you'd still be unhappy and unfulfilled." He took a sip of his drink. "Let's say you could find a role that would keep you active in the group. What other kind of teaching might interest you? For example, what if you were able to do guest lectures about your work as a professional? Might that interest you?"

Noah thought about it as he sipped his own drink. It wasn't a bad idea, and it would give him a chance to be with his peers in the field.

"I'd just need to find colleges interested in hiring me to do that," he said. "I mean, I don't think I can just invite myself to be on their roster of speakers."

Jax grinned. "No, I think you'll need to be just a tad more subtle and professional than that. Which brings me to my next question ... when was the last time you revised your resume?"

# Chapter 20

## *Jax*

*"What do you think about moving in here?"*

"I had a good time, thanks, Elise."

Jax smiled at his boss, who was clearly pleased that he had finally remembered to call her by her first name. She was waiting with him for their cars to be brought around for them. The retreat had been over for an hour, everyone else had said their goodbyes, and theirs were the last two cars to be retrieved from the back parking lot where they'd been valet parked at the beginning of the weekend.

"You may not know this, Jax, but your colleagues are super impressed with you already. I can tell you, since they're gone, that the few who may have been a bit of a challenge in that department have retired with all our blessings."

Jax laughed, understanding what she *wasn't* saying. While age might really just be a number in certain areas, when it came to teaching in the music department, and probably in any college department, age was often resistant to change, set in its ways, and generally difficult to live with. Jax was impressed by the number of people under forty who worked in the music department, some of them in their very early thirties. He thought that it bode well for the health of the program.

"I'm happy I'll have one less thing to worry about, then."

A silver Saab approached, and Elise turned to shake his hand. "Well, here's my ride, young man. I'll see you in the department tomorrow morning. Faculty meeting's at 9:00."

Jax returned her goodbye wave and watched as she drove rather speedily down the long driveway. His car stopping in front of him brought his attention back to where he was standing. Tipping the valet, he took himself off, heading toward his new home. He had moved in only a couple of days before the retreat and most of his things were still in boxes. Thankfully, everything he had had in storage had arrived intact, and the heavier items had already been placed where they belonged.

There'd be no time to cook dinner, as he was expecting Noah by late afternoon and he wanted to unpack a few more rooms, including the guest room, in case he wasn't ready to share Jax's space with him. Stopping into what was sure to become his favorite Thai restaurant, he bought Pad Thai, pot stickers, and bubble tea, then hurried home to get to work. His office and the master suite were already set up, and the guest room still needed fresh sheets, pillows, and the bedside lamps to be plugged in.

Once the food was in the refrigerator, he set to work, starting with Noah's room. Once the cool blue bedding was spread on the queen-sized bed, he fluffed the pillows he'd brought in, plugged in the cute lamps he'd bought at a yard sale, and straightened the painting on the wall. Drawing up the blinds, he let sunshine into the room and opened the window so the sweet late summer breeze could flow in.

He worked steadily, not thinking about anything except getting the house set up. When Noah had left on Monday, he hadn't known when he'd see him again. They'd spent the last two weeks together but hadn't had time to do more than steal some heated kisses when they could find a secluded spot to themselves. And though his young lover had wanted to come up with him when he was moving, he hadn't been able to switch his tutoring appointments.

The grandfather clock he'd had repaired before putting it into storage chimed four times. And as if on cue, his cell phone vibrated in his pocket. Noah's name flashed on the screen.

"Hey, how far away are you?"

"About an hour. Want me to stop for takeout?"

"No. I bought Thai food on the way home. Just get here soon."

Shedding his clothes, he showered, changed into a pair of comfortable old jeans and an equally well-worn t-shirt, and went back down to ensure that everything was ready for Noah's arrival. He felt unaccountably nervous, but he swallowed the irrational feeling, calming himself with deep breaths. Noah loved him, and he loved Noah. Whatever else there was to say and do, nothing could take that away from them.

He timed it so that when Noah rang the doorbell, their food was warmed through, and after a heated kiss that didn't last nearly long enough, he led his lover into the kitchen where he'd set the table. Noah's belly rumbled, and they both laughed.

"Bubble tea's in the fridge," Jax told him. "I'll just put the food out."

Another hot kiss as they passed each other to the table, and then they sat down to eat. Conversation could wait until their bellies were full, but once they'd cleaned their plates and were replete, they took their bubble tea and went into the den.

"So, any news?"

Noah had met with his friends in the quartet to discuss the future of the group going forward. They had come up to see him on the day Jax was moving, and he had introduced Jax to them. They'd seemed like very nice young men. He already knew that they were super talented, and he hoped that whatever decisions they came to regarding the future of the group, they'd find a way to keep Noah as part of it.

Noah settled into the armchair that Jax remembered had been his favorite seat—when he wasn't straddling Jax's lap or resting his head on it as he dozed—when they'd been together before and crossed one leg carelessly over the other. He really would have preferred to have Noah sit on him, but he could wait a little longer for that. They had the whole night, more than twelve hours, before life intruded on their time together again.

Noah's voice interrupted his musing. "We've decided that the best thing for us, going forward, is to remain together as a unit, but with me in a non-performing role. Since I will no longer have the heavy demands of daily rehearsals or the touring responsibilities, I'll be freer to compose more unique pieces for The Barrington Strings."

Jax smiled. "Nice. Love the subtle name change. How will you manage that in the media?"

"We'll meet with Richie, our manager, next weekend to iron out the plan as well as the rollout of the new format. We'll work out what he'll put on our social media page together, and he'll help me with what I put on my personal page, which I have neglected since the accident. I'll probably need to grovel a bit." His face flushed at those words, and Jax could see the shame in his eyes.

Jax remembered visiting the page earlier in the summer, after he'd first bumped into Noah, and wondering what had happened to him, as well. He hadn't gone there since. He had the real thing in his life … no need for substitutions. But Noah was right. His fans deserved an explanation and an apology. He resisted the urge to go to him. If he touched him before they were finished with the conversation, he knew it would become much more than an encouraging hug, and he wanted nothing to interrupt their lovemaking. He used his words instead.

"I'm sure you'll say the right things, babe." He sucked down some bubble tea before continuing. "Did the guys have any suggestions for what else you might do aside from composing for the group?"

"Well, that's the other thing we're going to discuss with Richie. I showed them the revised resume you helped me with, and we decided that Richie will know how to get the word out that I'm available for commissions, guest lectures, and anything else that a former violinist with an interest in paying it forward for younger musicians can do to keep body and soul together."

"You sound hopeful. I'm happy for that."

He had hated how broken Noah had felt when he could see no light at the end of the tunnel. He didn't know how he would have handled not being able to perform if he'd been in Noah's position.

"That's on you," Noah replied, surprising him.

"How so?"

"I had no reason to hope I could make a fresh start after the accident. My work was all I had after you … after we broke up. I immersed myself in it completely. I was only ever with someone to scratch an itch, and they knew that. My work was my solace. When I lost it, I felt like I had nothing left."

Jax watched him swallow some of his own drink, turning the glass in his hands. He waited, knowing that there were still a lot of things he didn't know about the Noah he'd bumped into just a month earlier. He was still getting to know that man, though his feelings had only grown deeper as a result.

"I'm even thinking I might go back to college for a master's degree in composing. It can't hurt, right?"

"No, it can't. As long as it'll make you happy."

He watched as Noah's Adam's apple rose and fell when he swallowed more of his drink, and the desire to hold him took prominence in his brain again. He wanted to do much more than hold him, but that would do for starters. He needed to get them closer for that to happen, though, so he put the rest of his drink down on the coffee table and crooked a finger at Noah.

"You're too far away. Join me?"

He patted the empty spot on the loveseat and watched as Noah's cheeks bloomed in a sweet smile. He stood up, putting his own glass on the coffee table next to Jax's and sat next to him, turning his body so he could see him. Jax reached out and took his hand, lacing their fingers together and leaning in.

"It's been too long," he murmured before he claimed Noah's lips, doing his best to keep the kiss just this side of consuming.

He wanted to build up to their lovemaking, to increase the level of seduction to where Noah would never question Jax's feelings for him, where he would know with absolute certainty that they would never be apart again because of any unilateral decision that Jax made. He'd been wrong to break them apart without talking it over with Noah, and he'd learned the hard way that that kind of alpha arrogance never paid off when it came to matters of the heart.

Noah's mouth was pliant, almost submissive beneath his, his body leaning against Jax with complete abandon. They explored each other's mouths, then left the warm confines to rediscover those spots where tongue and teeth and nibbling lips drew sighs and groans and gasps as they raised the heat level between them. When Noah turned and lifted himself to straddle Jax's lap, both of them sighed, recognizing that this had been the endgame of their foreplay all along and the beginning of the final stretch to the fulfillment they sought in each other's arms.

"I missed you, Jax." Noah's voice was strained, his eyes hot with truth and lust.

"No more than I missed you, Noah."

Jax wanted to shower him with endearments, but this time it seemed necessary to call him by his name, to cement the truth in his heart.

"I want you like I did way back when I was twenty-one and thought the world was mine and I could have anything I wanted. Like I've wanted you for eleven years." Noah's voice was harsh with emotion. "The wanting never left me. It had anger and sadness and hurt with it, but it stayed when the rest dissipated."

He rolled his hips, sliding his clothed cock against Jax's, and the groan they both let loose echoed around the room. Jax gripped the back of his head and pulled his mouth in, kissing him greedily, as though he was going to disappear in the next moment so he had to get everything he could before then.

"Strip," he grunted, dislodging Noah from his lap to stand.

Clothes went everywhere before he drew Noah down to the floor, pulling cushions off the couch to put behind his head. There was no time for finesse after all the teasing earlier. He ravished his younger lover, starting at his ears and sucking and licking his way down to his cock, which stood at attention like a soldier on guard.

"Jax!"

His name on Noah's lips was a plea he couldn't ignore. "I've got you, babe. Open for me."

Noah obeyed, spreading his legs and lifting his ass so Jax could sink his fingers into him. He gasped and writhed on those invading digits, sending Jax's temperature soaring at the erotic sight. He wanted to do so many things to Noah, but he didn't intend to blow his load before he was inside him.

"One more?"

At Noah's nod, he pushed a third finger in, aiming for his prostate and pegging it over and over, watching as Noah leaked precum in a steady stream. Needing to taste it as much as he needed Noah to come with him, he pulled his fingers free to wrap them around the hard length before his eyes and then he sucked him down to the root. Noah's ecstatic cries made his own precum flow freely.

Quickly pulling a condom from his jeans pocket, hating every second that he wasn't touching Noah, he covered his shaft and pulled Noah's knees over his shoulders, then dove into his willing body, pausing only for Noah to relax so he could push past his tight ring. Then he slid all the way home, gasping at how good it felt to nestle against his lover's body, hip to hip, balls to ass.

"Oh fuck, Jax!"

"I know, babe, I know. Feels so good!"

They stayed still a moment, each savoring the feeling of filling and being filled, and then Jax began to move. He couldn't hold out any longer, and he prayed that Noah wouldn't be sore tomorrow. Flesh against flesh, breath into breath, grunts, moans, and sighs kept the rhythm of their lovemaking, building in intensity as Jax rocked into Noah, fast and hard and deep.

"Oh g...aaaahhh!"

Noah came without touching himself, a shocked burst of sound breaking free, and his body shot cum between them. Jax looked down, watching the head of his lover's dick spurt cream, jerking with each shot, and he roared out his own release into the condom. He slammed into Noah's ass relentlessly, unable to stop the pistoning of his hips as his seed jetted from him, staying inside at the last and burrowing as deep as he could as Noah's muscles contracted around him and pulled every drop of semen from his cock.

When Jax tried to pull away so as not to crush him, Noah wrapped his arms around him, keeping him close. He gave in and lay atop him, their legs tangled, their harsh breathing easing together as they rested from their orgasms. His cock slid free, and he must have dozed for a minute, because he opened his eyes to find Noah smiling at him. He had rolled them onto their sides, the condom removed, and his arms were still around Jax.

"Welcome back, Prof! Did I wear you out?" he teased.

Jax chuckled. "I plead the Fifth." His smile widened when Noah reached over to kiss his lips, slipping him some tongue. "Shower?"

Noah nodded. "Otherwise, we'll really be joined at the hip."

Jax laughed, and they rose from the floor. Would sex with Noah always be this much fun? It went without saying that it would always be this hot and heavy, sparking and snapping fire at every turn. But he'd never laughed during and after sex until Noah came along. This kind of lovemaking would always have his seal of approval.

Morning came much too soon, despite Jax's best efforts to hang onto the bliss. He'd taken Noah again before they went to bed, and now, after two messy, fiery blowjobs, they were showering again. Noah was in a guest bathroom because they already knew if they washed up together, they'd never make it out on time, and Jax had to be in a meeting by nine.

In the kitchen, Noah eyed Jax up and down as they sipped coffee and munched on bagels and cream cheese.

"You look hot as hell, Prof!" he said, licking his lips as though Jax were a treat he'd just been enjoying. "I could hit that."

Jax laughed. "You're ridiculous." He liked that Noah found him attractive. He wasn't a vain man, but he was still eleven years older than his lover, and his ego would never refuse the boost that Noah's words offered.

"When will I see you again?" Time to focus on more important matters.

"My dad and I are getting the house ready for the winter regulars, so I'm having to figure out where I'll live at the end of the month. I gave up my apartment when the lease ran out five months ago."

Two emotions warred in Jax. The despair that Noah must have felt to do what he'd done hurt Jax's heart, but the counterbalancing spurt of excitement at the opportunity it opened up for him was equally undeniable. He hadn't really given much thought as to when he'd ask Noah to move in with him, but it seemed the Fates wanted it to be now, at this moment, an hour before he reported for duty at his new job. He swallowed the last of his coffee and inhaled deeply, breathing a silent prayer that Noah would be receptive. He didn't want him thinking this was Jax feeling sorry for him.

"About that, what do you think about moving in here?"

There … he'd posed it as a suggestion, not a request. He hoped Noah would think quickly, but he wouldn't say that aloud. Noah's smile gave him hope, but he tamped it down. He'd wait to hear the words before he went there.

"Anyway, I need to get a move on. Meeting's at nine and I don't know how parking goes on the first day or whether I'll even be able to park close to where my office is. Lots of first day things to get through before then." He reached for Noah, brushing his lips gently with his own. "I hate to rush away, babe, but it's time. Text me when you're on the way, okay?"

"What about the spare keys?"

"Keep them till I see you again. I have my own."

They parted at the front door, kissing as if their lives depended on retaining each other's flavor. Jax eyed Noah one more time, dressed only in an open robe and a pair of pale blue boxers, his half-hard cock tenting the thin material just enough to be noticeable. He dragged his gaze back up to his lover's eyes.

"I'll call you later?" Noah's words were a question, but his eyes were hot with promise.

"Can't wait. But text me when you leave."

# Chapter 21

## Jax

*It felt good to be so in sync.*

This first day was going to be odd. Jax already knew that. He couldn't remember the last time he'd had a first day of work, and back then, it had been in a big city university with as stellar a reputation as the one he was starting in now, but with nothing like the support he had already experienced here. Happy to find a spot in front of the building that housed the department and his office, he hurried in, dropped his bag and pulled his tablet from it, then made his way to the auditorium where he'd been told the faculty meeting would be held.

"Ah, Jax, good morning!"

Elise's cheerful voice warmed him as he stepped through the door, already buzzing with the voices of his colleagues.

"Good morning, Elise."

"Help yourself to whatever you need." She gestured to a table laden with food. "The bigwigs will be starting in about ten minutes."

She handed him a paper agenda, and he managed not to raise his brows in surprise. In this day of PowerPoint presentations, who dealt in paper anymore? He got himself another cup of joe, thinking that for all future meetings, he'd bring his own mug so he could keep the drink hot. Then he took a seat in the section where it seemed the music department were all gathered and waited.

The meeting was like all first of the year faculty meetings. There was the usual welcome back, the introductions of new faculty members—"Dr. Knox, we're beyond thrilled to have you join our staff!"—and the reminders about things like holidays, campus-wide activities and the like. Then came the business of reviewing opportunities for working in the community, which departments would have to vote on, and research grants that the college was considering applying for. Staff were invited to reach out if they were interested.

The roster of speakers for learned events was also discussed, and they were informed that there were still two spots open if any faculty member was interested in filling the gap. Jax took note of when they were and once the meeting was over, he found his boss and asked for more details about each event.

"Walk with me please, Jax. The president of the college has invited the heads of department for lunch, and I have some things I need to do before then."

"This won't take long. I was just wondering about the two remaining college lectures with missing speakers. Is either of them music-oriented in any way?"

Elise turned to glance at him before striding ahead again. "As a matter of fact, one of them is especially so. It's the annual Dr. Ralph J. Havisham Lecture that our department sponsors in honor of the first chair of the music department when our college was still in its infancy. The professor who was supposed to be the speaker had a heart attack over the weekend, and we have no one as yet to take his spot. We've never had this happen before and normally one of us would substitute in the event of a cancellation, but so far, no one is biting. I would do it myself, except I did it last year, and I'd prefer to let my staff share the limelight."

She stopped for another moment, turning to ask, "Are you interested in filling the gap, Jax? I know everyone in the department would be happy, not to mention relieved not to have to do it." She chuckled as she moved off again. "Apparently, I've inherited a bunch of shrinking violets. Still, it would be a useful way to get your feet wet in our lecture series."

That hadn't been where Jax's head had gone, but he hedged, not wanting to refuse outright. She was right, after all, and as he was, in fact, the new kid on the block, it behooved him to show that he was a team player. A lecture would also give him the chance to show his mettle in ways other than musical performance. And anyway, he had to run the idea by Noah before he even hinted at having a possible new recruit.

"I'll think about it," he said. "It might help me decide if I knew what this year's theme is."

"Shoot me an email and I'll send you the details."

He spent the rest of the day prepping for his classes, including sending out the emails to the students on the finalized class lists with his syllabus and practicum require-ments for upperclassmen, as well as his office hours and the like. Lunch was a hurried sandwich before he had a department meeting, in which the subject of the lecture was raised, and his name was fronted as a possible substitute.

He resisted the urge to be irritated. Elise Mann was his boss, after all, and if she gave him a direct order, he wasn't going to refuse. It wasn't worth it at this stage of his life to pick fights about minor matters. He knew she respected his professional autonomy. He listened as his colleagues cheered as though his agreement was a foregone conclusion and pasted as genuine a smile as he could muster on his face when he received a few back slaps from some.

He hadn't had a chance to check his text messages before lunch, when he'd seen that Noah had left at ten, so he'd be home already. He cleared his desk after the department meeting and agreed to go out for a final before-we-meet-the-students drink with a few of his single male colleagues. He didn't want to be alone for longer than he had to be. Being with Noah had been a wake-up call about how lonely he was and how much he wanted to have him as a constant companion in his home.

When his cell phone rang, an hour into his hangout session, he excused himself to take the call outside. It was Noah, and Jax didn't want anyone listening in to his conversation.

"Hey, babe. How was the drive?"

"I made it home in under three hours. Not even a cop in sight, and no one driving like an idiot to tie up the highway."

Jax chuckled. Noah was impatient with the way his fellow drivers handled their vehicles around him, and his irritation with the highway patrol was no less acute.

"I'm glad you're safe and unticketed. There's something I'll need to talk to you about but I'm out with colleagues right now. I'll call you when I get home."

"Sure. Enjoy yourself. Talk later." He was gone before Jax could answer.

"Everything okay?" Ted Parsons, one of the piano professors, asked.

"Yeah, everything's fine." He picked up his beer, signaling that he was done talking about his call and thankfully, they followed his lead.

"So, Jax, a few of us were wondering what made you choose to come here. After all, where you were previously is among the best music schools in the nation. Up there with Curtis and Julliard. So, why?"

Jax had been surprised that the question hadn't come up over the weekend, when he'd had a prepared speech to answer it. Now, two beers and the memory of some sweet lovemaking in, he was damned if he could remember the finer points. He went with the easiest response.

"I needed a change, and I wanted to stay at the same level. This was a no-brainer. Same high standards, less competition, more time to do what I love."

"Small college town universities can be as messy as big city ones, though," Stuart McKoy, another younger colleague and a flutist, said. "It took me a while to get used to everyone knowing my business."

Jax's ears perked up. "Your business? What do you mean?"

McKoy grinned. "I'm gay. I wasn't sure how well that would be received outside of the music department, which thankfully is honestly inclusive. Turns out, that wasn't what I should have been worried about."

The others laughed at that, and Jax turned curious eyes to McKoy. "What *should* you have worried been about?"

"Matchmakers. Everybody's mother, grandmother, aunt, and even a few grandpas suddenly knew a guy. I kept having to head them off at the pass. I even thought a little bit about hiring someone to pretend to be my man, so they'd stop accosting me in the supermarket to ask me how my date was, because of course they'd seen me the one time I was with a guy."

He was laughing as he told the story, but Jax could feel his frustration. He understood the feeling, though he didn't get it from outsiders. He got that from his family, particularly his mom.

"So, how did you escape that?"

"I got married."

Jax's eyes shot up in astonishment. "What? You just up and married some random dude?"

McKoy laughed long and loud. "Nope. I fell for my husband at first sight, if you can believe that, but he's an older man and I didn't think he'd be interested. Turns out I was wrong. Eighteen months later..." he held up his left hand, "I'm matchmaker-free and loved up by a silver fox I wasn't even looking for."

"Congratulations!" Jax raised his empty beer bottle in a toast.

"So, what are you planning to do to escape the matchmakers?"

"What makes you think they'll go after me? They don't even know I exist!"

"A babe in the woods, boys," Parsons chimed in with a smirk. "College students are the biggest gossip mongers in the world. Their mothers and grandmothers and aunties are gonna know you're single by the end of the day tomorrow."

"Stop it! That's just not credible!" Jax shook his head and ordered another beer and some loaded French fries.

"Don't say we didn't warn you," McKoy said, draining his beer. "One more round, guys? Dave's coming back from a business trip soon, and I want to be home when he gets there."

Whoops and teasing followed that revelation, and before he knew it, Jax was heading back to his new home. He had updated his address with the post office and with his department, and already he had mail in the box when he got home. A card from Noah and his dad welcoming him home, and one from Jim, with photographs of the family. His mother had sent him a letter with a hundred-dollar bill in it, widening the smile he already wore from the other things his friends had sent him.

It was a ritual she'd started with each child when they first left the nest, as she called it. Every time they moved, she sent them a hundred dollars for groceries, "Because you'll forget to eat, and you need your strength to move." He'd call her after he had a bite to eat. And then he'd FaceTime Noah.

"How was your day, Prof?"

Jax took in the sight of his lover sprawled across his bed wearing nothing but boxers, and his heart sang.

"Long, but it's better now that I've seen you. How about you?"

"*Papi* and I have started the big clear out. I've never had to do it with him before, but I persuaded him to save the money he normally spends on cleaners."

"Ah, free labor!"

"Isn't that why our parents keep us around?" He laughed softly, then added, "We should be done by the end of the week."

"So are you free for the whole weekend?"

"I am."

Jax watched as Noah's smile turned seductive, and he wagged his brows. Playful Noah was as much of a treat as passionate Noah, and he needed to have him for more than a random weekend now and again. If Noah agreed to live with him, he'd have his wish. But he'd only just asked him to move in the night before, and he didn't want to seem too eager or pushy. He was the older man, and he was expected to have better impulse control.

"I've been thinking about what you asked me."

Jax let out a soft sigh. Was Noah reading his mind now? Didn't that level of connection between partners take a longer time to happen? Whatever the reason, he was grateful that at least they'd both been thinking about it.

"And?"

"I'd want to pay my way."

Not what Jax was expecting to hear next. He had no ready response aside from "No," and he suspected that that wouldn't go over well with Noah. But he didn't want him paying rent. He wasn't interested in being Noah's landlord. He wanted a forever lover. Would Noah understand that?

*Maybe you need to be clear, Jax.* "Look, Noah, I know you need to be independent, and I understand that you don't want to be a kept man, but I don't feel comfortable with the idea of you paying your way. What does that even mean? I'm not asking you to be my tenant, and the thought of taking your money never crossed my mind." He sat forward, needing Noah to understand. "I want you with me as my partner, Noah."

"Don't partners share expenses?" Noah lifted a brow.

"I suppose they do, but I don't think it's negotiated like a business arrangement. It's an agreement they come to when they choose to cohabit with each other.'

"Well, if I choose to cohabit with you, I'll want such an agreement."

Jax sighed again. He wasn't going to win this argument. "We'll discuss all of that later. But the discussion would be moot if your answer to my invitation isn't yes. So do you choose to cohabit with me?"

"Yes." A cheeky grin accompanied the word.

"Tease!" Jax chastised him.

He didn't really mind because he'd gotten what he wanted. All that was left was the proposal. But that would wait. They'd have to see if living together would work for them beyond a night of wild sex. He didn't think it would be an issue, but he would wait until he'd had a chance to prove that his theory was accurate. A Christmas proposal sounded nice and romantic. Four months was surely enough time to know if they were compatible outside of the bedroom.

"Prof?"

Jax blinked. "Sorry. Got a little bit sidetracked."

"Care to share?"

"Not worth it. I prefer to talk about what time you'll be arriving on Friday."

"Maybe around five. I have to teach two sessions first."

"I can't wait to have you in my arms again, to have all that delicious flesh at my disposal."

"All this, huh?" Noah slid his free hand down his chest to the waistband of his boxers. "You sure know how to seduce a guy," he murmured.

"Something you need, babe?" Jax watched Noah's cock jerk at the word, and he chuckled.

"Anything you want to give me," Noah answered at once. "Maybe we can help each other, Prof."

He slid his fingers under the band and teased the head of his cock which Jax could see peeking over the edge. His own shaft lengthened, and he reached for it, ready to play any game Noah wanted.

By Friday, Jax had learned two things. First, Ted was right … college students were the nosiest people on the planet, and they couldn't mind their own business any more than they could pass his preliminary quiz, which was rigged. Rumors had already begun to spread about his marital status, his sexual orientation, and his shoe size. He refused to think about why that last question was so important to them.

The second thing he'd learned was that he wasn't nearly as grown up and patient as he'd thought. He'd been looking out for Noah for the last half hour, and he was at the front door by the time the key sounded in the lock. The second the door closed behind him, Jax had him up against it ravishing him with kisses. He basked in the overwhelming joy of Noah's hands roaming his body, of his cock pressed against Jax's, of their mingled breathing as they kissed and kissed. And when they were forced to release each other so they could catch their breath, Jax found he couldn't stop the slight trembling that had taken residence in his limbs.

"Go up and wait for me. I need to shut off the stove or dinner will be ruined."

Not that he cared really, but he'd rather not start a fire in his new home because he was horny. Afterward, when the urgency of their need had been satiated for the moment, they stood at the kitchen island in their boxers eating the reheated meal and smiling quietly into each other's eyes.

"So good, Prof," Noah said, humming as he took another bite of the shepherd's pie.

"I know."

The wink that Noah sent his way told Jax he knew Jax wasn't talking about the food. It felt good to be so in sync. Jax knew then that he would do everything to protect what they had, which meant that he wouldn't ask Noah if he was interested in doing the lecture. It wouldn't be a good look for him to suggest the man he loved as a guest speaker in a place where he hadn't been working a month. It would put them both in an awkward position, and he wasn't prepared to do that.

So when Noah asked what he wanted to talk to him about, once they'd gone into the den to cuddle and watch mindless television, his answer had been easy.

"I was going to ask if you'd be interested in doing a guest lecture this semester, but I don't think it's any better of an idea than you coming to the retreat had been. It's fine … Elise asked if I'd like to fill in the gap and it's not a bad idea, so I think I will."

Three weeks later, Jax drove down to say goodbye to Noah's dad, and to visit with Jim and his family. When he got to the Santiago house, Alvaro's suitcases were at the door, and the old man smiled widely when he opened it to Jax.

"Come in, *Profesor*. It is good to see you again."

Inside, the house was pristine and felt curiously empty. Noah's instruments and the beautiful leather loveseat that he had brought with him when he had run away after the accident, had already been delivered to Jax's house. All that remained were his suitcases. Noah walked out just then, a suitcase in each hand.

"Need any help?" Jax asked.

"My backpack and one more suitcase are in my room."

Jax went to get them while Noah spoke to his dad. Once the luggage was all packed into the bed of his truck, Noah said, "Well, it's time to go, *Papi*." He leaned in to hug his father and they kissed each other's cheeks. "Are you sure you don't need me for anything else?"

"I am sure, *mijo*. I always spend my last night with the boys, sleep in one of their houses, and that friend takes me to the train in the morning. It's our goodbye-for-now ritual. I don't want to change it. We're old men, and rituals bring comfort to our hearts."

Before Noah could speak again, a knock sounded, and Alvaro hurried to answer it. A tall, burly black man stood on the threshold with a bright smile on his face.

"You ready, Alvaro?"

The old man smiled. "Yes. I'll be right out."

He picked up his suitcases, which the man promptly took from him before heading back out to the SUV he'd parked at the curb. Alvaro turned back to them.

"I'll see you for Thanksgiving, *si*?"

"*Si, Papi.*"

"Jackson," Alvaro had taken to calling him by his full name. "Welcome to the family."

He reached in and hugged Jax, who wrapped his arm around him for a moment.

"Thank you, sir."

Then Alvaro pierced them both with his fatherly gaze. "Take care of each other. I will see you in two months."

After he left, Noah took the keys next door to Carrie, whom Alvaro paid to handle the housekeeping when he was away. They left after that, stopping in to visit Annie and Jim. He held his new godchild in his arms with a kind of awe. After a month, she was a robust and gorgeous infant, with rosy lips and cheeks.

"You're a sweet pea, aren't you, baby girl?" he cooed at her, placing a soft kiss on her forehead as he swayed with her against his shoulder.

Jim smirked at him as he danced with her and when he glanced over at Annie, her eyes were warm with amusement and affection.

"What?" he asked, not pausing in his baby dance.

"Nothing," Jim said. "You look good. It's been eight years since we've had this visual, that's all."

He pulled out his cellphone and snapped a couple of pictures before Jax could protest, ignoring Jax's glare.

"I'll make sure your mom and your man get these," he promised gleefully.

"Why are we best friends again?" Jax asked, but he wasn't really mad.

Having the baby in his arms was doing all sorts of things to his heart. What would it be like to have his own child to dance with, to swoon over, to care for and love? And to have that with Noah ... he couldn't imagine a better gift.

Noah's eyes widened when Jax handed over the baby. It was clear he didn't have any experience holding infants, and he sat down and held her in the crook of his arms, looking down at her with such tenderness and awe that Jax couldn't stop himself from recording it for posterity. Jim winked at him as he put his cellphone away. Noah hadn't even noticed Jax taking his picture.

"We'd better get a move on. Now that I live closer, we'll definitely see each other more often," he promised.

After hugging Annie and admonishing the boys to be good, they made the three-hour journey home. Home ... that sense of belonging with the man who parked his truck to one side of the garage so Jax could pull in beside him. He let the feeling wrap around him as he exited his car and went around to Noah to help him with his luggage. They met at the tailgate and kissed as if by mutual prior agreement, exchanging breaths and tastes, their moans growing louder as the kiss grew in intensity.

Jax pulled away reluctantly. "Let's go in, babe."

They made it all the way into his bedroom before he turned, dropping the bags he held, and reached for Noah again.

"Welcome home, Noah," he said, then kissed him again.

# Epilogue

## *Noah*

*Only one thing remained …*
*to make Jax his permanently.*

"Hey, calm down, Santiago. Everything's gonna be fine." Noah looked over at his new friend. Stuart McKoy had been one of the first members of Jax's new department to recognize him at the Halloween party that the music department put on for its students every year at the college. It was the first time he'd been formally introduced to Jax's colleagues as his partner, and the thrill of that moment still lived like a flame in his soul.

"I know he was wondering why I needed to go back down in the week before Christmas, and I'm not exactly the world's best liar."

"Well, he bought your story about needing to check on the house because the last tenant left unexpectedly. Anyway, everything's in order. Dave and I will be out of your hair in ten, and he'll be home in thirty. Stop wringing your hands and finish getting dressed. Do you have everything you need?"

"Yeah. The ring is in my pocket." He patted the side pockets of his dress pants. "The flowers will be here in the next ten minutes. His family, the Bells, and my dad are settling into the guest rooms, and they'll be down before he gets here."

"Then you're all set, my friend. Go, go. You don't have a lot of time."

Noah still hesitated. "Are you sure you and Dave won't stay, McKoy? You guys have done so much to help me and to make Jax feel at home."

"I'm sure. We'll see you at our New Year's Eve party. This time should be for just you and your family." He leaned in to give Noah a bro hug. "Go on. We'll find you before we head out."

McKoy and the rest of the department, with the full knowledge and cooperation of his department chair, had managed to persuade Jax to go out for drinks before coming home. That gave Noah time to bring all the guests for the party that Jax didn't know about, where he would propose to him in front of their family and friends. He was beyond nervous, but also excited to finally have what he'd always wanted with his professor ... forever, a happily ever after, like they got in romance novels.

His lover had been throwing around broad hints about them settling down, but Noah didn't know when Jax planned to do more than suggest they think about it. He was ready to move on, and he hoped Jax wouldn't be angry that he'd stolen his thunder. He just couldn't wait any longer. No time was better than the present to act on the desire that had been filling his heart almost from the day he'd moved in.

The doorbell rang ... that would be the flowers. He smoothed his hand down the white silk shirt he'd chosen, the mandarin collar hugging his throat softly. His black dress pants were pleated and cuffed, and his polished dress shoes shone in the light. Pulling the matching jacket over his shoulders, he headed back down the stairs where his and Jax's family were waiting in the living room.

McKoy was about to head up to get him. He and Dave stood at the foot of the stairs, watching him walk down.

"Looking sharp there, Santiago." McKoy reached in to give him another bro hug, and Dave, his husband, did the same from the other side. "Congratulations, man! The next time we see you, you'll be an engaged man."

"Everything's ready and where it should be. You'll need to serve dinner as soon as you pop the question so every-thing will still be fresh and warm."

Dave was a chef and had gifted Noah the evening meal so he would have one less thing to worry about. If Jax liked the food, maybe they could hire him to cater their wedding. Something to discuss with his lover, later ... much later, after everyone was asleep and he had given Jax at least one orgasm. Nope ... not going there. He didn't need to get all worked up with so many people around.

"Thank you, Dave. I really appreciate this."

"Well, we're going before he gets here. Text me after, to let me know how it went." McKoy paused a second, then added, "Or, even better, have someone record it so we can see for ourselves."

Noah smiled. "I'll think about it. Not sure I want to die before my wedding."

They laughed, and he watched them leave before going in to make sure everyone had a drink. Two charcuterie boards graced the coffee table, and his dad was in an animated conversation with Jax's mom, little sister, and Annie, while Jax's brother and brother-in-law were laughing over something Jim had said.

He wished Teagan, Joel, and Blair could be here, but they were finishing The Barrington Strings' second tour. They'd be back after Christmas. He'd send them the recording as well, so they could share in his joy. His manager had secured so many offers for him that they would need to discuss which ones were realistic for him to take on in the new year. Jax's boss had indicated that she'd be happy if he would spend an evening with the performance majors and had suggested that he might look into doing some adjunct lecturing in the new semester.

He had a lot to be grateful for and he knew it. Only one thing remained ... to make Jax his permanently. When lights on the driveway signaled his arrival, Noah shushed his guests, and went out to meet his man. He was glad that Jax was never less than well dressed for work, so he wouldn't have to do much to spruce up, though he might want to change his shirt. He'd see how that went. He knew Jax would want to know why *he* was all dressed up.

The door opened and Jax walked in, dropping his briefcase and his coat before gathering Noah into his arms.

"Mmm. I missed you today. Was everything okay when you got down there?"

Noah nodded and kissed him, needing to shut down the conversation. He didn't want to lie anymore, even if it was a harmless one.

"Something smells good," Jax observed next. "Did you order out?"

"Yeah." Well, technically, he'd had a chef cook it, but that was almost like takeout, right?

"Why are you all dressed up, then?"

"I just wanted to make it special. I felt like it." He really was a terrible liar. "You can stay in what you have…"

"No. I'll go change my shirt. I want to be dressy with you."

Another kiss and then Jax went up to change. Noah moved his coat to the closet and his briefcase to his office and then went back to wait for him, this time with drinks in his hands. When Jax came back down, he had changed into a white shirt like Noah's, only his was open at the collar.

"Let's go sit and have a drink. Dinner will take just a few minutes more to warm up completely."

The lights in the living room were on but Jax wouldn't see anyone until they walked in. Noah let him go ahead of him and grinned when Jax paused as he walked in and saw all the people gathered there.

He took a few more steps in as the others said, "Surprise!"

"It's not my birthday, babe," he said, turning to look for his lover and finding Noah down on one knee.

The look on his face was everything Noah could have wanted. Joy, love, desire … all the things that said the answer to his question would be "yes" shone in Jax's eyes. But before he could ask it, Jax was also kneeling and withdrawing something from his pocket. Noah's eyes immediately welled up. He'd been right … Jax had been planning to propose, as well. The room and its occupants faded away, and only he and Jax remained.

"You go first," Jax said.

"I didn't go anywhere today," were the first words from his mouth. That hadn't been what he meant to say, but it was too late now. "I wanted to make this memorable for us, so I needed to have the people we love the most here with us when I asked you the most important question I've ever asked anyone."

He pulled the ring from his pocket and opened his palm so Jax could see it. Out of the corner of his eye, he caught sight of someone—he couldn't tell who—moving close enough to take pictures. He refocused on the man on his knees before him.

"I love you, Prof. I've loved you for almost twelve years. I hated every second that we were apart, and Google says that that's almost 378,432,000." Quiet laughter filled the room, but Noah ignored it. "I think it's safe to say I will always love you, so will you please put me out of my misery and marry me, Jax?"

He watched as tears filled Jax's eyes, though he didn't let them fall. They were both a mess, but he didn't care.

"That's a whole lot of seconds, babe," Jax replied, swallowing hard. "And I know how every one of them without you feels. I never want to feel that way again. So yes, I'll put you out of your misery, because selfishly, it puts me out of mine."

More laughter ... Noah loved the feeling as he slid the gold ring onto Jax's finger. It fit perfectly, because he'd borrowed one of Jax's rings to get the right size. Then it was Jax's turn.

"I've been walking around with this ring—literally—for almost three months, Noah. I didn't want to rush you, but I knew, long before you moved in with me, that you would be the only man I'd ever ask to be mine. You've always been mine, from that first moment when you walked into my music room and gave me the eye. I should have known I didn't have a snowball's chance in hell of escaping you. I didn't want to then, and I don't want to now. I'm glad you want me, because I want you. So, will you stay mine forever?"

His ring also fit perfectly, and Noah didn't have to wonder how Jax knew his ring size, because he'd been trying on jewelry in a pop-op shop when they'd gone on one of their weekend excursions to a neighboring town. He had bought a costume piece with a big red stone for the Halloween party that he'd attended as a vampire with Jax.

"Forever," he promised and squeezed Jax's fingers when he slid the ring on.

They leaned in together and kissed each other, just managing to keep it PG. After the joyous congratulations of their family and friends, dinner was a happy, noisy affair, with dancing following it. Noah couldn't think of a time when he'd been happier and only one other day could top this one. He had a plan for that day, too, but this time he'd be the only one who would know it ... he and the officiant.

On a hot day at the beginning of August, a year after they first found each other again, Noah and Jax invited their family, friends, and colleagues to bear witness to the beginning of their marriage. Jax's boss, a notary public with the necessary license, married them in the gazebo down by the water. The Barrington Strings played all the music, from the walk down to the water's edge through to their walk back to the house as a married couple. And, in among all the other songs, was one piece that Noah knew no one would forget.

As he stood playing the song he had composed for his love, Noah's heart swelled with gratitude. He was only able to play the first movement, but he'd been practicing and doing his PT routine diligently so he would be prepared. The sound was rich, warm, romantic, and vintage Noah. He couldn't hold back the tears when he received a kiss from his man and a standing ovation from the guests. And even after the group took over and played the entire work, he was still buzzing from the high of that achievement.

"Are we staying for the party?" Jax whispered in his ear as they walked to the head table afterwards. "Because I can think of a lot of better things to do than eat a bunch of food and cake and smile for the cameras."

Noah laughed. "I'll bet you can, but you can't ditch the party until after dessert. Your mom made me promise." He looked into Jax's eyes and winked. "Seems she knows you a whole lot better than I do."

Jax shook his head. "If I'd known you were going to gang up against me with my own mother..." He cut himself off and sighed dramatically.

"Yes?" Noah grinned, daring him to say anything more.

"Nothing," he answered. "Because really, anything I said now would be a lie."

Noah chuckled. "That's what I thought," he replied with a self-satisfied smirk.

After dinner, the first dance, the cake—they smooshed each other's lips with frosting and then licked it off, to whoops and wolf whistles and catcalls—and dances with their parents, even Noah's patience had worn thin, and he was ready to disappear. Still, he waited until the guests all got up to dance to some stirring, sexy Latin rhythms before he pulled on his husband's arm.

"Let's get out of here now, Prof," he whispered in Jax's ear.

They were going to Niagara Falls, mostly because it was close by. They had nothing planned for the first week of their honeymoon. They'd just go where the mood took them. The second week, they'd fly down to Jamaica and spend two more weeks sunning themselves and discovering Jamaica, as the ad suggested. Then they'd come back to spend a few days with family before the new semester began.

But tonight, they had booked a room at a nearby inn and had already packed their suitcases for the drive up to Niagara Falls. All they had to do was get to Jax's car. Making discreet eye contact with Jax's mom, Noah pulled his husband along, making dance moves as he did until he got into the house.

"I'll be sure to lock up, boys," Mrs. Knox told them. "Get out before they notice you're gone. I love you both. Call me when you get to Canada."

"Will do, Mom. Love you too."

Hugs and kisses, and they were off. The sun had just gone down, the night was theirs.

This night, and forever.

**The End**

# Book Discussion Questions

1.  How does the Prologue prepare you—or not—for what happens in the rest of the story?

2.  Do you find Noah and Jax to be credible characters? Why/Why not?

3.  Is this second-chance story different from others you've read? In what way(s)?

4.  Would you have preferred to know more about the two towns in which the action takes place aside from their general location in upstate New York? For example, would it have increased your enjoyment to have known their names, real or imagined? Why?

5.  Of the important secondary characters, whom do you most appreciate? Why?

6.  What is the best thing about this love story?

7.  What is the worst thing about it?

8.  Of the secondary characters, whose story would you have wanted to read in a separate novel or short story?

9.  Did you find the story realistic? Why/Why not?

10. Did Noah's and Jax's motivations seem reasonable or far-fetched? Explain.

11. Does the epilogue satisfy your need for an HEA? If not, what else would you have included?

12. If this novel were to be made into a movie, whom would you cast in the important roles?

13. What do you think of the book's title? What other title might you have chosen?

14. How did you find this book's pacing? Was it consistent throughout?

15. Did you find the storytelling stronger in the beginning or in the end? What made it so?

# About
# The Author

A. J. Buchanan has been writing MM love stories since 2017, but she was writing them for clients and could take no credit for them. With over twenty ghostwritten MM romances ranging from short stories to full length novels—including a five-novel series—under her belt, she's more than ready to tell stories in her own name.

*Orchestrated Love* is A. J's debut novel as a gay romance writer. It is the first in her series, *No Strings Attached*.

When she's not creating worlds with men who grow to love each other, A. J. (and her equally romantic-at-heart alter ego, author K. T. Bond) reads romance voraciously, hangs out with her grown children, and plays Redecor, Word Crossy, Bingo Story, and Solitaire on her phone. She is a proud member of the Romance Writers of America.

# Social Media

https://www.facebook.com/authorajbuchanan
mybookdates.wordpress.com